Helen J. Rolfe writ
with characters to re

Before she started wri ....en J. Rolfe
worked in I.T. until she ....e to her senses and
studied journalism and writing. She wrote articles for
Women's Health & Fitness magazines as well as
newsletter content and media releases for a not-for-
profit organisation. In 2011 the fiction bug bit and
Helen has been writing fiction ever since.

After fourteen years of calling Australia home, Helen
has returned to the UK with her husband and two
children.

Handle Me with Care is her second novel.

Find out more at www.helenjrolfe.com, and follow
her on Twitter @HJRolfe.

Also by Helen J. Rolfe

The Friendship Tree

Handle Me with Care

Helen J. Rolfe

For my husband and my girls

curls should he let it grow longer, and the stubble that had settled across his jaw only added to his appeal.

As Maddie made eye contact, she noticed the same look of mischief in Evan's eyes as the little old lady's. 'Maddie.' She cleared her throat as her words failed to come out clearly, and she returned his smile with difficulty when his eyes – a deeper, seventy per cent cocoa version of Jem's – refused to look away.

Jem peeked into the box again and beckoned over a male friend of a similar age.

When Evan leaned closer, he took Maddie by surprise. 'I hope they're not doing any sort of comparison.'

She was only able to breathe again when he moved away; meeting him had left her unusually flustered.

'Do you make cakes like this for a living, Maddie?'

'It's just a hobby, cake-making—' Not penis-cake-making, she wanted to say. She felt as though her entire mouth had been filled with cotton wool. 'I'm a physiotherapist,' she offered instead.

'Well, I wouldn't tell half of this lot.' He indicated the crowd, most of whom were closer to Jem's generation than Evan and Maddie's. 'They'll be talking about their hips, their arthritis, their knees and backs and all sorts. You'll never get out of here.'

'Don't worry, I won't let it slip.' Uneasy beneath his gaze, she said, 'Jem looks remarkably well for her age.'

'She is. Apart from some mild arthritis in her wrists – which she says gets in the way of her doing so much around the house – she's as fit as anything.

She's a bit slower moving than she would've been twenty or thirty years ago, but she's lucky.'

Jem closed the box and turned to Maddie. 'You've made my day, dear. It's certainly a novel way of showing one hundred.' She giggled. 'The penis could be the *one*, and the testi—'

'That's enough, Jem!' A girl with the same smile, dark eyes and dark hair as Evan emerged from the crowd holding a yellow balloon between her fingers, ready to be blown up. 'I'm Holly, Jem's granddaughter and Evan's sister.' Unlike Evan, Holly had let the curls of her hair tumble out of their own free will.

Maddie introduced herself and was grateful to be released from Evan's scrutiny when two energetic little boys dragged him on to the dance floor. Both wore miniature suits, each with a tie she estimated had another ten minutes of shelf life before being yanked off and discarded on the floor.

'I'm really sorry about the mix-up, Holly.'

Holly finished blowing air into the long yellow balloon and tied a knot at the end. 'Between you and me, I think you've made Jem's day.'

When the double doors to the hall sprang open and a more professional looking caterer entered, Maddie swiftly shifted her cake out of the way to make room for the new, more appropriate square cake with white frosting.

'I rather preferred yours.' Jem appeared beside her, and Maddie couldn't ignore the way the old lady's mouth tugged at the corners when she spoke. 'Your cake is much more fun. Even the chocolate curly bits are very well formed. It's a professional job.'

'You mean professional apart from the fact that it's a penis.'

Jem's face danced with mischief and a chortle escaped. 'Oh, do please stay for a slice of cake, Maddie. It's not every day I turn one hundred, and it's not every day I meet a fresh young face like yours.'

'Of course I will, but I'd better deliver my cake to the bachelorette party first, or there'll be some angry ladies out to get me later.' Not to mention the need to remove her penis cake from the prying eyes of the rampant pensioners and inquisitive children who had again gathered around the creation.

Promising she'd return and uncomfortable beneath Evan's gaze from across the room, Maddie carried the cake out of the party, concentrating on putting one foot in front of the other as she crossed the car park. She prayed that she didn't stumble and fall flat on her face into the giant penis. She'd had enough embarrassment for one day.

Maddie found the correct venue easily enough, and as the bachelorette party wasn't set to be in full swing until much later, she headed back to Jem's celebrations. It was the least she could do after she'd disrupted the start of the party so spectacularly.

At Jem's party, Holly welcomed Maddie into the crowd that had at least doubled in her absence. They joked about the cake again, and it wasn't long before Jem noticed her return.

'I'm glad you came back,' said Jem, linking Maddie's arm with her own and leading her into the throng. 'You're just in time.'

Maddie realised how frail this little old lady really was, despite her energy. She was ever so slightly stooped at the shoulders, reducing her height to just below Maddie's, and the skin on her arm felt papery. Maddie suspected what kept this woman ploughing on through life was her enthusiasm and obvious appetite for merriment. From her vivid cardigan to the little grey curls that danced from the top of her head all the way to the nape of her neck, her laugh and the twinkle in her eye, Jem radiated warmth and fun.

The sound of tapping against a glass and the cessation of music brought the crowd to a standstill, and Jem was ushered to the middle of the room to say a few words before the cake was cut.

Maddie stood at the side of the dance floor feeling conspicuous as that-girl-who-brought-the-penis-cake. But the other guests appeared to have moved on to more exciting things, and she joined in as they sang Happy Birthday.

During the final round of applause, Maddie felt Evan's eyes settle on her from the other side of the room. They'd only exchanged a few words, but it hadn't lessened her reaction to him. Had her knees really weakened? Surely not, that was just a fallacy wasn't it? Had she really needed to concentrate on breathing in a rhythm that calmed her down and didn't let her heart thump against her chest? Or maybe the heat from the crowd was getting to her and that was all.

Maddie was rescued from Evan's gaze by a paper plate with a generous slice of cake being thrust in front of her. Since Riley, no other man had made her this nervous and her mouth was so dry that each bite of the lemony sponge formed a hard ball in her oesophagus.

Jem scurried over to her again. 'Come on, I need a cuppa.'

Maddie followed Jem to a longer table set against the far wall upon which was an obedient line of tea cups, saucers and labelled urns.

'Here, let me.' Maddie noted the size of the urn compared to Jem.

'Don't be silly.' Jem swatted away the offer of help. 'How do you think I stay looking so youthful? This is my weight training.' She smiled impishly. 'My brain stays in check with this Nintendo DS thingamajig Evan and Holly bought me for my 95th.'

Maddie could well imagine her using one, and it made her smile as they took their cups of tea over to the chairs lined up against a wall at the edge of the dance floor.

'I don't condone all this screen time youngsters have nowadays,' said Jem, slurping the top of her tea, 'but I'm old. I'm supposed to sit down a bit.'

Jem's family and friends seemed a lively bunch, but given the choice between this crowd and twenty girls making pottery penises and downing shots, Maddie knew this party was the lesser of two evils.

'Are they your great-grandchildren?' Maddie nodded towards a group of kids on the dance floor who looked as though they were auditioning for *The X Factor*.

'Most of them, yes.' She pointed to a little girl dressed in a silky, bottle-green and white polka dot dress with an enormous bow tied at the back. 'That's Ava, Holly's daughter. She's four going on fourteen. Reminds me of when I was her age.'

'She's gorgeous, quite the little lady.' Maddie watched as Ava pulled Evan in from the sidelines and pleaded with him to twirl her around in his arms. She hadn't thought it possible to be jealous of a four-year-old before.

'She's already got her eye on this.' Jem patted the butterfly brooch pinned to her dress. Tiny circles of crystal made up the wings and two thin antennae poked out, curling at the top.

'It's beautiful.'

'My late husband gave it to me. But I'm not daft. I won't be taking it to my grave. I'll let her have it.'

Raucous laughter erupted as party poppers exploded across the room with streams of yellows, pinks and reds landing on unsuspecting partiers. The kids dived on to the floor, grabbing at the strands.

'And are you with anyone, Maddie? I don't see a ring.'

Maddie laughed at the bluntness as she pushed her cup to join Jem's on the table next to them. 'No, I'm single.' If Riley had still been alive, her answer would probably have been 'married with children'.

'What, a lovely slip of a girl like you?' Jem shook her head. 'What's the world coming to?'

'I'm getting on a bit now. I'm thirty-six.'

'That's young by my book. Ah, look out, here comes trouble.'

Maddie followed the direction of Jem's gaze to see Evan fast approaching in an attempt to escape the rigours of the dance floor. Pink's 'Get the Party Started' was blaring out at this far-from-average tea and cake birthday celebration.

'Are you coming to request a dance with the birthday girl?' asked Jem cheekily. 'Because if you are, I'll have to take a rain check. My bladder isn't quite what it used to be, and that tea has gone right through me.' She excused herself but not before she put an arm on Maddie's, looked at Evan and said, 'Don't you let this one go anywhere. I haven't finished with her yet.'

Evan took the vacant chair, and Maddie tried to keep her composure when his thigh brushed against her own.

'What did you think of the cake?' he asked.

She gulped as his question conjured up the image of him watching her so intently just before she was offered a slice. 'It was lovely.'

'Now I know you're being polite. It was dry, even Jem said so.' The corners of his mouth tugged in amusement in the same way Jem's had moments ago. 'She's still hankering for a slice of that gigantic penis, you know.'

His laughter was enough to set her at ease when she flushed at the sound of the word 'penis' tumbling from his mouth. She wished she could hide behind her wavy caramel-coloured hair that usually hung midway down her back between her shoulder blades. But she always tied it up whenever she was baking for fear of producing the dreaded hair in the dessert one day.

'Thank you for the compliment … I think. But unless Jem wants to come to a feisty bachelorette party, she'll have to make do with her own cake.'

'Don't even suggest it to her or she'll be there in a flash, probably out-dancing half of the younger crowd.'

He pointed to another lady who had taken to the dance floor at the insistence of the younger ones. She had the family traits: dark hair, dark eyes and a smile that dazzled anyone in its path. 'That's my mum, Martha. She's been trying to persuade Jem to move out of her unit and into the granny flat at her place for years now. Mum's off on a holiday to Canada as of tomorrow, but I know she's hoping Jem will finally give in when she gets back.'

'Does Jem still live alone?' Maddie tried to ignore the way Evan's eyes continually dropped to her mouth.

'She does, and she sees moving out as admitting that she's old. And from what you know of Jem already, I think you'll probably be able to see she doesn't want to do that.'

'Does your mum live alone too?'

'Yes, and between you and me, I think she gets lonely. Dad died years ago and then eventually Holly and I grew up and moved out, too.'

Before Maddie had a chance to ask him more about his dad, a rainbow of streamers exploded from a party popper at the edge of the dance floor. Seconds later a pink streamer floated down from the ceiling and landed on her knee. She caught her breath when Evan lifted it off and handed it to the young boy who already had a multicoloured collection scrunched in his fist.

It was a long time since she'd reacted like that to a man's touch, and it left her dazed.

The palms of Evan's hands settled on firm, strong legs that were long but not lanky. His dark hair had a delicate sprinkling of greys just visible when he dipped his head to look at her, reminding her of George Clooney in his late thirties. She watched as he fiddled with his collar, loosening it around the neck where his tie held it firmly in place.

'You look uncomfortable,' she said.

'I'm not used to this kind of get-up. Suits are strictly for weddings and funerals. And Jem's birthday parties.'

'Don't you wear a suit for work?' She could see him as a lawyer or a manager of some sort, poised and self-assured, ready to argue his case.

'I'm a teacher, so I can't be overly scruffy, but it's definitely a smart-casual dress code.'

So much for the lawyer theory, but as he spoke about his occupation, Maddie realised that, as well as his obvious physical appeal, he had an approachable demeanour, was easy to talk to and was a good listener too. In fact, by the time they finished chatting, she realised how much being a teacher suited him.

Jem appeared beside them as Evan began to fidget with his shirt collar again. 'I told you to wear whatever you wanted, Evan. But you do look gorgeous in a suit. Doesn't he look gorgeous, Maddie?'

What was she supposed to say to that? Was she supposed to admit that her insides had flipped over when he first introduced himself? Or should she say she found it difficult to look at him without her mind running on spin cycle, wondering whether her words would come out as gobbledegook or not? Luckily, she didn't have to answer as Ava appeared, barefoot after dumping her shoes and socks beneath a chair.

'Uncle Evan, will you dance with me again?'

Maddie wasn't sure anyone could resist Ava's smile and the two honey-coloured bunches that swung from their bottle-green bows on each side of her head.

'How about you start and I'll be over in a sec?'

Jem turned to talk to a gentleman dressed in a tweed jacket with leather pads on the elbows.

'Are you hanging around, Maddie?' Evan asked.

'I'd better not.' She glanced at her watch. 'I'm due at the bachelorette party right about now.'

Ava was at Evan's side again, tugging at his hand.

'Give me a minute, Ava.' Evan ignored the pulling. 'Well, it was lovely to meet you, Maddie.'

His words cascaded through her body with every syllable.

Ava pulled some more, as though Evan's arm were a rope in a tug of war. And as Maddie collected her bag, he remained rooted to the spot as though he wanted to add something.

'I wonder if my wish will come true,' said Jem, scurrying over when she realised Maddie was leaving.

'What wish?' Evan successfully won the tug of war battle when Ava dropped his arm in lieu of following this more interesting development.

'What wish, Grandma Jem?' asked Ava.

'The wish I made when I blew out the candles on my sensible cake.' She winked at Maddie.

'Tell me what you wished for.' Ava grabbed Jem's arm this time but didn't attack it with anywhere near the severity that she had with Evan's. Lucky, as

12

Maddie suspected Jem would be the one to come off worse.

Jem smoothed down the child's bunches and stooped to whisper something in her ear.

'Uncle Evan? Are you going to make Maddie your girlfriend?'

Evan and Maddie stood aghast, but Jem sniggered. 'Come on, you two. You're both single, you're both around the same age. Make an old girl happy. I don't have time to beat around the bush at my ripe old age and I want to see my grandson happy. I hope to see you again, Maddie.' And with that, she took Ava's hand to the dance floor and left Evan and Maddie to deal with the words that still hung in the air.

Maddie felt her cheeks burn. It was impossible to look up at Evan.

'Well, that was embarrassing,' he said.

They stood side by side watching Ava and Jem dance; it was far easier than looking at each other.

'Embarrassing? I don't think anything can trump unveiling a huge penis cake at a one-hundredth birthday party.'

His laugh warmed her right through. 'True. So, what do you think?'

'What do I think of what?'

'Jem's wish. Do we make it come true? Can I ask you out?'

She pretended to be engrossed in watching some of the more senior guests getting their knees up the best they could to 'Party Rock'. She opened her mouth to answer his question but nothing came out, so instead she tried to flick off the party streamers caught up on one of her ballet flats.

Evan bent down and pulled the yellow and pink strands away from her foot, and when his hand grazed the skin on her ankle, she felt excitement ripple through her body. She so desperately wanted to say yes.

'Evan, I …'

He stood and held up his hands as though pre-empting her words. 'No offence taken.' His eyes held hers for a moment longer. 'Enjoy the bachelorette party.'

When other men asked her out, it was easy to turn them down, or she'd go out with them once and then never called them again. This was new to Maddie. *This man* she wanted to see again, and she scolded herself for not being able to think of anything to say.

She left the function room for the second time that day. Baking cakes let her lose herself in a world she was in control of, a world in which the boundaries were only determined by her. But today she felt more out of control than she had felt in a long time. Evan had rattled her. Past casual flings had never made her nervous like this; they had never left her tongue-tied. And she hadn't experienced such powerful chemistry with anyone since Riley.

A little voice inside her head told Maddie it was time she let another man into her life, but it had spoken up too late and she had missed her chance.

Some said it was better to have loved and lost than never to have loved at all, but Maddie wasn't so sure. Perhaps not letting anyone else in was the right thing to do. That way she would never expose herself to the type of pain she had experienced before and hoped she never had to go through again.

Chapter Two

When Evan woke the next morning with only the slightest headache from the party the day before, he was relieved to be in the familiar surroundings of his own apartment. Following Jem's celebrations he had ended up in a bar with his brother-in-law, Ben, and he could remember a blonde – Sadie? – leaving him in no doubt that she wanted to spend the night with him. She was gorgeous, had a smoking hot body with legs that went on for miles, but it still hadn't been enough for him. He couldn't push Maddie out of his mind, and he began to wonder whether the desire to be with one special person was something that came with age. Maybe that was it; at the ripe old age of thirty-eight, perhaps he was finally heading towards maturity.

The faultless autumn morning in Melbourne couldn't be overlooked. He had time to head out for a run before he went over to Jem's place to put up the painting he had bought her for her birthday.

A light breeze caressed the back of his neck as he pounded the pavements from his apartment block just behind the Exhibition Centre down to Albert Park Lake.

The sun, suspended between broken clouds, splintered the surface of the lake as he ran past the sailing club. He ran wide around a swan with her waddling cygnets, and then he fell back in step beside the shimmering section of the water's edge again.

Running always gave Evan the space to think, and the only thing on his mind this morning was Maddie. Last night, she hadn't blatantly turned him down; he hadn't given her the chance to actually say the word *no*, but he suspected that was going to be her response. Perhaps that was the attraction. Perhaps if she'd said yes, he wouldn't be so obsessed by her, by the thought of her bum in those figure-hugging jeans, the allure of her caramel-coloured hair tidied into a neat ponytail he wanted to release and run his fingers through.

*

When he arrived at Jem's place, Evan pulled his toolbox from the boot of his swish black Audi TT and then pressed the remote on his key ring to lock it and set the alarm. Holly thought his car was unnecessarily flashy and that he would always love it more than any woman; sometimes he was inclined to agree with her.

'Evan!' Jem pulled open the door to her unit that sat a couple of streets back from the beach in the trendy suburb of Albert Park. She enveloped her grandson in as big a hug as she could manage, considering she only came up to his chest.

'Before I set you to work, have a slice of cake.' Jem disappeared along a narrow corridor until she reached the open-plan kitchen and lounge. 'It's a lemon drizzle, freshly baked this morning,' she added when he set down his toolbox.

'You're a star. Now tell me, is it better than the birthday cake?'

She scrunched up her nose. 'I didn't complain too much about that as your mother arranged it from a caterer, but next time I want Maddie's number.'

'Don't we all?' He had known it wouldn't be long before Jem mentioned Maddie.

'You know, I could've sworn she'd jump at the chance to go out with you.' She cut a slice of cake for Evan and a smaller one for herself. 'You need a woman in your life.' She made her point with the knife still in hand.

He was glad he had a mouthful of cake so she couldn't see him smirk. The lecture sounded all too familiar because the women in his family had formed a united front to get him married off. Last week it had been Holly telling him he was going to be forty and alone if he wasn't careful; a few weeks ago his mum had taken him aside and asked him whether he had anyone serious in his life. He hadn't prolonged the conversation with either of them because there was nothing to tell.

'Don't worry about me.' He devoured the cake, including the final crumbs, then slipped the plate into the hot soapy water in the sink. 'Now where do you want me to put this new painting of yours?'

Once Jem showed him the section of wall where she wanted it hung, he said, 'I'm glad you like it. It took me forever to think of something for you.' He rummaged through the toolbox to find a spirit level. 'What do you buy the girl who has everything?'

When Jem laughed it was like music to his ears, always had been.

'Where did you find the painting?' she asked.

He tapped his nose. 'Let's just say that your friend Stan tipped me off.' He'd found it in an unassuming tiny gallery not far from Melbourne's Central Business District, but he would never have known it was there had it not been for the covert detective phase prior to her birthday.

'Well it's bright and colourful. Exactly what I wanted.'

Evan pencilled marks on the wall and used the spirit level to get the position of the hooks just right before he assembled the electric drill and pushed in the correct attachment.

After he lifted the painting into position, he stood back alongside Jem to admire the scene of Melbourne's Brighton Beach bathing boxes sitting proudly on golden sands. Although they remained as they did over one hundred years ago, licensees often differentiated the boxes by painting them different colours, or by adding their own design. In this painting, one bathing box had the Australian flag painted on its door; another had a mermaid; others were an array of banana yellows, turquoise, baby blues and pillar box reds.

'It reminds me of some good family times,' said Jem. 'Grandad Bernie and I used to watch you play in the ocean for hours, and then we'd all bundle into our little bathing box when the sun got too much, or when the summer rain started, and we'd play cards. Do you remember?'

'Of course I do.' He hugged her. 'I must say thank you to Stan when I next see him.'

'He's home from hospital now.'

'Stan?' Evan shooed away Jem's offer to sweep up the debris and crouched down with dustpan and brush in hand.

'He had a growth removed from his leg. He was lucky, mind.'

'Why's that?' Evan ran the brush along the ridge of the skirting board and knocked the dust he had created with his handiwork into the pan.

'The lump turned out to be nothing, but it could have easily been worse. Getting older you have to be careful of these things. I've always been good at getting myself checked. You know, women's checks.'

'Yeah, I don't need the details.'

'All I'm saying, Evan, is that it's better to be careful, and you need to act quickly if anything is amiss.'

He wondered whether Jem really did have a sixth sense when it came to knowing things about her family. She had known when Holly fell pregnant with Ava, even before Holly had taken the test herself; she had been the one to leap on his instant attraction to Maddie by instigating him asking her out. And now, the poignancy of her words were a reminder that nobody, young nor old, could afford to be complacent about their health, least of all him.

When he left that day, he knew Jem's words had given him the kick up the arse he needed. It was time to stop burying his head in the sand; it was time he had that lump checked out.

Chapter Three

Maddie squeezed past the group of teenagers huddled beside the doorway of the tram and tracked down the last spare seat towards the back, next to an open window. She watched the suburbs pass by as the breeze delicately toyed with her hair. Her hand rested on her Kindle, but instead of tapping in her password and diving into her latest book, she found her thoughts drifting back to last weekend.

When she had finally made it to the bachelorette party, a whiff of alcohol had snaked through the air, and she'd laughed with the gaggle of girls crowding round and pointing at several peculiar-looking attempts to fashion a penis out of clay.

But that wasn't the party that had stuck in her mind.

Jem's party had taken up a considerable amount of her thinking time over the last few days. She could still picture Evan's smile, his height, the stubble that hypnotised her when he spoke.

Typical. The girl opposite was talking into her phone at a volume more suitable for a nightclub than a tram full of commuters.

'Did you see the news feature on Ground Zero this morning?' The girl spoke with an American accent.

Maddie's heart quickened. She pulled her iPod from her bag – perfect for this sort of emergency – as the girl's voice rose above the volume of the other commuters.

'I still think of all those people, their families …' the girl continued.

The American accent, combined with the topic of conversation, felt like tiny hammers beating away inside Maddie's head as it brought everything flooding back to her. Her hands shook as she fumbled with her headphones, and she only relaxed when the sounds of Pink belted out so loud that the girl shot her a turn-it-down-I'm-trying-to-talk-here dirty look.

As the tune pounded her eardrums, Maddie was right back there on the morning when she had woken to the terrible telephone call, that split second when her life moved from what was so familiar to what she never imagined it could be.

On September 11th 2001, the world's worst terror attacks in New York had changed her life, and so many others', unequivocally. Maddie's boyfriend, Riley, was working in New York, and that morning he had an important meeting in the North Tower of the World Trade Center. He had spoken at length with Maddie the night before about his excitement. His firm had given him the reins, and he was leading the meeting and presenting to an important client who was looking to employ Riley's team of management consultants.

Maddie had assumed it would be Riley calling, nervous about the interview, and she'd answered the phone with a smile. But it was Caitlin, his mum, and as Maddie had listened to her urgent voice, she flicked on the television to see the news filling most channels; the news that shocked the entire world.

Even now she could remember those images vividly: the smoke and dust billowing out of the North tower; debris raining from the skies; sirens blaring in the background; the screams that filled the streets.

'I love you.' Those were her last words to Riley, and as the tram spat her out on Collins Street in Melbourne's Central Business District, Maddie remembered Riley repeating those exact words back to her. They'd been each other's pasts, they were supposed to be each other's future, but in the blink of an eye all that had disappeared.

Feeling empty inside, Maddie crossed the road and pushed through the glass entrance doors of the building where she worked on the fourth floor at Palmer's Physiotherapy. She pulled out her headphones and muttered hello to Tilly, the receptionist, who called out her compliments for the chocolate mud cake Maddie had supplied for her birthday over the weekend. Usually she was prepared for exactly what had just happened on the tram. On the anniversary of Riley's death, she always started the day armed with her iPod and a playlist full of loud rock songs that obliterated the world around her; she would leave the television switched off for a few days either side of the actual date; she never so much as glanced at a newspaper or the billboards that graced the little kiosks on so many street corners in Melbourne's CBD; she avoided Facebook, Twitter and all other social media.

But today she had been caught out. Today was nowhere near the anniversary of 9/11, and it was on occasions like this that she wasn't quite the prepared Girl Scout whom she wanted to be.

Throwing herself into her work was always a great antidote. A busy morning focusing on sore knees, back problems and neck issues helped Maddie block out thoughts of Riley and the day that would haunt her forever. But in the staffroom at lunchtime, as she released the elastic band from around a plastic tray of sushi, her colleague Stuart dumped a newspaper right beside her and familiar words and pictures hit her in the face like a giant slap. The headline of the article about the opening of the new National September 11 Memorial & Museum taunted her, and she pushed her food away.

Maddie wondered if the coverage of that day, or anything to do with 9/11 whatsoever, would ever be relegated so far to the back of the newspapers and the backs of the minds of the media that it fell out of the news altogether.

Maddie's phone pinged with an incoming text message. It was Adam, a mistake she had made almost a month ago. She hit delete. Unfortunately, he hadn't yet realised she wasn't interested in a repeat performance. Short, sharp flings had become a habit since Riley, and men like Adam lasted barely as long as a litre of milk before she pulled away. Getting attached and relying on someone was where it all went wrong; that was where you risked leaving yourself open to hurt, open to pain.

*

After work Maddie stopped at the supermarket. It was Ally's mum's birthday this Friday and she had promised to bake a cake for her. Flour was the last item on her list, and she wasn't thrilled to see half of the packets had white dust leaking from the bottom.

She stood on tiptoes to try to reach one from a higher shelf, and her fingertips gradually worked the packet towards the edge.

'Here, let me do that.' A familiar voice came from behind her as a hand stretched up and deftly plucked the package from the shelf.

'Evan.'

He gripped the large package in the palm of his hand and laid it carefully into the basket looped over her arm. She watched him eye the rest of the items she had collected. Thank goodness she didn't have tampons or condoms in there or she knew she would be going a lot redder than she was right now.

He looked thoughtful. 'You're not making another penis are you?'

'It's a birthday cake for a friend, and a lot more tasteful. It'll be a gift box with plain chocolate and white chocolate bows around the edge,' she babbled.

Evan watched her intently, and it gave her the same giddy feelings she'd had at the party last weekend. He leaned against a shelf full of packets of sugar, his hands pushed into a faded pair of Levis. 'You turned me down when I asked you out.'

'I didn't turn you down, I just didn't answer.' Her heart quickened as she noticed his manly arms that hadn't been on show last time they met. His skin was lightly tanned, and subtle-yet-definitely-there biceps sat beneath dark-grey T-shirt sleeves.

'It's the same thing.'

His eyes looked as though they could get their way whenever he wanted, the way a magician could move an object across the table by staring at it for long enough.

'I'm going to go out on a limb here,' he rushed on, saving her from providing an explanation. 'Can I take you out to dinner? I promise I'll behave and I won't even mention that cake. If you really don't have a good time, just don't go out with me again.'

He made it sound so simple.

'Okay,' she said before she could talk herself out of it.

'Okay what?'

'Dinner sounds good.'

'Fantastic.' He pulled out his phone. 'If you give me your number, I'll text you and then you'll have mine. How does Friday sound?'

'Friday would be great.' She reeled off her details and he tapped them into the device.

He picked up the empty basket down by his feet. 'I'll see you Friday.'

As Maddie made for the checkout and Evan headed in the opposite direction, she wondered when it would hit her that Evan was no different from the other men that had come along since Riley. Sure, there was a strong attraction, but was there really anything that separated him from the rest?

When she boarded the tram, her phone pinged to signal an incoming message:

It's a date. E.

Short and to the point, but it was enough to make Maddie smile; not the fake smile she sometimes put on, either, like the smile she sometimes forced with men who lasted no more than one or two dates.

She sat back in her seat as the tram began its battle through the rush hour traffic along the grand boulevard of St Kilda Road towards her apartment. If Evan was just like all the rest, then why was she so agitated every time she saw him or when she found herself thinking about him as she was doing now?

Maddie had known pain plenty of times before. She'd had her appendix out when she was eight, her hamster died when she was ten, and she remembered being clobbered accidentally by a baseball bat when she walked behind the batsman at an interschool match. But those types of pain were short-lived. They hurt for a while, but with a bit of tender loving care, she got over them. Riley had been the love of her life, and she was his; when he died the raw yet numbing pain had never left Maddie's side and part of her had died too. The only difference was her body remained above ground.

Maddie wasn't sure whether anyone got two chances at real happiness, but maybe, just maybe, Evan was the man to make her take a risk and try again.

Chapter Four

Maddie lifted the plastic cover and revealed the gift box cake. 'Well, what do you think?'

'I think it's totally awesome.' Ally leaned in to smell the chocolate creation. 'It smells like heaven. Thank you so much. Mum will love it.'

Maddie dropped the fondant ribbon cutter into the sink. 'You can borrow that cake carrier to take it home with you if you like. And let me know how the party goes tonight.'

'I will, on one condition.' Ally clipped down the plastic sides of the carrier.

'What's that?'

'You fill me in with all the juicy details about Evan when I next see you.'

Maddie rolled her eyes. 'Of course, now off you go or you'll be late.'

After Ally left, Maddie headed for the shower. She laughed at her reflection – she had flour on one ear lobe and across an eyebrow and dried white chocolate on her wrist. As she let the water wash away the evidence, she wondered whether tonight's date with Evan would be as successful as she wanted it to be. Perhaps tonight it would be her attitude that could make all the difference. Perhaps being open to possibilities could finally enable her to move forwards.

She blow-dried her hair and then pulled on her favourite Stitch's jeans, an ink-coloured top with a twist in the neckline and slipped into navy ballet flats with a crushed velvet appearance to complete the outfit. She adopted the obligatory mascara-pose with eyes wide and mouth open as she stroked the wand against her eyelashes, and she applied the faintest stroke of mocha eye shadow. With a dash of berry lip gloss that highlighted straight, white teeth – courtesy of dental plates and train-track braces that had coincided with puberty blues – she was ready to go.

She pulled a cardigan from the wardrobe, and it was then that her eyes fell on the shoe box on the shelf above the clothes rail. She rarely opened it these days, but Evan had stirred up feelings Maddie had thought she would never know again, and tonight she was drawn to its contents.

She pulled off the tatty lid to reveal the few mementoes she had kept from her time with Riley, including a bundle of letters dating back to when he first arrived in New York and a collection of postcards from the Big Apple. She didn't read those, and she didn't pull out the movie stub from their first date, either, nor the friendship bracelet he had given her on their first holiday up to Noosa. Instead, she took out the single, framed photograph – she had heaps of photos from their years as a couple, but they were stashed away within albums. Deep-green, trusting eyes looked back at her from beneath a light-brown fringe; a chiselled jaw harboured lips she had kissed a thousand times or more. This was the picture she kept for such times, times when she needed to run her hand across the glass of the frame as though she could feel his skin, the warmth from his mouth, the softness of his breath.

The autumn light had already begun to fade, and with a sigh Maddie replaced the lid of the box and pushed it to the back of the wardrobe. She was about to go on a date with a man who excited her, who made her heart do somersaults. She hoped tonight she would be able to smile and laugh freely without doing what she usually did, which was to imagine it was Riley sitting opposite her instead, laughing at one of their in-jokes nobody else understood.

The tram whisked Maddie from outside her apartment block to the historic Flinders Street Station, which dominated the banks of the Yarra River and basked in a sandy-coloured glow beneath the lights of the city. The grand station, topped with an enormous dome that shone at night like a golden beacon and visible for miles, was a cultural icon of Melbourne that linked suburbs to the big city.

Maddie passed underground, through the station, and over the pedestrian footbridge to Southbank, where the Crown Entertainment Complex, home to a casino, restaurants, cinemas and bars, lined one side of the river. Dotted along the boardwalk were tall, chimney-like towers which stood at around ten metres high. The start time was dependent upon the season, but usually when darkness descended, powerful orange fireballs would launch high into the air from the top of the towers, on the hour, every hour, and light up the night sky.

Maddie stood and watched the water run down from the grooved granite faces of the towers and listened to the gas stir inside as the time crept towards eight o'clock.

'We can come back on the hour to see the flames,' a voice said from behind her.

'Hi.' His gaze made her even more nervous than the time she had played the piano to the entire school in assembly.

The lights from the casino interrupted the velvet of the night sky and gave Evan's hair a subtle sheen. Her eyes briefly dipped to his strong jaw and the stubble that looked comfortable and exactly where it should be.

'Any thoughts on where you'd like to eat?' he asked. 'What's your favourite food?'

She was relieved that he hadn't asked her to name a restaurant because right now she felt sure she would struggle to remember her own surname. 'I love seafood,' she said instead. 'That is … unless you hate it?'

'I know the perfect place.' He tipped his head in the right direction and held out his arm for her to go first before the crowds descended in anticipation of the flame extravaganza. She felt his hand rest lightly in the small of her back as he guided her away from the water's edge and towards the restaurants. It was a presumptuous move, but one she didn't mind from him.

'How was the birthday cake for your friend?'

The flames launched into action as they walked away, and she felt her own temperature go up a notch. 'She loved it. Anything chocolate and we're both happy.' She tried to subtly take in his outfit. He wore a mid-blue, checked dress shirt beneath a lightweight navy jacket, and she was happy to see he had favoured jeans too. The cut suited him, and when she dropped back slightly to avoid colliding with a cyclist heading their way, she noticed a nice bum hugged by the denim.

'Any more orders of the 'interesting' variety?' He waited for her to catch up alongside him once again.

'No, not yet.' She smiled. 'Last year I did make a rather naughty Santa for a Christmas in July party.'

'Tell me more.'

She felt her tummy tie itself in a knot, not wanting to list the details now, wishing she hadn't blurted that out for something interesting to say.

'All I'll say is that there were some elves doing some pretty indecent things.'

'You're an interesting girl, Maddie.' His eyes lingered on her a moment longer than was comfortable.

At the restaurant the menu was overwhelming, or maybe it was the company that had thrown her. Maddie flicked to the second page and then the third, processing options of barramundi with lemon butter, seafood linguine, mussels in tomato and chilli sauce or crab ravioli.

Evan looked up from his menu. 'How would you feel about sharing something?'

'Honestly? I'd feel relieved. I'm having a hard time trying to decide what *not* to have.'

When the waiter appeared and made a fuss of shaking out the starched napkins from their swan shapes, Evan ordered the seafood platter for two. Maddie watched him all the while: the sneaky glimpse of his wrist as his fingers stretched out to point to a menu item, the firmness of his torso beneath his shirt. She couldn't drag her eyes away.

'Red or white?' asked Evan. 'Wine,' he added for clarification when she looked blank.

Had he seen her gawping at him as though he was the first man she had ever seen?

They settled on a bottle of Sauvignon Blanc and when the waiter left them alone, Evan asked, 'So how was your day?'

She flicked her hair behind her shoulder and tried to relax. 'Busy.'

'That makes two of us. Although, I bet you didn't have to separate two males getting physical over a whiteboard eraser.'

'True,' she smiled. 'Do you enjoy being a teacher?'

'Mostly, yes, although some days are more challenging than others. But hey, where else can I go to work and be greeted by twenty-two co-workers who are ecstatic to see me?'

'That's a good point. So where do you teach?'

'I teach at Huntley Primary School not far from Huntley High Street. I've got year ones this time round, which is a bit easier than the newbies.'

The waiter returned and held out the wine bottle for Evan's inspection. Evan shook his head at the offer to taste.

'I hate it when they do that,' he said when the waiter took their bottle away to put it on ice.

'You mean when they ask you to taste?'

'Well that, yes, but I meant when they whisk the bottle away and top you up discreetly so you've no idea how much you've had to drink.'

'And you have no idea why you end up totally sloshed?'

'Exactly, but at least I don't live far so I don't need to worry about driving.'

'Me either.'

They launched into a conversation about the merits of living in the city as opposed to the suburbs.

The seafood platter arrived and Maddie's eyes widened at the enormity of it as the waiter laid out some tools of the trade.

'Sorry, you first,' said Evan as they both went for the same Moreton Bay bug.

'Thank you.' Maddie lifted the red-shelled crustacean that had been cooked in garlic butter with parsley on to her plate and Evan took the other. She bit into the white, opaque, firm flesh from the tail.

Evan lifted an Oyster Kilpatrick next, and as he tipped his head back to swallow the tangy sauce from the shell, Maddie tried to take her eyes away from the flesh of his neck where the stubble stopped to reveal bare skin. She noticed his tongue moved briefly between his lips to catch any remnants.

'We're spoilt in Australia with all this seafood.' As a distraction she reached for an Oyster Kilpatrick and savoured the flavour of the bacon and the sauce, which brought out the sweetness and saltiness of the food.

'You're not wrong,' he agreed. 'Mind you, I went to Sri Lanka a few years ago and had an out-of-this-world squid curry.'

'Have you travelled much?'

'Not a huge amount. I was never one of those people who went backpacking for a year before they found a job. After University I completed my work experience stint, and that was that. Money permitting, I try to see a bit of the world in the holidays though.'

'The holidays must be a perk.'

'They are, but contrary to what many people believe, teachers do have to put in extra time at home for planning, marking, keeping on top of the latest education developments. So what about you? Did you do the backpacking thing?'

'I've only travelled in the holidays, and even then it's expensive. I wanted to buy my apartment so that put a stop to any more worldly experiences for a while. And I'm a bit of a homebody, to be honest.'

'You don't have to be embarrassed by that,' he admonished.

'I'm not.' She'd taken herself by surprise at how easy the conversation was flowing. 'Don't get me wrong, I'd love to see more of the world one day, but I also love this country and we have so many beautiful places right on our doorstep.'

'Here, here.' Evan raised his glass and Maddie chinked hers against it.

'Mind you, I did have a very bad experience in Tasmania once,' said Maddie.

'Do tell.'

'I went over there with my friend Ally and we stayed in a bed and breakfast over the Easter weekend. We went to a beautiful seafood restaurant and Ally had a steak – she isn't a fan of anything fishy or seafood-like – but I had the garlic prawns. Anyway, that night I was up vomiting and it carried on until three days later when we headed back to Melbourne.'

'I bet that ruined the weekend, didn't it?'

'Not only that. It was freezing and rained the entire time, and the owner of the bed and breakfast was a complete cow. Ally had asked her to stay out of the room because I was sick, and eight o'clock one morning when Ally had gone for a walk, there she was vacuuming in the hallway, bashing the blessed thing into the door. I couldn't wait to come home after that.'

'It sounds like she had it in for you two.'

'Oh, she did. The night of the food poisoning, Ally got wasted on wine and ended up falling into the table in the hall and smashing the vase on it. She was so drunk that she insisted we wake the owner to tell her what had happened. The owner was none too happy with us.'

Amused by the disaster story, Evan told one of his own. 'I once went to Noosa with my girlfriend at the time, and we got so drunk on the first night that we went skinny dipping.'

'Oh no, please tell me you didn't get caught.'

'We did, by the hotel manager. But he was male and when he saw Kate – she had a pretty good body – he let us off with a warning.'

'Ah, a bit like when a woman flutters her eyelashes at a parking inspector and he lets her off?'

'Exactly,' said Evan.

'So why was it a disaster if you didn't get into trouble?'

'Kate ended up copping off with the manager the following night. I fell asleep after a day at the beach and she'd left me a note to say she had gone to the bar. She probably didn't think I'd join her, but I did, and there she was kissing the face off of him.'

'Surely he should've been disciplined.'

'It was his night off.'

Maddie sniggered. 'I'm sorry, it's not funny.'

Evan couldn't help laughing either. 'It's okay. Kate was only ever a bit of fun anyway.'

Maddie wondered whether tonight's date was just a bit of fun too.

'So when was your last date, Maddie?'

His question took her by surprise.

'It was a blind date.' She cringed.

'Bad?'

'Worse. The guy took me to a curry house.' She relaxed as the wine took effect, and she began to worry less and less about Evan's agenda and whether this would lead anywhere. 'When I asked what was in the sauce, the guy pointed out a few of the ingredients including a long, green vegetable and told me it was a runner bean. Anyway, I bit off a great big chunk of it. It turned out to be a chilli and a bloody hot one too.'

He couldn't hide his amusement. 'You mean you couldn't spot that it was a chilli?'

'Call me naïve, but I was never that into curries and the sauce disguised pretty much everything in the dish. I'd had a few drinks by then as well – I needed to, the guy wasn't exactly my type – so I believed him. He thought it was hysterical, which is the other thing – he had a laugh exactly like a seal, and I had to listen to it all the way home. He thought he was so funny. He tried to kiss me too, but by that point I couldn't even stand being near him.'

The fact that Evan couldn't stop laughing now just made her grin all the more. 'Stop it, it wasn't funny.'

When he had himself under control, he asked, 'So what exactly is your type if it wasn't him?'

Maddie swigged on her wine so she had a chance to think of an answer. 'I don't really have one.' All she could think of was that right now she was looking at the prime candidate, and it was then she realised she hadn't thought about Riley all evening, she hadn't pictured sitting opposite him instead.

Maddie took some blue swimmer crab from the seafood platter and pulled out the flesh using the seafood cracker. Evan seemed impressed with her prowess, and after the crab it was on to the delicate white-fleshed snapper.

'Are you from Melbourne originally?' Maddie rinsed her fingertips in the tiny bowl of water as the waiter appeared with two dessert menus.

'I am. Melbourne born and bred. I like my Victoria Bitter and I like my footy. My family is here too, which I guess makes all the difference. How about you, are you a Melbourne girl?'

She tore her eyes away from his lips. 'I was born in Sydney, in the Northern Beaches, and my parents are still there, but I've been here for over fourteen years, so it feels more like home now.'

The waiter took Maddie's order for the sticky date pudding, and Evan chose a liqueur coffee.

'You make me feel greedy now,' she chided.

'Don't be daft. I like a girl who eats rather than one who pretends not to and then pinches half of my food.'

Most of the evening had flown by with ease as though they were on their fifth or sixth date rather than their first, but every now and again Evan's attention caught Maddie off-guard and reminded her of how new this all was. They talked some more about their workplaces, Evan regaling stories of amusing kids, naughty kids and the frustrations he sometimes faced as a teacher. Maddie talked about her awkward experiences as a physiotherapist, careful not to betray patient confidentiality, but at the same time amusing him with tales of body odour issues and excessive hair problems.

'I can't imagine you being a physio for rugby players, you don't look butch enough.' He seemed surprised when she told him Palmer's Physiotherapy was the first port of call for a well-known and very successful local team.

She flexed a bicep, spurred on by the alcohol that had been topped up as discreetly as expected. 'These muscles have a lot of power, you know.'

'I'm sure they do.'

The arrival of the dessert broke his stare at her across the table.

'Do you enjoy being a physio?' Evan asked.

'I do. I enjoy unravelling the mystery with anything from neck pain to back issues, and putting together a solution certainly keeps me on my toes. But I didn't realise how much baking excited me until I was at University. It became an escape from the books, away from the rigours of learning about anatomy.'

'I can understand that.'

'Baking became the dream and physiotherapy was the reality. When I'm baking I'm in heaven. Looking back I'm glad I chose the physiotherapy path, it's certainly a varied career. But I do dream sometimes of starting up my own cake business – maybe when my muscles get too tired of working with beefy rugby players I'll do it.'

He returned her smile. 'You could start a little side business now. Keep up the physiotherapy work but bake on weekends. That way you'll know if it's going to work before you chuck in the day job.'

She nodded, revelling in his support.

'You could build up your client base – even the biggest businesses had to start from somewhere.'

She looked down at the dessert she had almost forgotten was in front of her. Riley had said something similar to her the night before he died. He had vented about his presentation, she had let loose about how tired she was after an overflow of patients that day, daydreaming about what it would be like to bake all day instead.

'What's the sauce?' Evan's voice interrupted her reverie.

'Butterscotch. Here, try some.' She passed over her spoon filled with the rich, moreish sauce. She didn't realise the intimacy of the gesture until the spoon had passed between his lips and had been pulled out clean. It took her a moment to realise he was handing the spoon back to her.

She hid behind the pleasure of the sinful brown sugar-based sponge and the richness of the dates as she finished another mouthful of dessert. 'I'll definitely need a run tomorrow morning after this, it's a bit naughty.'

'You're a runner?'

'Don't I look like one?' She raised her eyebrows.

'It's not that, it's just that running is my thing too. It's nice to see we have things in common.'

Her heart skipped a beat because, so far tonight, it was all too good to be true.

He blew across the top of his coffee. 'Where do you run?'

'I do the Tan Track or run alongside the Yarra. Sometimes I head all the way down to the beach, up to Port Melbourne and Albert Park, maybe take in the lake.'

'That's quite a distance. I do similar routes, but you can't beat a run around the lake. Running around a big expanse of water never fails to make me happy. You should pop in and see Jem when you're next running through Albert Park. She doesn't live too far from the beach.'

Her dessert didn't quite slide down as smoothly as it could have as his suggestion implied that this had already gone way beyond a single date or a single night of unbridled passion with no strings attached.

'She likes having visitors. She complains that the only people coming round these days are religious door-knockers or real estate agents waiting for her to cark it!'

Glad that the wine hadn't yet reached her lips when she giggled, she asked, 'Were they Jem's exact words?'

'More or less.' He shrugged. 'But I'd suggest you go and see her after your run or she'll be feeding you cakes like that one.' He pointed at the last remnants of sticky date pudding.

'I'll try to remember that.'

He sipped his coffee and then said, 'Question time.'

'That sounds frighteningly like a challenge to a truth or dare game to me.'

'Not at all. At least not on our first date anyway.'

The way he looked at her sent ripples of excitement through her.

'Think of it as a getting-to-know-each-other game,' he explained. 'Right, first question: what's your most hated meal, ever?'

'Easy. Crappy breadcrumbed fish fillets from the freezer section of Coles supermarket with rank parsley sauce and peas.'

'That's pretty specific.'

She moved her hands as the waiter confirmed that they had finished and went to make up the bill. 'My mum used to serve it up every Friday, and I grew to hate it more and more each week.' She pulled a face. 'Okay, your turn.'

'Tuna and pasta bake – it's like vomit on a plate.'

'No it's not,' she chuckled. 'I quite like it.'

'That and vegemite, which I can't stand,' he added.

'You can't say that and call yourself an Aussie!'

'It's revolting. I reckon tar on the roads tastes better than that stuff. Okay, moving swiftly on … It's no use asking you about your favourite dessert as I think I know that already.'

'Actually, as nice as the sticky date was, I'd say chocolate mud cake was my absolute favourite. I didn't want to be too predictable though.' She didn't add that tonight she hoped to finally start down a new path, so the dessert had been in keeping with that theme.

Ignoring her pleas to pay half the bill when it arrived, Evan handed over his credit card. 'Mine is Jem's syrup sponge. You'll have to try it one day.'

She gulped at yet another reminder that he was in this for more than one date. He was so good looking, so sexy; he could have any woman he wanted, surely.

His eyes held hers. 'Next question: who's your favourite person?'

'Oh no, you're not expecting me to say *you* are you?'

He laughed. 'Present company excluded.'

'It's a tie between Mum and Dad.'

'You get on well with your parents?'

'Always have done. I don't see them as often as I should, but they're always in my mind.' She was lost in thought for a second. 'I always remember what a friend once said to me. She said she loved coming to our house when we were kids because we could make a mess. We used to cook, get muddy outside, and my parents were always so relaxed. And aside from the discipline they had to have as parents, I guess their attitude has always been relaxed towards me and my sister. They've let us make our own way in life and supported our moves, our decisions, but have always been there to pick up the pieces.'

Her parents had certainly been there to pick up the pieces after Riley was killed; she had been a total mess, still was in some ways.

'Who's your favourite person?' She asked before he had a chance to probe any further into her answer.

'Mum, of course, but equally I would have to say Jem.'

'Have you always been close?'

'We have. I suppose in much the same way as your parents, she was always relaxed and fun but certainly knew when to be strict and rein me in. Mum is a wonderful woman too. She can be a bit overprotective, but then what mum isn't about her kids?'

As Maddie pulled on her thin-weave cardigan, she stole a glance at Evan. His face had a softness sitting beneath the rugged exterior that she doubted many would be able to resist.

As they walked towards the door, his hand fell against the small of her back in the gesture that already felt familiar, surprisingly comfortable.

'You'd better let me pay next time,' she said.

'It's a deal.' He playfully nudged her arm. 'I'm not so chivalrous that I'll never let you pay, but it's not right on the first date. I'd never hear the end of it from Jem if she found out I'd taken you on a date and made you pay.'

'I can imagine.' Maddie chuckled.

'Come on, it's almost ten so if we're quick we'll get to see the flames.' She wasn't prepared for it, but when his larger, warm hand wrapped around her own as they picked up the pace, much the same as it had encased the packet of flour in the supermarket, she didn't resist.

A small crowd had gathered a few steps back from the mighty columns that were already whirring up, ready for their hourly performance. With a whoosh, great fireballs leapt into the air in quick succession, lighting up the ground beneath and warming the faces of onlookers, highlighting their smiles against the night sky. The heat between them as Evan stood beside her and his arm brushing against hers felt as intense as the flames themselves, and Maddie didn't ever want the moment to end.

'Pretty spectacular don't you think?' His voice flickered in her ear when he dipped his head to her height. 'I don't think I'll ever get tired of seeing those.'

'Me either.' She gulped.

They stayed there until the columns fell silent once again.

The autumn days were still bathed in sunshine, but come the evening Melburnians were reminded that summer had passed once again. 'Are you warm enough?' Evan asked as they continued along the banks of the river, away from the crowds and towards the steps that would take them back up to street level.

Maddie pulled her cardigan tighter around herself. 'I'm fine, thanks.'

They took the flight of steps leading up to St Kilda Road, and Maddie said, 'I'll wait for a tram, shouldn't be long.' She indicated the tram stop in the centre of the road where people jostled about checking the timetable against their watches.

'How about I walk you home tonight? Seeing as it's our first date.'

She hesitated, and then said, 'Come on.' She tilted her head in the direction of home.

As they left the city behind them, Evan said, 'Tell me a bit more about yourself.'

'What else would you like to know?'

She wondered whether he was going to say 'everything', but instead he said, 'You mentioned that you have a sister.'

'That's right. Jennifer. She lives overseas, in London.' She felt a jolt of electricity as Evan moved her in front of him to let two elderly gentlemen pass as the pavement thinned. 'Jennifer loves the London vibe, and her job in events means she's with a young, energetic crowd.'

'How long has she been over there?'

'It's coming up to two years now.'

'Do you miss her?'

'Yes, of course.' Jennifer had been there alongside Ally when Riley died and had shown such strength for a girl whose sister had fallen apart in front of her. Jennifer and Ally had held Maddie up for long enough so that eventually she took her own steps back into the world.

'We chat over the iPad when we can, we text, and she visited last April.'

'Have you been over to London?'

'I'm busy with work these days, but if she's stays on much longer then I'll think about it. Mum and Dad are thinking of going over there soon, now that they've both retired.'

'I bet they miss having their kids around though. I know my mum did when we first left home.'

'I'm not sure about that. They've downsized and moved up to Palm Beach, and I think the beautiful location probably makes it bearable.' She grinned.

'They've never had so many hobbies since us girls left: hiking, Mum has taken up yoga – Dad refused and got more into his golf – and the latest is pottery classes, which sound amusing. Dad says his creations are an embarrassment, but I bet they're not. He's always been good with his hands right from when I was a little girl, and he made me the best doll's house ever. He was so proud of it, said it was the best thing he'd ever done with his free time.'

'Do you still have it?'

'It's stored at my parents' place for now. I don't think I'd ever get rid of it.'

It felt like the right time to mention it. 'I hope you don't mind me asking, Evan, but how old were you when your dad died?'

'Eight.'

'I'm sorry.' She looked up at him as he passed beneath a street lamp. She didn't need to ask how much Evan missed his dad; she could hear it in the catch of his voice, see it in the tension of his jaw.

'It was a long time ago,' he said.

'That doesn't matter, I bet it still hurts.'

'Whoever said time is a great healer was right, but the wound never completely heals over. It's like when you fall down and cut your knee badly – there's a lot of pain and blood, a decent scab for a while, and when it falls off you're left with a scar that fades in time but is always there, always remembered.'

Maddie wondered what stage she was at after more than thirteen years had passed since losing Riley.

She waited for a tram to rattle its way past. 'So to continue the quizzing game from the restaurant, what would you say would be the best thing you've ever done?'

'Ah, we're back to that again are we?' His grin tugged at her insides. 'I don't think I can come close to the creation of a doll's house, like your dad.'

'It doesn't have to be something you made … it could be something you did.'

'Well, that's easier.' He thought for a moment. 'I ran a marathon in Copenhagen in 2010 to raise money for leukaemia research.'

'I'm impressed.' She looked sideways at him to take in his strong profile and towering presence. 'I love running, but a marathon is quite something.'

'It was an awesome experience. We raised almost fifteen thousand dollars.'

'Good on you!'

'My mum was a teacher too, and a little girl in her class was diagnosed with leukaemia when she was nine. It was different back then. Thankfully medical science has come a long way since.'

Maddie was sure she hadn't mistaken a wobble in his voice as he pulled on his jacket when the autumn chill crept in. She wondered if, perhaps, he had known the little girl, or maybe it was his profession that made the situation all the more real.

He nudged her. 'So come on then, your turn. What's the best thing you've ever done?'

'This is going to sound unbelievably selfish – and I'm thinking in a different way to you here, which I'm not sure is painting me in the best light – but the best thing I ever did was to do a bungy jump in New Zealand.'

It was Evan's turn to stand and stare in awe. 'Now that's impressive. I'd never dare do that … which makes me sound like a complete wimp and that's not the impression I want to give *you*.'

They chanced the next set of lights, running across as the red illuminated man flickered urgently.

'So was it the big bungy, or the teeny-tiny one on the teeny-tiny little bridge?' Evan asked when they were safely across.

'You've been reading too many kids books about teeny-tiny things. And would you do the teeny-tiny one?'

'Ah, you got me there.'

'For your information, it was the big one, *The Nevis*.' Her insides clenched as she remembered being on that platform, ready to shuffle her feet closer to the edge and plunge head first over the magnificent Nevis river.

His hand rubbed across the stubble of his jaw. 'I'm impressed. No, I'm floored. So was it the absolute thrill that made it the best thing you've ever done?'

She thought back to the nausea she felt that day, the tears that pricked at her eyes as she fought the urge to back down at the last minute. 'I think it was more the fact that I didn't want to do it and once I did, well, it made me think anything was possible.'

She hadn't shared the entire bungy story with him of course. The New Zealand holiday had been a getaway a year after Riley died, and it was almost as though she wanted to free fall from that great height, head first, to remind herself that she still had a life to live; she was the lucky one to still be alive with a future ahead of her. The bungy had been the single most defining moment since Riley's death and the point at which she felt she had at least started to gather up the fragments of herself that had shattered all over the place like a smashed Christmas bauble.

'Is it much farther?' Evan's voice broke into her reverie.

'One more block.'

She wasn't sure, but she thought she heard him swallow, nervously, before he said, 'So, what's the worst thing that's ever happened to you?'

When she looked up at him he was staring straight ahead rather than down at her, as she had caught him doing so many times tonight.

She hesitated because she knew the exact answer, but confessing all the details on their first date wouldn't be right. 'I had a friend who died suddenly.' It wasn't a lie, but it wasn't the full truth, either, and she felt guilty.

'I'm sorry,' said Evan.

'Thanks.' Maddie stopped outside her apartment block with lit up square windows dotted about like open doors on an advent calendar. She dug around in her bag for her keys. 'So what's the worst thing that's ever happened to you?'

'I'm not sure it's happened yet.'

'Oh come on, that's against the rules of the game. You have to share.' Her hand shot to her mouth just as she found her keys. 'Oh no, your dad. I'm so sorry, I wasn't thinking.'

When he remained silent, she said, 'That was your answer, wasn't it?'

He leant up against a concrete bollard, unconcerned about the ivy which covered it and more than likely the creepy crawlies that inhabited it. She definitely hadn't mistaken the nervous gulp this time, and she watched the deep brown of his eyes search the night sky. They darted to her own and then away again.

'There's something else,' he said, and when he spoke again his words hit her like the tram ploughing through the centre of the road opposite the apartment block. 'I found out last week that I may have cancer.'

Chapter Five

The glass door in the foyer zipped open and shut, and they went inside the building. But out of the cold evening air Evan's announcement wasn't any less shocking. Without speaking they walked to the lift, and their silence continued as the lift crept up to the seventh floor, not daring to stop on the way.

'I don't have anything strong to offer you.' Maddie let the heavy door to her apartment thump closed behind them. 'I could make us a cup of tea?'

The atmosphere was stilted compared to only moments ago when they had chatted freely, in the heady phase of getting to know one another. Maddie blundered about the kitchen, pulling out cups, a tub of sugar, milk. Her eyes followed Evan, who took a seat on one of the two maroon sofas separated by a glass-topped coffee table.

When she sat down she watched him across the top of her cup as she blew the hot liquid. The tea wasn't quite the healer that so many people made it out to be, but it was a distraction nevertheless.

'I swear I didn't tell you that as a way to get you to invite me in.' Evan attempted to lighten the mood, but it didn't work.

Maddie realised she was shivering and put both hands around her mug of tea to try and stop her body's involuntary movement. She thought about how tonight was supposed to be different; different in a good way.

'Say something, please?' Evan put his full cup back on to the coffee table and the tap against the glass reverberated in the silence between them.

'I don't know what to say, Evan.'

'You're using my name when you talk to me. That's got to be serious.'

She felt some of the tension flow out of her body. Evan, like Riley, seemed to have the magical knack of being able to put her at ease. Before Riley left for New York, Maddie had been in charge of his cousin Eddie's eighteenth birthday cake. The pinball machine cake was the most intricate and unfamiliar design she had ever tackled, and she was overwhelmed trying to shape the flippers so they didn't resemble white sausages, trying to co-ordinate colours; basically trying to make it look realistic. Riley had poured her a gin and tonic – much too large a measure for a girl who was trying to hone her creativity – and patiently encouraged her as she pulled herself together and produced a cake that was a success with even the plunger, a steel ball and ramps.

'You're shaking.' Evan pulled the black woollen throw from the back of the sofa, doubled it over and wrapped it around her shoulders before he sat down beside her. 'I'm sorry to have laid all this on you tonight. Trust me to ruin the best date I've had in a long time.'

'It came as a shock, that's all. I mean, you'd been so – so normal all night. And to come out with that, I just—'

He leant back and locked his hands together behind his head as he gazed at the ceiling. 'Please believe me when I say that I had no intention of saying anything to you, especially not tonight. I should've kept my big mouth shut.'

'No, it's fine, really. Stop apologising.' She couldn't look him in the eye. 'I'm just not sure what to say to you now. I don't think I'd even know what to say to a close friend, let alone someone I barely know.'

He reached out his hand and grabbed hers, holding it firmly. 'Then don't say anything.'

For a while they sat quietly, hand in hand.

Maddie spoke first. 'What sort of cancer is it?'

He hesitated, exhaled. 'It's testicular cancer. God, it's even embarrassing to say the type of cancer. I mean, I barely know you, and I wouldn't usually talk about that part of my anatomy on a first date.'

She noticed his smile. It was a smile that reminded her of how she had tried to mask her own pain over the years. 'Don't joke,' she said.

'Sorry. I'm trying to recover from the clanger I've dropped tonight, that's all.' The corners of his mouth dropped and his mouth formed a hard line. 'The only way to find out for certain that it's cancer is to remove the testicle.'

As Evan continued to explain, words such as 'pathology', 'chemotherapy', 'operation', whirled in front of her eyes, and all she could think was that, with every step she took in a relationship with him, the pain of the unknown would get worse: the waiting, the wondering, the uncertainty of what lay ahead. Maddie knew what it was like to be so consumed in a relationship, so in love with the person who was your world, that when they were taken away from you the world stopped turning. When she was with Riley she knew herself, but when he died it took her a long time to find out who she was supposed to be without him. Did she have the strength to go through all that again? Could she go on, day to day, wondering whether Evan would be alive at the end of this?

Evan's shoulder was comfortably wedged against hers as they both sat staring ahead at the blank television screen, tall roman candlesticks on either side. Maddie heard the distant sound of a tram's bell ding as it moved away from the stop, she heard faint footsteps from the apartment above, she heard voices as people passed by in the corridor outside, shushing each other at this time of night. She listened to life carrying on all around them and wondering if hers ever would. She wished she could catapult herself back in time, back to the restaurant with Evan sitting across from her, each of them smiling while in that exciting getting-to-know-you phase that was so addictive, so exhilarating. Right now they should be sharing a first kiss; their only concern should be where to go on their next date.

But that Evan wasn't here now. The Evan who could die was sitting right next to her on the sofa, and all she wanted to do was to curl up in a tiny ball and for the fear to go away. She glanced up at him when he took the mugs over to the sink, turning the taps to rinse them. He looked strung out, fraught with worry, and Maddie didn't feel ready to help him. She watched him pick up his jacket from the back of the dining chair and his wallet from the coffee table.

'Goodnight, Maddie. I'm sorry for laying all this on you, I really am.'

She shook her head to stop his apologies, but no words came out as he crouched down next to the sofa where she still sat.

'I've had a great, great night with you. I'd love to see you again,' he said.

Maddie looked at him grasping his jacket tightly as though it could persuade her to give him another chance. It was a standard end-of-a-first-date thing to say, yet she felt numb, unable to give a response, like she had felt at Jem's party when he first asked her out.

Without waiting for an answer, Evan brought his face to hers to kiss her lightly on her cheek. She closed her eyes at the feel of his lips: soft and warm with the hint of more to come. She breathed in long and hard, hoping that the smell of his clean, crisp aftershave would linger long after he left her apartment.

'I'll be in touch,' he said.

The door clicked shut behind him, and Maddie listened to the faint ping of the lift arriving and the doors sliding shut, and she knew he had gone.

Chapter Six

The giant penis lay there in all its glory. The chocolate testicles were growing at an alarming rate until the right one became distorted and the chocolate turned as black as liquorice. The light bounced off a silver machete as a masked man sliced it down through the air and swiped both testicles away in one go and then attacked the penis until it was one splattered mess.

Evan jolted himself awake. His back was drenched with sweat, his mouth dry. He peeled off his T-shirt and, gasping for air, staggered to open the window. As he breathed in, breathed out, he watched trucks at the Exhibition Centre make early morning deliveries, the world continuing as though everything were normal.

It was funny how people took things for granted until they were forced to face up to their own mortality. Evan had never worried about his health, assuming that it wouldn't be a concern until he was old and grey. But Jem's comment the other day had been enough to convince him to get that lump checked out – a lump the size of a large grape that he had found on his right testicle a couple of weeks before but hadn't done anything about. He had done the usual reconnaissance via his good friend Google, of course, but contrary to his own hopes, the lump hadn't just magically gone away on its own accord. Rather than have the doctor examine him and tell him not to worry, send him on his way, he had faced a barrage of tests with a urologist. There'd been full bloods, a testicular ultrasound – the pretty, petite blonde operating the Doppler hadn't helped him maintain his feelings of masculinity – and when the results were reviewed, they indicated the high probability that it was testicular cancer. When a CT scan came back normal, Evan had assumed the next step would be a needle biopsy, but there was a risk the scrotum could be cut accidentally, making the cancer cells more likely to spread to other parts of the body. And that had left him with no option but to have the orchidectomy. An orchidectomy meant the removal of the testicle, but the only translation Evan understood was 'castration'.

In the bathroom now, Evan splashed cold water over his face and let it trickle down over his chest, the temperature helping to wipe away the nightmare. He shuddered when he thought back to how he broke the news to Maddie last night. He would never forget that look on her face: shock, denial, fear even. What the hell had he been thinking? He tried to imagine how he would have felt had one of his dates, whom he barely knew, pulled the same stunt with him. He would've run a mile. Heck, his past dates had never done anything quite so shocking, and he had still been disinterested in going for round two.

Evan wondered what it was that made you desperate to tell one person something so huge, yet not tell others. Was it a sign of trust? Love, perhaps? Or sheer stupidity? He couldn't say why, but he was drawn to Maddie, had been from the get-go. She was extraordinarily different in a way he couldn't describe, and if he tried, he knew his words wouldn't do her justice. He could see her clearly in his mind: sexy, long layered hair with teasing waves and strands of chestnut and gold, sometimes caramel depending on how the light of the day or night chose to present it. He loved long hair on a girl, always had – not that he didn't like short hair of course. Demi Moore in Ghost had been the sole reason to go and see that particular chick flick – but on Maddie long hair looked so right. She had a strong personality too, from what he could tell, and he suspected that she wasn't afraid to speak her mind, even if it was uncomfortable doing so. And underneath all that, Evan saw a certain vulnerability that showed Maddie wouldn't be immune to life's reality and the crap it could sometimes deal out.

What was Maddie thinking this morning? Was she even thinking about him? He hoped so, but more so he hoped she didn't pity him; he couldn't stand that.

He tugged the sheets from the bed and bundled them into the washing machine. He filled a glass with water from the fridge after stacking it with ice cubes, listening to them crack when the water made contact. He leaned against the fridge and watched the dust motes dance in a stream of sunshine coming from between the venetian blinds that hung in front of the balcony doors. His mind drifted back to his school days and a boy in his class, Stephen, who flew under the radar most of the time. Stephen had earned himself the nickname *Womble,* and for years Evan hadn't understood the joke – in his innocence he had thought that Stephen looked nothing like Uncle Bulgaria or Orinoco – but one day after footy training he had overheard some of the lads talking about it. Apparently Stephen's nickname derived from only having one ball.

Evan tipped his head back and let an ice cube tumble into his mouth. He never had found out why Stephen had one ball, or indeed whether the rumour was even true; kids could be unnecessarily cruel sometimes.

He opened the balcony door and leant up against the frame as he watched the clouds sauntering lazily across the sky. If this was cancer then it could mean chemotherapy following the op, which would mean going bald – and not only on his head. It would mean spending days and nights on end praying to the porcelain god. It would mean being bloody useless and about as masculine as a chorus line girl.

He idly flicked the door catch up and down and hoped that whatever happened, he would be able to kick the cancer's arse into the middle of next week. Then maybe, just maybe, he would still have a chance with Maddie.

Chapter Seven

'You've got to be kidding.' Ally's coffee failed to reach her lips as Maddie sat across from her in Jerimiah's café and told her about her date with Evan, or more importantly, how it had ended. 'No wonder you look like you haven't slept a wink.'

Maddie stared into the froth of her own skim cappuccino and watched the sprinkled chocolate powder hover on top, daring it to sink into the milk so it was as low as she felt.

Ally's blonde chiselled bob swung sideways as she shook her head in disbelief. 'You wouldn't wish the Big C on anyone. I'd say he's either gutsy for telling you after your first date or a little bit crazy.'

'He's not crazy.' Maddie ploughed her spoon across the chocolate-covered froth.

'What sort of cancer is it?'

'It might be testicular cancer, but he told me that the only way to be sure is to have the testicle removed.'

'Bloody hell – imagine how he must be feeling. Obviously we can't as we don't have balls, but you know what I mean. It's like … one of us losing our breasts.' She looked down at her own as though she could suddenly see their value. 'It would be devastating.'

'I feel like such a heartless, selfish cow.' Maddie held up her hand before Ally had the chance to mollify her. They had been best friends ever since they met at a taxi rank when Maddie first came to Melbourne, and Maddie knew Ally always gave her the benefit of the doubt. 'Let me finish. When he told me I immediately thought how awful it must be for him, but then my mind just started ticking over thinking about what it meant for me. We'd had so much fun on the date that all I kept asking myself was whether I've got the strength to deal with Evan, whether I've got the strength to cope with the possibility that I could lose Evan like I lost Riley.' She looked up at her friend. 'Now tell me that doesn't make me a heartless, selfish bitch.'

'I think it makes you human.' Ally gripped her friend's hand across the table. Ally had known Maddie before that devastating September, had known Riley, and more importantly she had known them together as a couple. And that was what made her more than qualified to be Maddie's go-to person in a time of crisis.

Maddie had thought about Evan non-stop ever since he had dropped the bombshell that had blown open the wounds from Riley that had never healed over properly in the first place. 'I really like him,' she said.

'Well it's about time. One-nighters and casual sex don't suit you,' replied Ally.

'Thanks … I think.'

'And for your information, I'd never think you were a selfish bitch, so stop being so hard on yourself.' Ally checked her watch. 'Now, I'm going to be late for a lecture if I'm not careful, and I was late this time last week because I overslept, so today I can't even miss it on compassionate grounds.'

Ally finished up her coffee and shrugged a rucksack on to her back. She paused to grab a takeaway muffin on their way out. 'I need to keep my concentration up in the lecture,' she justified. 'We mature medical students need all the help we can get.'

Maddie shook her head at the offer of food on top of the coffee; the thought of anything more in her stomach was plain unsettling.

'Anyway, back to Evan.' Ally pushed open the door to the café. 'Apart from the fact that the man has cancer—'

Maddie went to protest at the flippant comment as she held the door open for another customer, but Ally continued.

'Apart from that one factor, how was the date? You know, before he told you?' She took a bite of the muffin.

Maddie's grin widened for the first time that morning.

'Okay, so now I want details.' Ally pulled her sunglasses down from where they sat on top of her blonde, bobbed hair as the Australian sun came out in full force.

Maddie regaled the story about the dinner, the simplicity of the evening, the instant attraction to Evan both physically and emotionally.

'I haven't felt that way about anyone since Riley. Other guys have always been fun, good looking … but Evan is different. I knew it from the first moment we met. He's the cliché tall, dark and handsome, he's fit and sexy and, well—'

'Well what?'

Her smile disappeared, and as the clouds blocked the sun, she felt a tiny shiver creep its way across her neck, down her arms. 'Well, perhaps he was too good to be true.'

'Maddie, you've been through more than most when it comes to love and loss. Not to mention all the shit that went down with Riley's parents cutting you out of their lives after the memorial. You're stronger than you think.'

'So why haven't I moved on by now? I still can't even manage to watch the commemorative events every year. I find no comfort knowing that other people have suffered the same loss. And now, just when I think there's a man for me, he goes and announces that he has cancer.'

'Evan must see something special in you to share what he did last night.' Ally placed a reassuring hand on her friend's shoulder. 'Imagine how secure he must've felt with you to do that. Unless …'

'Unless what?'

'He wasn't wasted, was he?' She pulled a face.

'No, he wasn't wasted at all.' They had both consumed enough wine, but his strong body combined with the food would've left him clear-headed enough. And if it hadn't, his confession would have been like an icy bucket of water to sober him up.

Ally pulled Maddie away from the door as the café filled with morning coffee-seekers, people out for an early breakfast before work. 'I think your gut instinct about this man is right. Maybe Evan is different. You could always follow his lead and share about what happened to Riley.'

Maddie pulled out her car keys. 'Come on, I'll run you up to Uni. I've got time before my shift.'

Ally's five-foot-nine-inch athletic build blocked her way. 'Don't ignore me.'

Maddie sighed. 'I don't know if I'll ever be ready to explain about Riley, and I really don't know what Evan was thinking telling me about the cancer. I doubt he planned it that way, and I wouldn't be surprised if he's wondering why on earth he did.'

Ally shrugged a grey jumper over her white shirt, defining her student status indisputably. 'Maybe he feels better about telling someone. It must be a massive secret to deal with alone and sometimes bottling it all up makes things ten times worse.'

Maddie hadn't missed the subtext of Ally's remark, but she wasn't ready to talk about Riley with Evan. She wanted him to know her for who she was now, not as a woman who'd imagined a future with another man. And besides, Riley's mum's words still rang in her ears after more than a decade, and Maddie couldn't help but question her own grief and whether she had any right to feel this way, especially after all this time.

Maddie climbed into the car and paused, her key in the ignition. 'It's not the confiding in me that's the problem though, is it?' She did a head check before she pulled out into the traffic. 'It's the risk of losing someone I care about all over again.'

'It's pretty huge, I agree,' said Ally. 'But can I ask you one thing?'

'Sure.'

'Would you want to go on a second date if he hadn't told you about his testicular cancer, if there wasn't this looming cloud of loss hovering over you?'

Maddie drove on as the traffic lights changed to green, her mouth set in a defiant line till she finally said, 'Yes, without a shadow of a doubt, I would.'

Chapter Eight

On Monday morning, for the first time ever, Evan slept through his alarm. Last night he had tossed and turned, alternating between dreams of Maddie and their date with the worst ending in history, and dreams about the impending surgery and the lasting effects on his anatomy and manhood. But when he arrived at Huntley Primary, he had no time for tiredness or fixations on anything else other than his classroom full of energetic five- and six-year-olds.

Evan had been at Huntley Primary for the last nine years, and it was the job he had dreamt about during his study and his teacher training. His enthusiasm didn't wane when he had to raise his voice above the din to hush his class, directing them to the crates to deposit their lunch boxes, morning tea boxes and drink bottles for easy reach later; and it didn't wane when he pulled a few rambunctious boys into line as they began a game of kicking each other as a fun way to start the day.

At last the children took their seats at desks with individual name cards on each. 'Good morning, class,' said Evan.

'Good morning, Mr Quinn.' The class were well versed at the greeting now that they were well into the first term.

Arriving later than usual, Evan had seen another teacher usher his class into line just before he turned up in the playground. Had he been much later, then a change in routine that would've been minor to older kids and adults would've been a big deal to some of these children. Take Lainey for instance. Most girls were wary of men and found women more nurturing, but Lainey had practically clung to him for the entire first term. He watched her now, marvelling at how in the groove she was with another girl, Dexi, who had become a firm friend. He had been traded in and that, to Evan, was mission accomplished.

Glad to be there for his class, Evan moved between tables as the class beavered away adding colour to their projects on Australian animals. There were fierce looking crocodiles, questionably shaped koalas and peculiarly coloured kookaburras. Perhaps a few more educational images on the smart board wouldn't go amiss this term.

'Mr Quinn?' Paul, a child with a serious snot issue raised his hand. He sniffed, predictably.

'Yes, Paul.' Evan passed over the box of tissues and the boy reluctantly took one. It never ceased to amaze him why kids made such a fuss about blowing their noses when it was a million times more comfortable once it was all out.

'Why were you late this morning?' Paul waited expectantly for an answer.

The question, of course, was inevitable. Young kids liked their routines, and anything out of the ordinary had to be explained, sometimes to a painful degree. It was part of what he loved about being a teacher though. He loved that these kids were trying to make sense of the big wide world, and it was his job to help forge that vital connection for them.

Evan crouched down beside Paul. 'I overslept, that's all.' He also knew that telling kids anything before you knew for sure would set you up for failure: promise too much and you could fail to deliver; tell them anything negative and you could upset them for no reason. He leant over and pulled a picture book, *Possum on the Porch*, from the bookshelves surrounded by brightly coloured bean bags. He did his best to help Paul sketch something that resembled the Australian animal by using the illustrations, and the distraction served its purpose for now.

At the start of his career, plenty of his mates had been sceptical and teased Evan for doing a girl's job, or being a babysitter. But Evan's comeback was that he loved his job, and while they were working in silence at their desks, hunched over a computer, he was kicking a ball around in sports class, out on excursions or getting messy with paints. Of course, he only told them the good stuff. All the paperwork and planning side of being a teacher wasn't nearly as much fun, but he never tried to argue the point as they, like many others, couldn't see past the long holidays and the early finishes at half past three.

As he moved to the next table, Evan found his mind wandering to a place where it had never ventured before: he began to think about Maddie and how she would interact with these children. She would fall in love with Lainey, and Dexi would probably be relegated to the subs bench this time. He wasn't sure how Maddie would react to the two green lines of snot creeping down towards Paul's top lip again, but even he struggled with that one and he was a guy. He looked around the room. Maddie would take charge of Bill and roll up the bottoms of his school pants and fix his laces; and she would giggle at Maxine for no other reason than the little girl had this insane, infectious laugh.

Evan shook himself back to the present and passed Paul another tissue. His pulse raced, his palms were sweaty, and it was then Evan realised he was already in deeper than he could ever have imagined with a girl he barely even knew.

Chapter Nine

Maddie's first patient of the day on Thursday, Arnie, was always up for a good banter.

'How's your running going, Maddie?' he asked when she drew the curtain around the cubicle.

'I did a personal best at the Tan: seventeen minutes forty-three seconds.' She perused the previous notes.

'Awesome. What's your time around Albert Park Lake?'

'Twenty-three minutes. I can't seem to move past that.'

Maddie's bedside manner was a hit with her patients, and she suspected it was one of the elements of her job that had made her hold on to this career path rather than make the leap into the cake business. Riley always said she had a natural reassuring ability, but then he was biased of course. When he broke his leg, he milked it for all it was worth: meals in bed, massages on call, cupcakes made on demand. She hadn't minded, though. She had enjoyed playing nursemaid, especially when it allowed her to bake.

Arnie had come to see her for a classic case of runner's knee, and Maddie treated him with some light massage around the hip and the upper leg and sketched stick men drawings on a piece of paper to show him exercises to do at home.

'Are we all set with the graduation cake?' he asked as he tried some of the exercises. 'My daughter Jess loved the photos of your previous work, and the suggestion of the text book and mortar board was genius.'

'I hope she likes it.'

'You should go into business. Which reminds me, can I pass your details on to my sister? She's expecting a baby in a couple of months and fell in love with the cake with the pink bootees and white piping.'

'That was for a friend's baby shower last month. I'm happy for you to pass on my details, but keep your voice down around here or you'll get me fired!'

'Well then you'll have to take the leap, won't you? I've seen the sparkle in your eyes when you talk about baking. You don't fool me.' He matched Maddie's grin. 'So, in between all your personal bests, have you managed to find yourself a man yet? That was the task I set you months ago, or have you forgotten?'

'How about we find you some tougher exercises? That way you can't quiz me during your appointments.'

'Ah, where's the fun in that? Come on, spinster, tell all.'

Arnie had been calling her 'spinster' for as long as she could remember, and in all the time she had known him, she never once mentioned her history with Riley. She knew Arnie would be devastated about all his teasing if she did. Then he would pussyfoot around her, his appointments tainted with the sympathy that made her feel worse. By keeping

71

quiet, she got to enjoy the banter, the jokes that made her feel normal.

'Not yet.' She scribbled down notes on today's treatment and his progress.

'I'll have to fix you up with someone. It's the only way.'

Oh please, no. His idea of someone suitable was bound to be poles apart from what she was looking for.

'I met someone.' She silently prayed that he would forget the idea of fixing her up. 'It didn't work out.'

'What happened? Come on, Maddie, usually you'd be telling me how he spent the entire evening talking with his mouth full, or how he talked about himself non-stop, or that his breath reeked. What aren't you telling me?'

'Blimey! I have shared a lot with you over the last couple of years, haven't I?'

'Yes, and that's why I know you're hiding something.'

'We really hit it off,' she said. 'We had a fabulous first date: you know, the kind where you just talk and don't realise the time, don't realise that it's the first time you've ever been out with the other person.'

'I know what you mean. Even I'm not too old to remember that type of date. That's what happens when you meet "the one".'

She felt herself blush. 'Something tells me that you're an old romantic, really.'

'Tell anyone, and I'll have you disciplined for breach of patient confidentiality.' He pointed a finger at her in jest. 'So what happened? Did he make a move on you? Come over all sleazy?'

'No, it was nothing like that. He was a perfect gentleman. Let's just say he told me something at the end of the date, and I think it was a deal breaker.' She wasn't sure if that was the case from her point of view, but it certainly seemed to be the way Evan was thinking as he hadn't been in touch.

'Is he married?' Arnie spoke quietly even though they were as good as alone.

'No.'

'Gay?'

She sniggered. 'No!'

'You took him to your place and found him dressing up in your clothes?'

'No!' This is what she loved about Arnie and why she would never tell him about Riley.

'So he must be a conjoined twin, then?'

'Arnie, that's enough.'

'So come on then, spinster. Tell me what it is that's so bad.'

Her mouth twisted awkwardly. 'I can't. It's not my secret to tell.'

He whistled and his eyebrows arched at the same time. 'It must be something pretty dark to make you so secretive and to convince you not to see him again.'

'I'll leave you to get dressed.'

'You've got a good head on your shoulders, Maddie,' he called after her. 'Whatever this guy is, or whatever he's done, you'll know the right thing to do.'

*

When Maddie arrived home at her apartment on St Kilda Road, she pulled on her running pants, a striking violet singlet and a new pair of runners that had been worn in and finally felt comfortable enough to go the distance. She got through a pair at least every six months, more so if they had taken a battering in winter weather or on muddier terrain. She opened up the balcony door and breathed in the cool evening air as she fastened her pink Garmin watch round her wrist. She went through a stretch routine she would repeat when she arrived home again to cool her body down and give it a chance to recover before she hit the shower.

She thought back to that afternoon with Arnie and wondered whether anyone really got a second shot at finding 'the one'. Right now, any second chance felt as though it were on the other side of the Berlin Wall, and she had no idea whether she or Evan had the stamina to climb over it, or whether it was even an option anymore. And if she ever did find that person, would it mean Caitlin had been right all along?

Outside the apartment block Maddie let the light breeze blow away thoughts of Riley's mum as she pushed her headphones into her ears. She pressed the button to start the GPS on her watch, and it signalled the start of the route that would bring the feeling of freedom with every step she took.

As she pounded the pavements the familiar running playlist ran through Pink's 'Raise Your Glass', Taio Cruz's 'Dynamite', Survivor's 'Eye of the Tiger' and more. Running had been her saviour in the early days after Riley's death and every day since. Whenever she felt the walls closing in, she pounded the pavements, the promenade, even the sand on the beach when she wanted to work off her anger at the sheer unfairness of it all.

She ran along the pavement to the end of St Kilda Road, across at the lights and onwards to where Fitzroy Street met the beach. A rollerblading pair split up and zipped past on either side of her as she kept on running, beneath towering palm trees on the promenade, soaking up the last moments of light as the sun gave up for the day. She tried to match the beat of the music as she ran down the concrete slope and on to the sand, but even with the frustration inside of her and the eagerness to block out memories, the challenging surface rendered it next to impossible.

And then it was as though the sand had suddenly thickened, and no matter how hard she tried, she couldn't lift her feet to move anymore.

She looked at Evan coming towards her. His feet seemed to have stopped working too as he pulled a black and red cap down tighter over his forehead when the sun headed straight for him.

'You look well,' said Maddie and immediately regretted it. He had hardly been at death's door last time she saw him, and her comment sounded as pathetic as she felt. 'Sorry, I just meant …'

'No worries.' His smile was forgiveness itself, and his words came out between breaths as he let his heart rate recover. 'How are you?'

'I'm fine, I'm good.' She was making a right mess of this conversation. 'Have you run far?'

He wiped the back of his hand across his upper lip. 'Not really, but I thought I'd add the sand challenge today for something different. I'll run all the way to the end and then do a big loop through St Kilda.'

Maddie pushed her sunglasses further up her nose; they had slipped from the sweat and the sunscreen, and although the sun was behind her now she daren't take them off because she knew that if he could see her eyes, she would feel even more vulnerable.

'Have you heard anything?' she asked.

'You mean, about the operation?' He shook his head. 'I kind of want it over with, but on the other hand I want to be normal for a bit longer.'

Normal? Maddie hadn't felt normal in such a long time. Meeting Evan had made her believe that eventually she would, but here she was barely able to manage more than a stilted conversation. It was completely different to how they had gelled in the restaurant and on the walk home.

'I really did have a good time the other night.' The intensity of his stare could have burnt a hole right through her sunglasses.

'I did too.' Riley's name was on the tip of her tongue. She thought about explaining why she was so shocked at his news, why she wasn't quite the rock he probably needed at the moment.

But he spoke too soon. 'I'll see you around.' And with that, the moment was gone. Both Evan and Maddie carried on running in different directions, both struggling their way through the sand as though their lives depended on it.

Maddie took a slope up to the promenade and the relative ease of concrete in comparison. Her pace had increased, her determination was fierce, and she continued all the way to the pier. But instead of continuing past as she usually would, across the road and doubling back to go down the other side, she ran all the way to the end of the wooden structure. She stopped, bent over, hands resting on her thighs, trying to catch her breath. She yanked the headphones from her ears as the music started to sound like voices in her head, taunting her that she couldn't get a grip on reality.

Was she relieved that she hadn't told him about Riley? Did keeping Riley a secret keep her precious memories under lock and key? Did mourning him still after all these years, and chasing away any man who showed more than a passing interest, prove Caitlin wrong? Her behaviour for more than a decade had been Maddie's coping mechanism, so much so that she barely knew how to behave any differently.

She stood for a while beside a man sitting on the edge of the pier, legs dangling over the edge with a hopeful line cast into the water. She watched the sea lapping around the posts beneath her, listened to the seagulls squawk overhead as they penetrated the fug in her mind, let the sea air into her lungs and hoped it would flush out the confusion. But it didn't.

Puffed white clouds meandered across the sky as she looked back the way Evan had gone, but of course there was no sign of him. Was he still running? Or was he, like her, thinking about what might have been? Her and Riley's friends had drifted off one by one after he died – perhaps not consciously, perhaps simply moving on – so why couldn't she do the same after all this time? She thought about how close she'd come to telling Evan about Riley this afternoon. Maybe she'd had the same urge that he felt the night he told her about the cancer. Did they have a connection that made them instantly trust one another, made them immediately want to share the details of their lives with one another?

Maybe Evan actually was her second chance to be happy. But it still didn't stop Maddie's niggling doubts that the pain of the past could be happening all over again.

Chapter Ten

'Ava, guess who's here?' Holly lunged at him and dragged Evan inside the moment she opened her front door. 'Please, please rescue me,' she said, hands clasped tightly together, pleading. 'Ben's still at work and Ava is having one hell of a tantrum. I thought she was getting too old for this, but she's having a complete meltdown and won't take any notice of me.'

Now this was something Evan felt sure he could handle: a four-year-old girl who was totally besotted with her cool uncle. This would be a breeze compared to what he had been trying to get his head around these past few days.

He pulled Ava's favourite bunny, Mr Snuggles, from Holly's hand. 'Reinforcements,' he assured her.

Tentatively, he turned the door handle to the bedroom, crouched down, and pushed the bunny's nose, then cheeks and whiskers around the side of the door frame. He chuckled quietly; the light relief felt as though he'd had a sprinkling of fairy dust at Ava's door – the dust that she made out of glitter and torn up rose petals, insisting it was magic. What he would give right now to go back in time and have that childhood innocence all over again.

The sobbing continued, but when he heard a couple of stunted gasps, Evan knew Ava had seen Mr Snuggles. He poked the bunny's front paws around the door until a giggle told him he'd done it. In a squeaky, girlie voice he would never, ever do in front of his mates, he said: 'Mr Snuggles has a special guest and would like to invite him in for a tea party.'

The door flew open, and Ava ran at Evan. 'Uncle Evan!' He scooped her up and hugged her tight as she clung on like a koala on a gum tree, legs and arms tightly clasped around his torso.

'Thank you,' mouthed Holly with eyes closed and a nod. She left them to it and escaped to the other end of the house.

Evan sat cross-legged on the floor in Ava's bedroom, grateful that the lump was only uncomfortable, not painful. He wondered how much of the discomfort was in his head rather than his groin; was it only uncomfortable because he knew it was there?

Ava pottered around her bedroom in the compact house that sat in Port Melbourne, a stone's throw from the beach. She arranged bright pink plastic tea cups, matching side plates with Barbie designs on the base, a few plastic slices of cake, which looked more than a little used, and a questionable brown plastic burger she insisted was a camel slice; he assumed she meant 'caramel', but it was cute listening to words she was convinced were the right ones, and so he hadn't started an argument when she refused to accept his correction.

When they'd had their tea, Evan sat with Ava and Mr Snuggles on her purple beanbag and read a story. Ava's head lolled out of exhaustion from the tantrum, and when they finished he tucked her in, and Holly went in to say goodnight.

'You've got the magic touch,' said Holly as she crept out of Ava's bedroom. 'I think the tantrum really wore her out. She's fighting to keep her eyes open.'

'What's the matter, sis, can't handle the pace?'

'Hey, don't knock it until you've tried it. Parenthood is hard work, and all those people who think a stay-at-home mum has it easy need to come and spend a day in my shoes.'

He pulled a face as his sister went off into a familiar rant.

'Sorry.' She lined up two wine glasses. 'It's been a long day, that's all.' She toasted his glass, and not waiting for a return clink, she took a generous gulp of the rich Merlot and closed her eyes.

'Number two not on the way yet, then?' he joked.

She opened one eye. 'Not yet.'

'Ah, so you're thinking about it?'

'I wish I'd done it sooner to be honest. But it just didn't happen.'

'Oh. I didn't realise, sis. I assumed—'

'Everyone assumed the same, don't worry. Everyone thought we were content with one child, and I didn't want to tell anyone that we weren't having any luck, because if Ava is all we have, then so be it. It's just that I had visions of at least two siblings running around together – you know, like we did.'

'We used to fight too. Don't you remember?'

'Of course I remember.' Holly's voice bubbled as she opened up a packet of Tim Tams and proffered the smooth chocolate-coated biscuits to Evan.

'What?' he asked.

She nodded towards the stack of three that he had taken. 'I'm wondering how you stay looking so fit and healthy when you put away alcohol and chocolate biscuits?'

'I only indulge when I'm here.'

'Rubbish.' She gathered her long, dark ringlets together and wound the pink band that had been lying on the table around three times to secure it in place.

'Can I ask if there's a medical reason why you guys haven't been able to have another baby? Or is it a case of not enough sex with Ava running loose?'

'*Eurgh*, Evan! You're my brother! Ask all you want about the medical side, but steer clear of any questions about sex.'

'It's a deal.'

She sighed. 'They call it "secondary infertility", which is code for we-don't-know-why-the-hell-it-didn't-work-this-time. Apparently it's more common than you'd think. And between Ben's work, and Ava and everything she needs, some things, like sex, just take a back seat.'

'I thought we weren't mentioning sex?'

'Oh, be quiet.' She sipped her own wine thoughtfully and a lot slower than her brother. 'Besides, maybe you could provide a cousin if things work out with Maddie? Then I wouldn't need to go through all this again.' She gestured at a mountain of washing folded at one end of the table and the toy corner, which was no longer a corner but had spilt over to most of the lounge room.

It wasn't only the mention of Maddie's name that made Evan feel as though he had just balanced all his apples on top of a cart in a perfect pyramid shape and one had been yanked out from the bottom, causing the whole lot to topple over. It was also the double whammy that, as well as losing one of his balls, he could lose his chance at fatherhood. The fact that the doctors insisted one healthy testicle was all he would need did little to reassure him. Funny, he had always thought of himself as a positive person, a glass-half-full type of guy, until now.

He helped himself to a fourth Tim Tam. Seeing Maddie on the beach yesterday had been an unexpected pleasure and a source of great pain: pleasure because he knew his feelings for her already ran as deep as the ocean that crashed right beside them; pain because his future was too unsure, too risky to allow himself to fall for her completely. When they first met he had envisaged a quick fling, no strings attached. But from their first date and from the moment he had stood watching her profile lit up by the flames outside the casino, he knew she was a girl who was worthy of so much more. And it killed him that he couldn't be the man to give that to her; at least not until his operation and whatever came afterwards was out of the way.

Evan grinned when Holly followed his lead and reached for another biscuit.

'I don't feel so bad when I see you do it,' she justified.

'How are those spinning classes going?' He topped up both glasses. 'How's the hot instructor?'

'Don't tell Ben, he'll stay in meetings late on purpose so I can't get to the class anymore. And I need my sanity twice a week, believe me.'

'Don't worry, your secret's safe with me.'

83

'Good sidestep on the topic of Maddie, by the way.'

'I've got no idea what you're talking about.'

'You know exactly what I mean. I touched a nerve when I mentioned her, so come on, out with it.'

Holly, much like Jem, rarely missed a thing. 'Seriously, sis, it's nothing.'

'Bullshit.'

'Hey, talking of which, do you have any cards?' Evan began to raid the shelves at the side of the kitchen next to the table. 'I still reckon I can beat you at a good old-fashioned game of bullshit.'

'Come on, Evan. What's bothering you? Don't tell me she's dumped you already after one date?'

'Aha!' He triumphantly pulled out a pack of cards lurking beneath a *Dora the Explorer* backpack shoved in between a *Wiggles* DVD and a textbook about how to raise girls. He untwisted the elastic band. 'Is it a full deck?'

'I think so, but no guarantees in this house.'

'Okay, then. I'll deal'

Holly whipped the pack away from him.

'Hey!'

She held the pack behind her back as he tried to make a grab for them. 'Not until you tell me what's going on. It can't be that big a deal even if she has dumped you – although it's a shame, she seemed lovely.'

'Holly,' said Evan, exasperated. 'She didn't dump me. Forget about it, and give me the cards … please.'

She stared him out.

'I said it's nothing for fuck's sake!'

She gestured for him to mind his language with a child in the house who may or may not be asleep yet.

He snatched up his wine. 'Fuck!' Most of it missed his mouth and splashed down the front of his white T-shirt.

Holly didn't give him a look this time. Instead, she watched him as he sunk into his chair, unconcerned at the stains on his clothing.

'I'm your sister, Evan. Talk to me, please. I may have a mummy-brain, but I know something's going on. What is it?'

'I … I …'

His eyes filled with tears and he couldn't look at her. He was a grown man. He didn't cry, and certainly not in front of his sister. He hadn't cried since his father died, and he wasn't going to cry now, damn it. His chair scraped back angrily, and he marched to the bathroom, shutting his sister and the world out while he pulled himself together.

He took deep breaths, purposely avoiding the mirror above the sink. He didn't want to see how much of a wimp he looked, how much of a coward. That was how he felt now, and he wondered how much less of a man he'd feel once they took away one of his balls. Balls produced testosterone, the essence of a man, the reason they had their features: facial hair, deep voice, muscles. One testicle was supposedly capable of producing sufficient testosterone to do all that, but doctors were wrong all the time.

Evan flushed the toilet even though there was no need and went back to face Holly, who was sitting at the table rotating her wine glass stem between her fingers. The mother in her had discreetly mopped up the splashes of red wine.

She passed him a shirt. 'It's Ben's. Pop it on while I wash yours.'

Evan did as he was told, and Holly took the T-shirt away to work whatever magic she could. 'You can wear that one home and I'll let yours soak,' she called from the laundry hidden behind a door at the end of the kitchen.

'Thanks,' he said, his head hung.

When she took a seat opposite her brother again, she said, 'Whatever it is, please tell me. I shouldn't have teased you about Maddie. I didn't realise how much you liked her.'

'This isn't about Maddie.'

'Well what, then?'

Evan felt his lip wobble when his sister reached out and held his hand over the table. They were close, but holding his hand made him realise how real this thing was. He pulled his other hand through his hair.

'I went to the doctor for some tests.' He cringed as he remembered his GP's gloved hand checking his scrotum, then later the clinical ultrasound that seemed to go on forever, the sharp needle piercing his skin to take his blood.

Holly's hand moved to her mouth, and when he uttered the word *cancer*, it was no longer *his* tears that were the problem. He wrapped his arms around his sister as she grabbed a hold of him through her husband's freshly laundered polo shirt and sobbed.

When Ben arrived home almost an hour later and had made the usual pit-stop at his daughter's bedroom before continuing to the kitchen, Evan and Holly were on to strong cups of coffee, and Evan had sunk his fifth Tim Tam.

'Oh, I see,' Ben joked. 'Late home from work one night, and another bloke has already got his feet under my table, drinking my good coffee, eating my Tim Tams.' He placed a firm hand on Evan's shoulder and gave him a shake in jest. 'Good to see you, mate.'

He moved around to the other side of the table to greet Holly, but before he could take off his tie and leave his day at the office behind, Holly leapt up and wrapped her arms around him.

'Hey, hey, hey, what's all this?' He looked back at Evan. 'What's going on?'

*

Evan and Ben sat at a table in the pub. Holly had ushered them out for the rest of the evening, insisting she wanted a hot bubble bath and an early night. She was a good sister to him, sensing that what he really needed tonight was another guy to talk to.

Evan stared into the amber liquid in his glass and after a large mouthful said, 'Think I'll be catching the tram home tonight, with this and the wine I put away at your place.'

'Does that mean the Audi TT is mine for a joyride?' Ben whistled through his teeth. 'That's so cool.'

'I'll leave it to you in my will.'

'Don't you let Holly hear you talking like that, you hear me.'

'Sorry, mate, it's just …' Evan traced a finger down the condensation of his glass.

'When's the operation?'

'Don't know yet. I'm standing by for the good news from the doctor. Should be any day now.' Evan's voice dripped with disdain. He glugged back his beer.

'Are you sure you should be having a skinful if you've got an operation coming up?'

'Probably not, but I'm about to lose one of my balls, Ben, so I'm thinking I should make the most of every remaining moment I have left as a man.'

'Evan, this doesn't make you any less of a man.'

'Doesn't it?' When Ben frowned at him, Evan softened. 'I guess you're right. But if I don't make jokes I may actually start thinking about how real this all is and the possibility that it really is cancer and I could die.'

Evan bought two more beers. It was quiet tonight with a handful of punters dispersed around the room, leaving them at one end of the bar in relative peace as Evan explained why the doctors wouldn't perform a biopsy first.

'Unfortunately, the only way to be a hundred per cent sure of what I'm dealing with, whether the lump is cancerous, is to do the orchidectomy,' said Evan.

'Brutal.'

'Yeah, you could say that. Losing my ball is kind of a fait accompli.'

Telling the family was always going to be traumatic, but at least now he had another man to talk to. Since seeing Maddie on the beach yesterday afternoon, his head had been in even more of a spin than ever.

Evan pulled the snack menu away from Ben, who wasn't even focusing on the task in hand, and headed to the bar to order a bowl of wedges.

When he returned he said, 'Holly told me you've been trying for another baby.'

'Don't change the subject.'

'I have to, or I'll be a big girl and cry.'

'Yeah, I'm not sure I want you crying on me.'

'It wouldn't be pretty.'

'I'm sure it wouldn't,' said Ben, humouring him and changing the subject. 'It happened so fast for us with Ava I suppose we assumed it would be that way again. Mind you, back then we were having a lot of sex – good sex. Sorry …'

Evan made a face. 'Yes, thanks for that image of you both going at it like rabbits. I was hoping you'd had the Immaculate Conception with Ava.'

'I won't give you any more details, don't worry,' he chuckled. 'I guess Holly and I have this vision of Ava with a brother or a sister – you know, building hide-outs, getting muddy in the back garden. I do all those things with her, but it's not the same, is it?'

'The problem is, Ben, that you both had pretty idyllic childhoods with fantastic siblings.'

'Bollocks!'

Evan screwed his face up.

'Sorry,' Ben grimaced, 'bad choice of words.'

'My point is, it could still happen, especially if the medical professionals don't see why it shouldn't. And like you said, you have Ava.'

'So we should be grateful?'

'That's not what I meant exactly. What I mean is that you have a child who's happy and healthy, and if you don't end up having any more then, yes, you'll be gutted, but you only have to look at Ava to be reminded of what you do have.' He took a gulp and let the amber liquid slide down his throat. 'Who knows whether I'll end up having a family? I always thought I would, but …'

'So what's the deal with this orchi-whatever?'

'Orchidectomy,' Evan corrected.

'That was it, so how does that affect the likelihood of you being a father?'

Evan sank back into the maroon velour seat. 'Apparently with one remaining healthy testicle, it shouldn't be a problem.'

'There you go, then.'

Evan almost added that Ben's simplifying of the situation was easy to do when you were married with a child, but he knew the man was trying to put him at ease and not add to the worry that already swam around in his head with all the aggression of a piranha waiting for some flesh to sink its teeth into.

He pulled a hand through his unruly hair which, with everything going on, was starting to show its hidden curls in the absence of a haircut. 'I want a family, Ben. I can't believe how much I want it, how little I realised it until now.'

Ben shook his head, slumped back against the leather seat running along the wall of the pub as a bowl of steaming wedges was delivered to them.

Evan lifted out the small pots of sour cream and sweet chilli sauce. 'I have these images in my head of Holly and me as young kids, then teenagers, then adults.'

Ben nodded as he tentatively took a bite from the edge of a steaming hot wedge. 'Now do you see where I'm coming from when I talk about a sibling for Ava?'

Evan nodded. 'Mind you, Holly and I used to get into scrapes too. Did she ever tell you about the night we damaged Mum's car?'

'Holly? Do you mean my wife, Holly, who only last week was teasing me about reversing into a bollard outside work?'

'Yep, that's the one.'

'What happened?'

'Mum used to stress about us taking the car to the city full stop, thinking it would get damaged if we parked outside bars and the like. Anyway, we promised we would drive to the station in Huntley and park near all those posh houses and commute to the city. We missed the sodding train, and we didn't want to miss out on the live band at the Kitten Club, so …'

'You drove to the city,' Ben concluded for him.

'We figured what she didn't know wouldn't hurt her. I can't even remember whether it was my idea or Holly's; I really want to say it was hers, but I suspect we both egged each other on. Anyway, we parked as close to the club as we could, and when we got back to the car someone had driven into the side of it – we were in the end space of a group of cars – and they'd driven off, no details left or anything. I still remember shoving Holly into Mum's bedroom first and making her tell her. Holly was fuming at that.' He laughed. 'But I told her if she didn't, then I'd tell Mum she hadn't really stayed at her friend Amy's the week before.'

'Who was she with?'

Evan tapped the side of his nose. 'I really can't say.'

'I bet there are a thousand stories I don't know about you guys. I'll be asking Holly later, don't you worry.'

'Hey, what goes on tour stays on tour … I can't divulge everything or Holly would kill me.' He finished the other half of the wedge he had bitten into. 'I know that to you guys I'm just Holly's younger brother who's carefree, not tied down and never wants to be, but that's not the case, not anymore.'

'So now you're Evan, the responsible primary school teacher who's ready to settle down?'

'That's right.'

'Shit!' Ben dropped the wedge on to the table as it burnt the roof of his mouth. He took a sip of beer to take the edge off the discomfort. 'Glad you think it's funny.'

'Sorry, mate, a bit of light relief from the conversation, I think,' said Evan, still smiling.

Ben took another, this time a much smaller, cooler one. 'So, as much as I want to talk about your nuts all night, let's change the subject.'

'I'd be happy to.'

'What's happening with this girl, Maddie?'

Every time he heard her name, his body froze, his mind hovered on the memory of the little time they had spent together.

'Not much,' Evan shrugged.

'What does she make of the whole ball situation?'

'Nicely put, Ben, nicely put.'

'Does she know?'

'Oh, yes, she knows all right.'

'What does that mean?'

And then Evan blurted out the whole sorry story: the fantastic first date, the fact that he had never felt this strongly about a girl, how Maddie's face fell the moment he told her.

'She's awesome, Ben.'

'Bloody hell, you must've scared the crap out of her.'

'Thanks.'

'Have you called her, or texted her?'

'No. But I did bump into her down the beach.' He noticed Ben's hopeful gaze. 'I was out for a run, so was she.'

'And ...'

When Evan didn't answer, Ben shook his head. 'Why don't you call her?'

'How can I? How can I expect her to be with me when I'm having one of my balls chopped off and God knows what the test results will be? Firstly, she doesn't deserve that, and secondly, I don't want her to be with me because she feels sorry for me.'

Ben put both elbows on the table and scratched at his head with both hands. 'You need to call her, mate. If she tells you to get lost then you'll know she wasn't worth it, and you'll feel better. But if – and I suspect that this is more likely to happen – you talk to her, you might feel better when you realise she had a great time on your first date and doesn't want this to be the end either.'

Evan shrugged.

'Don't shrug like that. You're being defeated before you've even had the operation.'

'And what happens when she finds out I've got a fake ball?'

Ben almost spluttered his mouthful of beer across the table.

'I don't like the idea of hanging too loose down there,' Evan explained. 'I considered going back at a later date to have a fake ball put in, but I don't think I can go under the knife twice.'

Ben took a confident swig of beer now. 'Who cares? Remember Ashley Torrington?'

Evan pulled a face, shuddered. 'How can I forget? One shag and I couldn't get rid of her.'

'Yes, but do you *remember* Ashley Torrington?' This time Ben upturned both hands and gestured out from his chest as though he had a weight in each palm.

'Ah, you mean the enormous breasts?'

'That's right. And were they real? I think not. But it didn't put you off, did it? In fact, when she burst through the door of that bar in the city that night you were gaga over her. She just turned out to be a bit of a psycho, that's all, but you didn't get rid of her because of any fake part of her anatomy.' He sniggered into his beer.

'You're very funny.'

'Oh come on, my point is that, fake or not fake, it didn't stop her getting the men, and your fake ball won't matter one iota to Maddie or any other girl you end up falling into bed with.'

The problem now was that he didn't want to fall into bed with just any girl. He wanted it to be Maddie, and he wanted it to be right in every possible way. What was happening to him?

'She's a gorgeous looking girl,' said Ben.

'She is. She's funny too, and I feel as though I can trust her – I must've thought that to tell her. And she has a certain confidence that I like, but not so much that I don't want to pull her in tight and hold her.'

Ben pushed his fingers down his throat. 'Get me a bucket! You got all that from one date?'

Evan dug his brother-in-law in the ribs.

'It's sod's law, Ben. I really like this girl and now … well, now I don't know what's going on.'

'You need to get in touch with her. What have you got to lose?'

*

Over the weekend Evan tapped out text messages to Maddie and subsequently deleted them. His fingers had hovered over the keys to call her, but by Monday morning he still hadn't heeded his brother-in-law's advice.

'Well done, Oliver, but what's this one?' His first task of the week was to introduce his year ones to pastels and the task of drawing their dream garden. He crouched down beside a red-headed boy.

'That's my spaceship,' said Oliver.

Evan's raised eyebrows prompted him to explain.

'In my dream garden it would come down from the sky, land and take me off on adventures.'

How could you argue with that? 'You've got a great imagination, Oliver. But could you try adding some greenery, some flowers, maybe even a super cool water feature.'

Facing your own mortality opened your eyes to what was around you already. Cancer, or the possibility of cancer, was life altering and it made Evan subconsciously reassess his life, his routine. He'd had plenty of girlfriends, but none of them lasted, and now, the one he wanted to be a keeper probably didn't want to come anywhere near him.

Still, his personal life may be a shambles, but at least his professional life didn't need changing. He knew too many friends who were dissatisfied with their jobs: Jack, a Financial Advisor, was at odds with his lazy manager; Simon was restless and demotivated as a lawyer; and Will never knew whether he had done the right thing by setting up a building company with his brother. Evan classed himself as one of the lucky few in a job where the only clock-watching he did was when he flew into a panic that he would run out of time for everything he wanted to teach.

Of course, there were the down sides of teaching too: constant colds when he first took up his post, to which he developed an immunity after a while; the time he got nits and Holly had kindly treated his hair with stinking shampoo and picked each of the little buggers out; the admin side of the job, which nobody could claim to love.

Evan rolled up his shirt sleeves and moved towards a table at the back.

'Millie, this is great.' They were studying bugs in the garden this week, and Evan marvelled at her creative streak. He looked down at the ginormous snail painted in brown with purple spots. 'And who are they?' he pointed to the two small people up against this dinosaur-like creature.

'That's me,' she said, dipping her brush into the sunshine yellow paint and adding a strip to either side of one of the heads to represent her blonde, straight hair. 'And the other one is my sister.'

Evan tapped Gabriel on the shoulder as he sat, tongue jutting out between his lips in concentration, painting streaks of brown for the trunk of a tree. 'You need to do up your shoelace so that you don't trip over.' The boy obediently crouched down and did a pretty good job of it. The best lesson Evan had been taught at the school where he began his teaching career was to never tie a boy's shoelaces if they were wet. There was every possibility the child's laces had trailed along the floor in the boy's bathrooms.

Come five o'clock, Evan was exhausted. He'd dealt with stragglers running in for forgotten lunch boxes, left-behind cardigans and school hats; he'd had back-to-back meetings for lesson planning; and he'd gathered together the marking he needed to do tonight. By the time he left school, his tiredness hit like a tidal wave as he passed a few children making the most of the sunny, still afternoon by whizzing on the supernova and clambering up and down the climbing net.

As he drove home his mind churned with the two women in his life he knew he needed to speak to, to explain. Jem knew something was up already, she had quizzed him over the phone, but he knew he would have to tell her about the cancer face-to-face, and tonight he didn't have the energy to manage it.

The other woman was Maddie. He was still fighting the inner battle as to whether he should contact her, or whether it would be fairer, easier all round if he didn't. But when every spare moment seemed to feature her, how could he possibly ignore that?

Chapter Eleven

Maddie reached out and found the glass of water beside her bed. Each swallow echoed around the room as she sat upright and pulled her sheets around her as a shudder took hold. When she lay down, the colours of the parachute in her dream were still there: red, gold, lime green and a white that matched the clouds. She had been skydiving in her dream, with Evan and Riley. All three of them had been holding hands in a circle, smiling as wide as the biggest rainbow as they fell through the air with a feeling of freedom and peace. Then Maddie had pulled open her parachute, but the men fought over the single parachute remaining, wrenching it back and forth, and when Maddie saw the burst of colour and one man floating safely towards the ground, she had no idea who had survived, Evan or Riley.

That was when she woke up, and lying there now, big fat tears rolled out the corners of her eyes and on to the pillow. The nightmares had passed over the years, but ever since Evan appeared in her life, they had resurfaced. It was even getting to the point where she dreaded going to bed, knowing when she shut her eyes, she may see things she wished she wouldn't. Last week she had spent a quiet night watching *The Wizard of Oz,* and she had fallen asleep part way through, waking with tears already streaming down her cheeks. She had dreamt Riley was walking around Oz when Maddie's house fell, trapping him beneath it just like the witch wearing the ruby slippers.

Her happy-ever-after felt as though it was getting further out of reach all the time, and some days she wondered whether it would ever come.

Maddie checked the clock: almost 4 a.m. Her alarm was already set for 4:30 a.m., anyway, with her next masterpiece awaiting decoration so she could deliver it to her patient, Arnie, when he came in today.

She switched off the alarm, and in the kitchen she pulled out ingredients, clattered around in the utensils cupboard and pulled out everything she needed to make the icing. She did her best to ignore the dull ache behind her eyes that reminded her of her nightmare and the resulting lack of sleep.

The night before, she'd made one sponge using a pudding basin – this would form the domed part of a mortar board for Arnie's daughter's graduation cake – and another sponge in an oblong tin to make a textbook that would have 'Congratulations Jess!' piped along its spine.

Once she'd wiped down the surfaces to clean up the icing sugar that had escaped during weighing at this incredibly early hour, Maddie spread each cake with the butter icing. She used a decorating comb to pull along the edge of the oblong cake to create the effect of pages. She carefully balanced the chocolate slab on top of the domed part of the hat and attached the fondant tassel to complete the mortar board.

Maddie wondered what other things she should add to her shopping list if she wanted to launch this hobby into a real business. She already had plenty to fill her kitchen – tins in all shapes and sizes; spatulas large, medium and small; stainless steel kitchen scales as well as a digital scale for when small, precise quantities were essential; piping nozzles; a decorating comb; a fondant ribbon cutter; half a dozen moulds with everything from a Santa face and reindeer heads, to a Halloween mould. Since Evan's confidence boost at dinner that night, she had dared to dream of one day owning her own premises: a shop where people could buy over the counter, sample before they placed an order. But for now, if Rachel Khoo of *The Little Paris Kitchen* fame could run The Smallest Restaurant in Paris from a tiny studio flat, then Maddie Kershaw could make do with her apartment.

Satisfied, Maddie clipped the cake carrier in place, ready to transport the cake to Arnie when he came in for his appointment today. The distraction of baking had worked wonders yet again, and for that Maddie was grateful as she headed to the shower to wash away the final traces of last night's nightmare.

*

'Thank you for bringing me, Evan.' Jem linked her grandson's arm as they walked down Collins Street.

'Don't be silly, you should've told me before, and I'd have made the appointment for you.'

'I've hurt one wrist, Evan. I'm perfectly capable of making a telephone call.'

Evan held the door open to a glass-fronted building for his ever-independent, one-hundred-year-old grandmother as Jem checked a piece of paper with the address. 'Which floor?' he asked.

'Fourth.' She followed him into the lift and up they went.

It was only as they made their way along the carpeted corridor that he saw the sign saying Palmers.

'Jem, did you know this is where Maddie works?' He waited for her answer, but she came over all innocent.

The sensation of his heart soaring took him by surprise. Half of him hoped Maddie would be here, on duty, but the other half of him didn't want to see her. He hadn't called her since the day he saw her on the beach and now he felt like a prize bastard for the way things had worked out. She knew he had his reasons, but it still didn't seem like much of an excuse. 'In limbo' – that was what an ex-girlfriend, Bec, had said she'd been when he never got in touch. Bec had told him she couldn't care less if he never wanted to see her again, but it would've been nice to be told.

He gingerly pushed open the heavy glass door and held it for Jem, whose face wasn't giving anything away. She stood behind a man in the queue.

'Evan, would you look at this cake?' Jem was admiring the cake tucked inside a plastic container by the man's feet.

It had to be one of Maddie's, no doubt about it. Evan looked at the cake, clearly for a graduation. With talent like this, Maddie had a real shot at turning her hobby into a business. She'd be crazy not to, crazy to stay in a job for which she lacked a genuine passion.

She was close by, he could tell. His heart quickened as Jem launched into a repartee with the man about the cake and the talents of its creator.

Evan pushed his hands into the pockets of his jeans in case they were shaking, and he was about to take a seat when he saw caramel, wavy hair shining beneath the downlights as Maddie came into the reception.

'Evan?' She looked about as shocked as he was, and he had had prior warning given that they were about to cross paths.

'G'day, Maddie.'

He didn't have to think of something to say because Jem had already launched into fancy-seeing-you-here's and lovely-to-see-you-again's. Maddie took Jem through to a treatment room and Evan ignored Jem's request that he go too.

'I'm fine just here, Jem.' He picked up the broadsheet on the table and opened it to stop any more protests. He didn't focus on a single word.

Twenty minutes later and Jem was back in reception accompanied by Maddie.

'It's not broken, just strained,' Maddie explained. 'I've bandaged it up so that it's easier to rest it, and it should come good. If it doesn't'—she turned to Jem—'please come back and see me.'

Evan wondered whether Jem had really hurt her arm; it seemed a miraculous recovery given her insistence that it needed to be seen to.

'Jem, I've been thinking,' said Evan. 'Perhaps you should give more thought to moving in with Mum. You know, if you're going to hurt yourself like this.'

He noticed Maddie stifle a laugh.

'I'll worry about you on your own now.'

'I'll just go and pay, Evan. Thank you again, Maddie.' And with no reference to Evan's suggestion, and perhaps because she knew she'd been sprung with her engineered injury, Jem scurried over to the reception desk.

'That'll teach her to mess with me,' said Evan when Jem was out of earshot. 'The looming threat of – heaven forbid – accepting some help and moving in with Mum will teach her for trying to throw us together again.'

'She's a lovely lady, Evan.' Maddie smiled, her cheeks flushed. She spoke softly. 'You'd be surprised at how many elderly patients come in with ailments that really don't need attention from a physio. I think some of them are just lonely.'

He wished she weren't so nice; it would be easier to walk away then. 'I don't think Jem has that excuse. She has loads of people around. But it's nice to see you anyway.'

'And you.' He saw her swallow, hard. 'Does she know?'

'That we went out on a date?'

She shook her head.

'Ah, you mean the dreaded C word? No, haven't quite got around to that yet.' He wondered again what made it easy to tell one person and not another. 'I probably should've kept my big mouth shut the other night too.'

Maddie looked distracted as another patient pushed through the doors. 'I'm glad you were so honest with me, Evan. Not every man would be quite so bold.'

Or quite so stupid, he decided.

He cleared his throat nervously. 'I suppose what I'm really sorry for is that we hadn't had more dates before I told you. I would've liked to get to know you better.'

'Can I ask you something, Evan?'

'Go on.'

'Why did you go out on a date with me when you knew that you could have cancer?'

The truth was that ever since he met Maddie, he couldn't imagine *not* asking her out. Women had come and gone from his life over the years, but she was the only one who had ever stayed in his mind long enough to consider more than a casual encounter with. And it had thrown him.

'I didn't know before I asked you out in the supermarket that day. I probably did what most blokes do and hoped that the problem would go away by itself. I still can't believe it didn't.'

He watched her chew on her bottom lip. She had no idea how sexy that was. All he wanted to do was to put his arms around her, breathe in the smell of her hair and feel her body against his.

'I hope it all goes well for you, Evan.'

'Thanks.' He took a deep breath and then said, 'I need some time to get my head around this, you know?'

'I should go.' She put an end to their encounter and any hint at another date later down the track. She turned, waved to Jem, who had kept her distance, pretending to be engrossed in the pamphlets on the front desk, and showed her next patient through to the treatment area.

What he didn't want was Maddie's pity. He wanted her to fancy him, to look at him as though she couldn't get enough. He wanted her to see him as the dependable strong man he had always been, and he didn't want her to be witness to his weakness – what kind of a wuss would he be then, ball or no ball? No, when it was all sorted out, that's when he would make his next move.

Chapter Twelve

After school came to a close on Friday, Evan went over to Jem's place to sort out her garden. It had been three days since she'd pulled her stunt and taken him to see Maddie, and he knew he couldn't wait any longer to tell his grandmother what was going on with his health.

Evan folded in the wing mirror of his Audi TT so it didn't get sideswiped outside Jem's place – it had happened twice before in the skinny road – took a deep breath and clicked open the wooden gate. After he rapped on the door, he stood back so Jem would be able to see it was him through the peephole he insisted she use. He made the obligatory crazy face with his tongue hanging out to one side, cross-eyed and a big frown on his forehead, a tradition between them that he never grew tired of when it was met with laughter from his grandmother when she opened the door.

'Evan, come in!' She pulled him into a hug, his large frame enveloping her.

'How's the wrist? I'm surprised you didn't call me before today.'

'It's much better. Your Maddie worked wonders. And I can manage perfectly well on my own, young man, have done for years.'

Jem had no idea how much he wished Maddie was 'his Maddie'.

'It's a miracle.' He smiled. He had to admire her persistence in throwing them together, even when she knew nothing about their date nor about the bombshell he had dropped at the end of it. After the physio appointment the other day, Evan had called Jem and quizzed her enough to find out that she had phoned several physiotherapists in the city before she found out where Maddie Kershaw worked.

'I'll get started.' He made his way through the house and out into the rear courtyard – gardening first, explanations later.

'Don't you want a cuppa first?' Jem called after him.

'Best not.'

The tiny courtyard showed signs of neglect: the agapanthuses on the far wall were in a bad way; the small patch of camellias had seen better days. The entire courtyard looked as though it felt sorry for itself, much like Evan, and he vented his frustration in the small space now that the morning rain had stopped.

His emotions had ebbed and flowed this week from the thrill of seeing Maddie to the misery of adjusting himself in his running shorts that morning and feeling the lump. He took his frustration out on the spent purple agapanthus, ripping off the heads. He tore out the debris from the terracotta pot in the far corner of the courtyard and wrestled with wisteria vines.

'Don't you get rid of too much of that,' warned Jem, stepping over to the lavender flowers that grew from the vines littering the back fence. She leant in, closed her eyes and inhaled the fragrance.

'You should get rid of all of it.' Evan forced his foot hard on the spade to push it into the soil of the flowerbed that ran down one side of the courtyard.

'Fuck!' His hair caught on a vine that looped low. 'Sorry,' he muttered without looking at Jem. He wiped the sweat from his brow with the back of his hand and knelt on the ground in the middle of the dead plants and mud that was strewn all over the place.

He felt a hand on his shoulder.

'Don't.' His voice barely a whisper, he wiped the stinging tears from his eyes.

'What's going on, Evan? Is everything okay at work? Is it Maddie?'

He wished it were quite so simple.

Jem lowered herself into the wooden chair beside him in the courtyard. 'What is it, Evan?'

He didn't look at her when he said, 'I need to have an operation.' He felt a papery hand on his own. He knew Jem was trying to instil confidence, but her hand shook as much as his heart pounded.

'What sort of operation?'

'They think I've got testicular cancer.'

He heard her gasp, and when he looked up her eyes were filled with tears. Neither of them spoke when Jem pulled him closer, and he felt as comforted as when he was a child who'd grazed his knee and sat on her lap.

'I don't understand, Evan. You're so … you're so young, so fit and strong.'

He ducked inside the back door and came back with a box of tissues. Jem took one as he said, 'Whenever the next vacancy comes up, I'm having an operation to remove the testicle. It's the only way the doctors can see what's really going on, how serious it is. I was going to wait to tell you, until after the operation was over with. But I knew that if you found out I'd kept it from you, you would've had my other ball on the chopping block.'

She was smiling now, albeit through tears. Jem had always kept her family close, and for him to keep this a secret would've crushed her regardless of the prognosis.

'Listen, Jem. Let's not worry until I know what I'm dealing with. Okay?' He grabbed both of her hands in his own, her cool skin vulnerable beneath his. 'The best case scenario is that it isn't cancer at all. But I'm afraid that the bloods and the ultrasound strongly suggest it is, so the next best thing is that we've caught it early enough that it hasn't had the chance to spread.'

Had he been indoctrinated into talking like the specialists?

'Have you spoken to Martha?' asked Jem.

He hated seeing the pallor that replaced his usually rosy-cheeked grandmother when she spoke.

'I've decided not to tell Mum for the time being.'

'Oh, Evan, are you sure that's a good idea? She'd want to be here for you, you know she would.'

'Yes, and I know how great a time she's having in Canada and the U.S. She's had this travelling planned for such a long time, and she deserves the chance to see it through. She worked long and hard for us kids, especially after Dad died. Now it's her turn to do something for herself. Her racing home won't change the outcome.'

'No, I don't suppose it will. So if it's cancer, what happens then?'

'The doctor says that if we've caught it early enough, then a single round of chemotherapy should be all that's needed to eradicate the cancer cells.' He just hoped they were right, but reciting those words to Jem actually helped – without those words he would go crazy with the possibilities of what could happen.

'Listen to you.' Jem clasped both of his hands in her own. 'You're counselling me when it should be the other way round.'

'It's funny. Out in the courtyard I was so angry—'

'I did notice.' She managed a smile.

'Telling you calmed me down in a way, and putting the whole story into words somehow helps to rationalise what's going on in my head.'

He didn't discuss the ins and outs of the operation. If it were a different cancer, then he probably would have done, but he couldn't sit and talk about his testicles with his grandmother. She was pretty liberal, but he drew the line at that.

Evan began piling the garden debris to one side. 'It's made me think about the future, Jem. I never gave much thought to long-term, but now all I seem to be able to fixate on is meeting the right person, settling down and having a family. All the normal things in life.'

The smell of damp grass and foliage hung in the air as he busied himself with the rest of the courtyard. 'This Winter Daphne will produce white flowers

111

eventually.' He smiled over at Jem as he emptied potting mix into an enormous terracotta pot. He'd already lined it with a piece of plastic fly wire to prevent the soil from seeping out when it was watered.

Jem reached out to run a hand along the vines of the wisteria that had moulded to the fence over the years. 'You know, Bernie and I planted this when we first bought the house.' She didn't look at him when he stopped to listen. 'Oh, we were in a terrible panic that it would never take. Neither of us knew a thing about gardening, but we both had visions of a beautiful oasis out here where we could relax, be together. And look at it now.'

Evan looked around the tiny rear courtyard Jem had put her mark on over the years; he looked up at the thin, weatherboard house that had as much character as she did with its signs of determination to beat whatever went on around it.

'I'm sorry for snapping at you to get rid of the wisteria.' His comment got the smile he was hoping for and Jem squeezed his hand reassuringly. He calmed when he felt her familiar, cool skin. No matter how warm it was outside or in, Jem's hands always felt the same.

'Bernie and I were lucky, Evan. We married young, had three beautiful children and we got to enjoy our grandchildren and now great-grandchildren. I realise how lucky I am, but only because I'm so old that I have time to sit around and contemplate what life has thrown at me. I've done pretty well dodging any curveballs.'

He chuckled at Jem's modern saying that had to have come from watching too many American sitcoms or movies as she tried to stay in touch with the times.

'Is that what you think the cancer is, a curveball?'

'I think sometimes we can get swept away in the business of everyday life, and we forget about the big picture. Think of it as a problem that must be overcome, a bit like the wisteria.'

'You're comparing wisteria to cancer?'

'Of course not, but Bernie and I pulled together with that wretched wisteria. We had no idea about gardening, but we had our future dream. The wisteria represents something we had to learn about, to work our way through to get to the good stuff – the oasis we envisioned when we bought this place. What I'm saying is that you shouldn't let cancer have the last word as to what your future will be. Never, ever give up on what you want, Evan. The chances are you'll get it, cancer or no cancer. You're a Quinn, after all.'

Evan grabbed the broom propped up against the house and swept up the debris, piling it into the garden waste bin.

'I don't want to speak out of turn,' Jem began.

'But you will,' he teased.

'I was wondering whether your sudden frustration is about more than the cancer, whether it has something to do with Maddie. I saw the way you two were with each other at the party and at the physio the other day. Is she the reason you've suddenly started thinking about the future and what could have been?'

'Has Holly been talking?'

'She may have mentioned that you two went on a date.'

'We did, and I went and told her about the cancer.' He pushed the last of the debris into the bin and swiped a beetle surreptitiously creeping up his forearm. 'I want to see her again, I really do. But I don't want our time together to be tainted with talk of losing a testicle, having chemotherapy, a recurrence of cancer.'

'Evan Quinn. Since when have you been afraid to take a chance? Right from a little nipper you were all about taking a risk and dealing with the consequences later. Do you remember your first athletics carnival when you were nine years old?'

He squinted as the sun crept above the rooftop and fully graced the courtyard.

'Well I do,' she continued. 'You weren't the slightest bit nervous. Your friend Jack was in a terrible state, worried he would come last, worried he wouldn't be able to finish the longer races. I can remember you standing there, sipping from your drink bottle, telling him that he would never know if he didn't at least try. You told him to stop being such a big girl's blouse – admittedly Martha and I were in fits of laughter at that expression coming from a nine-year-old – and you told him to get over to that start line.'

'I sound like a bossy girl.'

'You're not so different to Holly, you know.' Jem chided. 'My point, Evan, is that you won't know how Maddie feels if you don't give her a chance to tell you, a chance to react and deal with what's going on.'

114

She puffed out her cheeks and exhaled. I knew that girl was meant for you the second I saw her.'

'Is that so?'

'Okay, enough of this chit-chat.' She headed back into the kitchen, calling over her shoulder, 'The rest of this can wait. You need a cup of tea and something to perk you up, and so do I.'

He very rarely needed a cup of tea. In fact, he mostly drank it to humour Jem, who he could have sworn had tea running through her veins like blood. But Jem's baking? Now that was another matter entirely.

How had he not detected the smell seeping from the pan on the stove? He must have been in another world when he arrived. The smell filled the kitchen, wrapping a cloak of familial love around Evan as he took a scrubbing brush to his hands and fingernails.

'What's cooking, Gran?' he asked.

Jem gave him a don't-mess-with-me look.

'Sorry, "Jem".'

'That's better.' The smile that could light the way for a thousand ships reached her eyes and reminded Evan she hadn't always been this age. The photograph on her bedside table was testament to that: a slip of a woman on her wedding day standing next to his grandad Bernie, looking beautiful, happy – her life ahead of her just as his should be now.

'Is this what I think it is?' Evan's eyes widened as Jem carefully lifted the pudding basin out of the water – no sign of any problem in her wrist, he noted – and untied the baking paper lid secured by a string.

'Syrup Sponge.' His mouth watered as he looked at a deep golden sponge, his childhood favourite.

Jem ran a knife gently around the edge of the pudding basin and then tipped it out on to the waiting serving plate. She warmed extra syrup in a milk pan and then tipped it over the top of the golden sponge, letting it ooze through the air bubbles. She cut a thick slice and placed it in a bowl in front of Evan.

He shut his eyes at the first mouthful, couldn't speak on the second, but managed a few words after the third. 'I still remember coming home from school on cold winter days, and you'd pull out a syrup sponge from the pan on top of the stove, cover it in extra sauce and finish each serving with a great big dollop of vanilla ice cream.'

When he finished, even though they were alone, Jem lowered her voice and said, 'Go on, I won't tell.'

He picked up the bowl and used his tongue to lick anything leftover. When he resurfaced he saw the sparkle in Jem's eyes and they both dissolved into fits of giggles.

'Mum always hated that you let me do that,' he said.

'I don't care. I wanted to see my grandson happy today.' The coolness of her hand met with his cheek, and he inhaled the familiar Lily soap she had used since he was a kid.

'I thought the cancer was bad enough, Jem. I thought having an operation and chemotherapy would be the worst thing that could happen to me, but it's not. It's the uncertainty of the future.' His voice wavered. 'I'm scared that the cancer will be my last journey, Jem. I'm scared I won't get all the normal things in life that I've always taken for granted.'

'As I said before, don't let it dictate the future. The doctors sound positive, so for God's sake stay positive yourself. Thank goodness I've never known cancer, but from what I've heard, you have to choose to fight it.'

Her firmness of voice took him back to his school days when he would sit in this very kitchen, dangling his legs from a chair as they chatted about what he'd been up to that day.

Jem picked up the knife and it hovered over the syrup sponge. 'Now, would you like seconds?'

'Do you even have to ask?'

'So tell me, how was the date with the lovely Maddie?' Jem placed a second generous slice in front of him and ladled it with extra warm syrup.

'I bet you've been dying to ask me that.' He chuckled.

'I'm nobody's fool, Evan. You think you can distract me with your big health scare, but you can't.'

'It was worth a shot though, eh?' He smiled and stretched his legs out beneath the table. 'She's fantastic.'

Jem adjusted a small brown clip that held one side of her hair away from her face. 'It was incredibly honest of you to tell her about the cancer.'

'Honest? Don't you mean stupid? I told her I need time to get my own head around everything that's going on. I think she thought I was just fobbing her off.'

'I'll bet she doesn't. And time to think, for both of you, isn't necessarily a bad thing.'

'Well, if a girl told me she needed time, I would take it as code for don't-expect-me-to-call-you-anytime-soon.'

'I don't know. You youngsters and your mind games.'

'It's too much to expect of her.'

'Don't give up on her. If you like her as much as I suspect you do, it'll be worth the difficulties now, you mark my words. And if she's half the girl I think she is, she won't be scared off easily.'

He plunged both empty plates into the sink full of hot, soapy water, and poured them both a cup of tea.

'I saw a lot of hurt and sadness in her eyes, Jem, when I told her. We're both so new to each other that I don't know anything about her past. I don't know what effect the word *cancer* had on her. How can I expect a girl who I know nothing about, and who knows nothing about me, to see me through this journey. I'm about to have my bloody ba—' He stopped his rant. 'Let's just say I'm not going to feel like boyfriend material for a while.'

'I think you'll always be more of a man than you know, Evan.'

'You're biased. But cancer, or even the possibility of cancer, is the sort of journey people face when they're properly together: married for years and years, or at least a hell of a lot closer to a relationship than one date.'

Jem set her tea cup back on to its saucer. 'Evan, they say cancer doesn't discriminate. It happens to anyone at any stage of their life. Don't try to fit it into some ideal box, some ideal way it should be, like one of your lessons at school that start from one place and end up in another. Be prepared for the unexpected and for things to unfold.'

What he didn't tell Jem was that he wasn't scared Maddie wouldn't stick by him; he was more scared that she would. And pity, or even overwhelming sympathy, wasn't what any real man wanted, least of all him.

Chapter Thirteen

Maddie scooped the last dollop of creamy mixture into the cake tin and pushed it into the oven, and before long the smell of baking filled the apartment. Wearing the worn cherry-red oven mitts her sister bought her from Covent Garden last Christmas, she took out two identical sponge cakes and set them on top of the cooker. The cake tester came out satisfactorily clean from the centre of both cakes, so it was all systems go.

Maddie waited until the cakes naturally drew away from the edges of the tins as they cooled, and then turned them out so they could cool sufficiently for decorating. Today she was making a cake for Joel, Ally's boyfriend, who was hosting his birthday bash. She wiped down the kitchen surfaces and sat and read a book for a while until the intercom signalled Ally's arrival.

'Your neighbours must love you,' said Ally as she breezed through the door. 'The smell hits you the second you step out of the lift.'

'Let's hope the cakes taste as good as they smell,' said Maddie, hugging her friend.

When her mum, dad and sister complained that her baking was making their waistlines expand too much, Maddie had started baking for friends, neighbours, colleagues. Like running and pounding the streets gave her an escape from normality, so did baking. She'd focus on the recipe, sort through ingredients, work out an intricate design, all the while getting further away from real life.

Ally helped herself to a glass of juice from the fridge and plonked herself down on a stool at the kitchen bench as they chatted. She didn't take long to work out that Maddie wasn't quite herself that day.

'Do you want to talk about it?' Ally asked.

'No, thanks.' Smiling, Maddie pottered around the lounge, tidying away a couple of magazines, the cake decorating books she'd flicked through. Evan had left her in a puddle of confusion for the last few days, and she didn't really know how to explain it to herself, let alone anyone else.

When it was time to decorate the cakes, Maddie set them on the bench top at the end farthest away from Ally.

'Oh relax, I won't pick at them.'

'I don't trust you. "Just a little taste."' She mimicked Ally's voice. '"You won't notice once the icing is covering it."'

'That does sound an awful lot like me. So are we still making the French Maid cake?'

'We sure are. And before you say anything, I don't even want to ask *why* this cake would be such a hit with the boys, because all I keep picturing is you, dressed in a little pinny and fishnet stockings.'

'There's nothing wrong with a bit of imagination in the bedroom.'

'I'm just glad you found me a simple picture from a magazine and didn't give me a photograph.' Maddie glanced over her shoulder at the clock hanging above the cooker. 'What time's the party?'

'Not until four o'clock, so plenty of time to get your glad rags on. Some of the boys will get there for early afternoon to reserve a good barbecue along the Yarra.'

'It looks as though we got a good day for it.' The sight of clouds that looked like churned white candyfloss drifting steadily across the palest of skies beyond the balcony doors told Maddie all she needed to know, and the welcome autumn breeze kept the kitchen at the right temperature as she worked.

The venue for this afternoon's party just happened to be one of Maddie's favourite places too. Down beside the Yarra River, she loved to hear the sound of the water rushing so freely beneath the boats as they slid across the surface, the sounds of the blades chopping the water before gliding back across. When she walked to work, she often paused on the bridge that straddled the Yarra, remembering how she had watched Riley row in the men's eight as it passed beneath, water swirling in its wake.

'It'll do you good to get out today,' said Ally.

Maddie rummaged for the appropriate piping nozzle in a kitchen drawer. 'I'm looking forward to it.' She plonked all the implements on to the stone bench top.

'Do you think Evan will call you again?'

Maddie had told Ally all about the encounter at work when Jem came in as a patient. 'I don't think so. I don't think he knows what he wants, and maybe when it's all over he'll lose interest in me anyway.'

'What makes you say that?'

'Maybe he just told me because he wanted some comfort, someone to turn to. Once it's all over with, I wouldn't be surprised if he's out trying to pick up any woman. I'm nothing special, Ally, even I can see that.'

Maddie swore when she knocked the cake knife on to the floor. She used both hands to tighten her ponytail, pulled it so hard it almost hurt, and then bent down to pick up the knife.

'Besides,' Maddie continued, 'if I'm struggling to get my head around what he has going on, then I'm sure Evan must be in a worse state. I'd say this is no way to start a relationship.'

'It's no way to end one, either,' Ally muttered, but not so quietly that Maddie didn't hear.

She rinsed the knife and laid out the pre-cut sections of baking paper that, when put together, would give the curvy outline of a French Maid. She laid one on top of the first rectangular cake and cut around the curves of what would become the breasts and along the bottom to give the short apron a frilly edge. From the other block of sponge, she cut two smaller rectangles using the paper outlines and positioned them on the cake board which, when sandwiched with the other shape, would represent the legs.

Maddie combined the wet ingredients for the fondant icing and added those to the icing sugar in the mixer. Using a dough hook, the fondant icing was formed into a smooth ball which she separated and added the appropriate food colouring to before rolling out to form each part of the design.

As Maddie worked, the saucy French Maid gradually took shape. A steady hand and a hushed silence allowed her to mix more icing and pipe on the frills of the skirt, the outline of the white apron and the intricate criss-cross pattern of the fishnet tights.

Ally came to the other side of the bench and put an arm around her friend's shoulders. 'It's brilliant. Joel is going to be stoked.' She lingered for a moment and then, pressing both palms together in prayer position, said, '*Now* do I get to lick the bowl?'

'You're such a big kid!' Maddie handed her a teaspoon, grabbed one for herself, and for the next couple of minutes all that could be heard was the clinking of spoons as they fought to get every last trace of mixture stuck to the bowl.

Ally disappeared at lunchtime and came back a couple of hours later into the apartment that still smelt sweet from the baking. She looked like a 1950's starlet. 'What do you think?' Her scarlet strappy dress with black trim twirled with her, and her blonde hair hung loose.

'You look amazing,' said Maddie, 'but I thought this was a casual barbecue on the Yarra.'

'It is. But it's also Joel's special day, and since I returned to student land, I never get to dress up. I'm damn well gonna make the most of my opportunity.'

'I wish you were staying over tonight,' said Maddie as Ally followed her down to her bedroom. She may not have been very forthcoming about her feelings for Evan, but she knew that post-barbecue, and with a few drinks inside of her, she would be ready to talk late into the night.

Ally winked as she sat on the lilac bedspread in the room Maddie had painted white with the slightest hint of rose petal. 'Sorry, boyfriend's birthday trumps best friend's need for company tonight.'

'That's a fair point.' Maddie sifted through her wardrobe, scrunching her nose up at various options.

'Here, let me.' Ally took over the wardrobe inspection and within seconds had pulled out a black cotton dress with a halter-neck and white edging. 'This is perfect. Try it on. It's a gorgeous day, and it's thicker cotton so you'll be warm enough. You can team it with that little black Alannah Hill cardigan,' she said, pulling said item from the back of the wardrobe. 'You'll look fabulous, trust me.'

While Ally pouted in front of the mirror and checked her lipstick in the same shade as her dress, Maddie took a shower. It was ages since they had been out, and she was looking forward to spending the day with Ally, her boyfriend and some of his friends. Sometimes it was easier to be in the company of strangers who knew nothing about you.

Thirty minutes later Maddie pulled on her dress, smoothed it down across her tummy and hips and stood next to Ally as they both looked in the mirror.

'Joel's a lucky guy,' said Maddie.

Ally gave her a cheeky nudge. 'He'll be even luckier later; I've got a French Maid's outfit in my bag.'

'You have not!'

'I have too!'

Maddie swished her hands in front of her. 'Okay, okay, no more sharing.'

Ally hugged her friend tight. 'The world can be a crappy place, Maddie. But it can also be a beautiful one. Let's have a great time this afternoon, eh? Get sloshed, forget all about Evan.'

After much giggling and spritzing of perfumes as well as topping up of make-up, Maddie grabbed the cake and they headed out of the apartment, emerging on to St Kilda Road to wait for the tram. Maddie had fallen in love with this iconic grand boulevard in Melbourne and snapped up her apartment almost the moment it came on the market. Trams hooked on to cables in the centre of the road trundled passengers from city to suburbs and the beach; majestic plane trees lined the median strips and turned a rich spinach colour in the lights from traffic and streetlamps overhead. St Kilda Road was home to the National Gallery of Victoria too, as well as the Arts Centre and the markets that lined footpaths on Sundays. Green spaces of the Royal Botanic Gardens and the Domain Parklands close by created an incredible juxtaposition to the mayhem of city life.

Outside Federation Square they followed the steps down to the river, passed by the rowing sheds and made their way along the line of barbecues until Joel called out their names.

Joel immediately tried to take a peek at what lay beneath the lid of the cardboard box in Maddie's arms.

'Not so fast!' Ally moved his hand away. 'It's a surprise, so no unveiling until I give the nod, okay Maddie?'

'Right you are, boss.'

Joel and his mates seemed to have everything organised, with trestle tables set up for food and drinks, eskies full of ice from which the tops of unopened champagne bottles poked out as well as cans and bottles of beer. Packages of meat sat beside the barbecue, raring to go.

Maddie stowed the cake away from the heat of the barbecue, a glass of champagne was thrust into her hand as introductions were made, and sun endorphins, alcohol and peals of laughter worked their magic. For now, she felt glad of the chattering crowd, grateful of the escape.

Her champagne almost went flying when someone behind her jogged her arm.

'Sorry,' said the guy. He held out a hand. 'I don't think we've been introduced. I'm Josh.'

'Hi, I'm Maddie.' She returned his gesture with her dry hand, then swapped the glass and shook off the drips from the other.

'Here, let me get you a refill.' Josh whisked the glass away and was back within seconds. 'Plenty more where that came from, don't worry. Thank you for the cake by the way, I haven't seen it yet, but rest assured that none of us would have a hope of making anything edible between us – our culinary competence extends as far as the barbecue and that's about it.'

On the banks of the Yarra, Maddie and Josh chatted about work, hobbies – all the usual small talk made when you first met someone. Usually, Maddie measured each man she met against Riley, but not this time, and it caught her off guard. She found herself comparing Josh to Evan: Josh was shorter, he was toned yet not as muscly and he had dead-straight, dirty-blond hair. Evan's voice was strong, yet gentle at the same time, caressing her ears when he spoke. Josh was a real Aussie bloke – not that there was anything wrong with him; he just wasn't Evan.

The afternoon flew by, and before long a chinking noise rose above their voices and all faces turned towards Ally. She made a toast to Joel before the grand unveiling of the cake, and the French Maid met with a unanimous roar of enthusiasm as Maddie stepped forwards to do the honours and serve it on to paper plates.

At the end of the afternoon, champagne corks, empty bottles and plastic plates were shoved into bin bags as the group cleared the barbecue area.

'Let me take that.' Josh took the cardboard cake box from Maddie's hands as she looked around for a recycling bin. 'I can't believe we ate the entire cake.'

'I thought it was huge when I made it, but with twenty partiers drinking alcohol, it never really stood a chance.' Bin liner in hand, Maddie threw out the remaining disposable champagne flutes as Joel and a mate folded down the trestle table and carried it towards the direction of a parked car. She wondered who the poor designated driver was today; she was glad it wasn't her and that she had been able to kick back and enjoy herself.

When Josh had emptied the esky upside down to drain it of any remaining ice cubes and the water created from those that had melted, he said, 'I don't know about you, but I could use a walk to work off some of that food.'

Maddie looked at him. 'That sounds like a great idea.'

They set off along the river and Maddie knew she was swaying from the champagne, made worse with the combination of the sun that had only just started to turn a rich orange hue as it fell slowly in the sky, preparing for dusk. Josh was good company today, and she knew he was interested in her – a brush of her arm here; a nudge there; a look that left her in no doubt. Maddie was flattered and she found herself longing to be held tightly, into the night, to be so close to someone that she couldn't breathe in the thoughts of her own life. Sometimes her head was so full of Riley, Caitlin, and now Evan, that she felt like a snow globe that had been turned upside down and shaken, her feelings scattering all over the place.

They followed the curves of the river, laughing as Josh regaled a funny tale of a work party and being stuck on a boat with forty people he couldn't stand. And when the night sky fell in a blanket all around them, they turned to head back, but Josh's hand on her arm stopped her. She knew what was going to happen, and when he moved in she allowed herself to fall into his kiss, a kiss that anaesthetised painful memories and watered down the uncertainty in her mind. And as they went back to his apartment together, Maddie hoped he would be the escape she needed.

Chapter Fourteen

'I'm sorry, Josh, I can't.' Maddie pushed him away as he undid the tie on her dress.

'What's wrong?'

'I just can't do this. It wouldn't be right.' It was Evan's face she saw when she closed her eyes, Evan's body she longed to have pressed against her own.

'Are you with someone?' Josh asked.

She saw no anger in his eyes, just a need for an explanation that she couldn't give right now.

'I'm sorry.' She picked up her bag, and his voice followed her as she ran from the apartment all the way home, adrenalin pumping enough to not worry about being out alone late at night.

When she dumped her keys on the stone kitchen bench, they clattered in the silence. She sat for a while, staring at the shadows cast from the furniture in the glow of the moon from the outside. She listened to the odd groan and creak of the building as it slept soundly.

She opened the balcony doors and shivered as the breeze kissed her bare shoulders, and outside, she stood engulfed in darkness, looking towards the lake which was barely visible. She wondered whether she could only see it because she knew it was there. Tonight the Albert Park Lake was innocent and still, silent; in March it had been the home to the Grand

Prix, alive and vibrant, completely at odds with what it was tonight. How quickly things could change in your world.

A siren in the distance made her recoil from the railing. She stumbled back, scared that she may fall despite the glass panels, that she might plummet into the blackness of the last decade from the moment Riley was killed. Tears pricked her eyes as she thought of Josh and what had just happened. He was a nice guy; he didn't deserve someone like her messing up his life because she had no sense of what was happening in her own.

Tonight, the temptation to have sex with Josh and lose herself in his arms had obliterated her mind of everything else. But for the first time in a long time, the reality had taken over before it could happen. And now, in the safety of her apartment, all she wanted to do was sleep in her own bed.

*

What time was it? Maddie sat bolt upright, confused. Why was the room so dark? She grabbed her iPhone, which once illuminated, told her it was 3 a.m. and it hadn't been her alarm at all, but a text.

She focused on the message; it was from Evan.

His name was enough to bring her to a sitting position beneath the duvet, and she anxiously grabbed each word in turn, as though it were a small jewel to treasure:

Been thinking about you – a lot. If it's not too much to ask I'd really like to see you again. How about tomorrow arvo, beneath the clocks at Flinders Street Station? Evan.

131

Her hands shook as she re-read the message four times. She felt like a teenager with her first Valentine's, trying to commit the words to memory. But any feelings of joy were quickly nullified when she thought of how close she had come to sleeping with Josh. She felt disgusted with herself, repulsed that she had been intimate with him when the only person she had been able to think about was Evan.

She left the iPhone perched on her bedside table, and despite it being the early hours of the morning, she headed for the shower. She turned the taps on full blast, stripped off her pyjamas and let the water drench her from head to toe, hoping it would wash away the guilt and the pain from the past. And along with the water droplets the tears fell. This was what she couldn't handle: the confusion, the not knowing, the thinking that one minute you knew where your life was headed, but the next, you found yourself travelling in a completely different direction.

'Fuck you, Caitlin!' She screamed, her head resting against the warmth of the tiles. 'Fuck you!'

When Riley died, the mooring that had kept Maddie a part of his family had been slashed, and Caitlin had drifted off into an unknown ocean, shutting down emotionally in her own grief and leaving Maddie all alone on the shore. But right now, inexplicably, the only person Maddie wished she had in her life to talk to was Caitlin. They had been so close for so many years that she wished she could see her, shake her, find out why she had said those words to her, why she had cut Maddie out of their lives.

Maddie wrapped herself in the soft, ocean-blue bath towel and sat on the edge of the bed, holding her iPhone. She blamed Caitlin for her inability to move on, for the comfort she found with men with whom she had no commitment. After all, there was no dishonouring of Riley's memory when she was with those men; they were no replacement for the love she once shared with Riley. Evan had been the first man with whom plans and dreams of the future had even entered her mind; he was so much more than an aid to forgetting the past.

She tapped in a reply to say that, yes, she did want to meet him, and his reply came through so quickly her insides flipped.

So, you can't sleep either, huh?

Maddie tapped away again, her fingers flying expertly across the screen.

It happens sometimes :-)

She added the smiley face and held her breath, waiting for his reply, enjoying the buzz the repartee gave her.

I'd better say goodnight as I've got a busy morning, but I'll see you underneath the clocks tomorrow at midday x

The kiss at the end stopped her mid-flow pulling her pyjama top over her head. The top sat around her neck, the arms hanging loose at the sides. She knew now that she wasn't ready to forget Evan, and, it seemed, Evan wasn't ready to forget her either.

*

Evan dumped his sweaty running gear in the washing machine. This apartment was the place he had called home for almost three years now. Bought off the plan and his first non-shared place, he had made it so much more than a bachelor pad. Oh, it had its signs: the latest plasma dominating the lounge area, the black leather couches and the stash of stubby holders taking up an entire shelf in one of the cupboards next to the fridge – designs included the Australian flag, as well as a fair few representing his footy team, The Demons – but Evan's apartment also had a coffee table, a rug in the centre of the lounge and paintings on the walls.

He pulled on jeans and a long-sleeved blue grandad top and grabbed his black Barbour jacket before he left his apartment and headed towards Flinders Street. He hoped the walk would help him to work out what to say to Maddie. He had run around Albert Park Lake that afternoon, and for the entire five kilometres he had pondered what he should, or shouldn't, say. Texting Maddie last night hadn't been something he had planned, but he was glad he had finally done it.

When he arrived at Flinders Street Station, Evan stood beneath the clocks that sat in a line above the main entrance to identify expected arrival times for trains on various platforms. He felt more nervous than he had on any date before, including his first ever date with Donna, the girl who was two years older than him, asked him out, and to whom he had lost his virginity.

He ran a hand through his hair and watched as a group of teenagers scrambled frantically up the steps to catch their train. And then, there she was. The waves of her hair lifted delicately in the breeze, hypnotising him. Her jeans did nothing to deter his eyes from her neat little figure, nor did the navy and white striped top with a sheer finish that made his mouth open and his groin awaken with longing. He hadn't been prepared for such a reaction.

Maddie pulled her black cardigan around herself as she reached the spot where he stood. Was she cold or had she seen him gazing at her like he had never seen a woman before?

'Hi.' How was it possible for one little word to sound so lame?

'Hey,' she replied.

Should he kiss her? Man, this was harder than he thought. He took the brave – or was it the easy? – option and bent down to kiss her on her cheek, but he knew he came off more like a nervous school boy than a grown man with a full-time job, an apartment and the ability to drive legally.

'It's good to see you again, Maddie.'

She scooped her hair behind her ears, but the wind refused to let it stay that way. 'It's good to see you too.'

'Let's head over to the laneways, find somewhere for coffee.'

They followed the steps down at the front of the station, waited for a tram to pass and then crossed the road to a small laneway filled with the aroma of coffee beans and the sounds of chatter and clinking cutlery against plates.

A waitress seated them outside at the first venue they came to, and they sat beneath an outdoor heater that hissed its bright orange circle of heat as Maddie placed her order.

'I'll have a large skim milk hot chocolate please.'

'Make that two,' said Evan, shutting his menu firmly. He could barely take his eyes off of Maddie, and wasting time looking at the menu was something he didn't want to do.

'I didn't place you as a hot chocolate drinker,' she said when the waitress left them alone.

Even the sound of her voice had the ability to get him excited, or was it watching her lips as she spoke? He had no idea but tried to keep his feelings under control, at least for now. 'I'm usually a coffee man – tea if it's with Jem – but hot chocolate is great in autumn and winter. It's a bit of a meal in a cup.'

His nerves had obviously got the better of him, and words raced out of his mouth at the same rate as his pulse hammered against his insides. He was talking utter bollocks.

'I like the way you think,' said Maddie. 'Although, I think it's probably soup that's a meal in a cup.'

Today felt far more intimate than their first date had been, and he was glad when she spoke again to save him from trying to think of something intelligent to say.

'How's Jem?' she asked.

'She's grand. Strangely enough, her wrist doesn't seem to be giving her any problems at all.'

'Funny that,' Maddie sniggered.

'It must be a miracle because she's talking about playing lawn bowls.'

'Well you can't blame her for trying,' said Maddie, who smiled at the waitress when she placed the decadent hot chocolates in front of them. 'I think you could be right about that meal in a cup.' She took her spoon to tackle what looked more like a sumptuous dessert than a hot drink. She scooped up some of the whipped cream – it was too much to take in one hit, and she stirred the rest into the hot chocolate that sat beneath.

'I've been for a run so I've earned this,' Evan said, doing the same with his cream. 'We should go running together some time. I know you said you're a regular.'

'I am. I can't stand pumping iron in a room full of sweaty bodies. I'd much rather be out in the fresh air.'

'I'm the same. I've got a spare room with a set of weights, but that's about it. Sometimes I attempt a session in the gym at the apartment complex, but fresh air will win for me every time. Maybe we could do the lake or the Tan Track some time.'

'I'd like that.' Maddie clasped her mug between her hands, halfway through the rich liquid inside. 'I ran along the beach this morning, but I'll go again a couple of times this week. I'm on the early shift on Tuesday so I'll finish at a decent time, how about joining me then?'

'Great. I'd better check that I don't have any irate parents scheduled for then and I'll confirm.'

'Do you really get irate parents?'

He skimmed the top of the liquid in his mug to get another mouthful of cream. 'Some of them can be a bit pushy, but on the whole they're harmless. I can handle them.'

'I'm sure you can.'

He loved the way her cheeks glowed when she spoke.

'Have you heard when your operation will be?'

The happy feeling he had inside dissolved with her question. Even watching her lips move as she talked and the way she scooped her hair away from her face wasn't enough to soften the blow.

He rubbed the back of his neck and found it hard to meet her gaze. 'Not yet.'

'I'm sorry.'

'Why?' Please, anything but pity. He could handle anything she dished out, but not that.

'I didn't mean to bring it up.'

'You mean the cancer?'

'Well, yes.'

'I'm trying my best to be positive, and that's why I've gone back on what I said by contacting you.' It was time to be honest now. 'At first I didn't want to start anything until after the operation, until I knew what I was dealing with. But seeing you at work that day, well it threw me. I couldn't stay away.'

Her eyes darted to his hand that had reached out across the table and covered hers. He didn't miss her sharp intake of breath when he showed no signs of moving it away.

'So what happens now? What will happen in the operation?'

His manhood had been very much the focus of a second date with other girls, but never in this way. He explained in layman's terms what the orchidectomy involved – he wanted to answer her questions, but it was hard when they were discussing his balls.

'Once the results go to pathology, I'll know what I'm dealing with.'

'Have you got someone to go with you? You know, on the day?'

'Yes, of course.' He hadn't, yet, but he wasn't sure he could face their third date being in a hospital room with his virility being tampered with and the woman he was falling for standing by as a witness. 'Would you mind if we didn't talk about the Big C? Can we pretend it's you and me, Evan and Maddie, out on a second date?'

The corners of her mouth moved upwards. 'Okay, but before we do, I need to explain why I found the cancer so hard to deal with when you first told me.'

'You really don't need to explain, Maddie. We were playing an innocent, fun game, and I ruined that by asking what the worst thing was that had ever happened to you. When it got to my turn I hadn't meant to blurt it out like that, I just did.'

'Well, when it was my turn to tell you the worst thing that had happened to me, I said that a friend had died suddenly. But what I didn't tell you was that he was my boyfriend.'

He kept hold of her hand until she eventually looked up at him. 'Why didn't you tell me that?' he asked. Did it mean she wasn't over this other guy?

'I don't tend to tell the new people I meet about Riley, because of the sympathy, the way they treat me.'

He nodded sagely. 'I've been there.'

'You have?'

'When Dad died I hated being pitied, being one of those Quinn children who had lost their father.' He hesitated. 'Can I ask why you're suddenly telling me about Riley?'

'Because I feel that I should. Because I know that losing Riley made an impact on how I took your news about the cancer. I think it would have been a shock anyway, but I think I would've handled it a hell of a lot better than I did.'

'You had every right to be shocked. I can't imagine what it would be like to hear that on a first date.'

He felt a warm feeling settle in his stomach when she relaxed and smiled up at him, the tips of her fingers curling upwards into the palm of his hand. He would ask her more about Riley someday, but not yet. It felt too intrusive this early on in their relationship and too much had been carelessly blurted out already. He wanted Maddie to open up to him in her own time because he had the feeling there were many complex layers to this girl, and he wanted to peel back each one in turn and savour getting to know her.

'Now,' he teased, 'you know the most intimate details about me, and I know some of your past, but I want to know more.' He watched a slow blush creep up on to her cheeks. 'Tell me what it was like to grow up in Sydney.'

'What do you want to know?'

'Everything,' he said.

They talked about her childhood spent frolicking on amazing beaches, her school days and his, her time at University and her family. When they began to debate the differences between her home city and his, he went into battle for Melbourne and she did her best to do the same for Sydney.

'Well our beaches are pretty spectacular,' Maddie declared.

'Listen to you: "our beaches",' he mocked.

'But … the harbour can be filthy. Have you ever looked down next to one of those ferries? There's rubbish, the water's murky. They don't show that on the postcards, do they?'

'Now that's true. They're both very different cities I think, each with their own merits.'

'I couldn't agree more.'

The more he got to know Maddie, the deeper he was falling. 'So, can I ask how the cake business is going?'

'It's hardly a business.'

'Don't be so modest. I saw the graduation cake the other day, remember. And don't forget the penis cake of course. You're a talented girl.'

'I got two more requests after the graduation party: one for a baby shower and another for a fiftieth.'

'See, what did I tell you?' He ran a hand through the air as though he were writing words on a sign. 'Maddie Kershaw, cake extraordinaire.'

'I was thinking I should get some business cards made up.'

'That's a great idea. Let me have some when they're done and I can pass them out to my colleagues, perhaps you could even make an ad and I can have it included in the school's community newsletter. I'm sure there are just as many mums looking to outsource the making of birthday cakes as there are mums who want to make them themselves.'

141

'I may just take you up on that.'

They talked about Evan's family, his mum's trip overseas and they sifted through his memories of Jem over the years.

'I can't remember it, but there are enough pictures to prove it,' he said. 'Honestly, the woman was petrified that I'd drown in Albert Park Lake every time I fed the ducks, and she would grasp hold of whatever clothes I had on, even if I was a good ten feet from the water's edge! I'm surprised I'm not too disturbed by childhood memories to go running past it so often.'

'She sounds like a lot of fun.'

'She was. She still is.'

'I couldn't believe it at the party when she told me she was a hundred years old,' said Maddie.

'It's bizarre isn't it? I think she's got more energy than the rest of us put together. If you tell her that though, she'll go on about how she didn't have all this fancy technology in her day; they played in the park and fresh air until their parents called them inside for dinner. Or she'll tell you that it's because she never stresses about food, never says no to cake.'

The conversation turned to holidays they'd both taken – or wished they'd taken – and then on to television programs they loved or loathed, and favourite bands. The normality soothed Evan, and once the bill was paid and the hot chocolates lined their contented stomachs, he held out his hand.

'Where are we going?' She looked almost as scared as he had been on his way to today's date.

His hand fell down to his side when he realised she wasn't going to take it. He watched her twiddle a set of keys in her fingers.

'What's wrong?' he asked.

'Evan, before we go anywhere else, we really need to talk.'

Chapter Fifteen

'Evan, I met someone else.'

They sat on a bench and both looked out over the water to the restaurants on the opposite side of the river.

'I had a lot of champagne at a barbecue and I got talking to this guy. I was convinced you would never get in touch with me again and—'

'So you moved on to the next? That didn't take long.'

'Now that's not fair.'

He was hurt, she knew, and he didn't speak for a while.

'I met someone, and I went home with him,' she continued.

'I don't need the details,' he spat.

'Evan, I'm trying to explain, please hear me out.'

His mouth sat in a hard line, and he refused to look at Maddie.

'Nothing happened apart from a kiss. Please believe me when I say that I wouldn't have got involved at all if I thought you and I were going to get together.'

Her words seemed to placate him, but when his silence became too much to bear, she said, 'Please say something. I know it sounds as though I just moved on to someone else, but that wasn't how it was, really it wasn't. I'd had a lot to drink at the barbecue, and I guess I felt lonely. And Josh … well he was just there, he helped me to forget.'

'Forget me, you mean?'

'Kind of,' she stammered and slumped back against the bench. 'I'm not making a very good job of this, am I?'

'No.'

She waited until a man walking his dog had passed them by. 'When I lost Riley, I didn't cope very well.' Her head fell into her hands as she grappled with the words. 'I fell apart, and since then I haven't had a proper relationship.'

'So you're not over Riley?'

'Riley died a long time ago.' She wondered whether Evan would feel second best if she told him that Riley was the love of her life, how he would feel if he thought he was in any way a replacement for the part of her life she had lost, a replacement for the togetherness and closeness she had shared with Riley.

She bit down on her lip, her heart pounding hard. 'Evan, there's something else.' She had to tell him. If they were going to start anything, if she was going to have a proper relationship again, she wanted him to know who she was. And if he didn't like it, then she would just have to deal with that.

'I'm listening.'

'I fell hard after Riley, and I didn't think of men in the same way.' God this was harder than she thought. How could she tell him without making him think the worst of her?

'I'm not sure I follow.'

'I have met men since, but I was never interested in anything more than …'

'Having a fling?'

She looked at him now, allowed those chocolate eyes to melt the stress away as he watched her. She couldn't read his face. Was he surprised, jealous, disgusted?

'I used to give out fake telephone numbers, avoid the guy like the plague if I saw him again.'

'Sounds like you could give any man a run for his money. I'm sorry,' he added when her face dropped.

'I wanted the company more than the sex.' She looked down at her bag on her lap. 'It was never about the sex,' she whispered.

Some said sex was the biggest bond you could have with another human being, but it was surprisingly easy to detach yourself and use the intimacy, the frisson of excitement as an escape, and that's exactly what Maddie had done. All she had wanted was to feel loved and cared for, feel safe in a man's arms, but the sex had become part of the escape.

Evan's warm hand closed around her own. When he spoke, his voice was calmer. 'Maddie, I'm not judging you.'

'But sleeping around is hardly an appealing quality, especially for a woman.' She hoped he wouldn't ask her how many men she'd been involved with over the years.

'You're only human, and I could get all high and mighty and jealous – which I am, by the way – or I could admit that, until you came along, I went in for the no-strings-attached approach too. I can't judge you when I'm no better.'

'When I met you, Evan, it was different. You were different to any of the men I've met since Riley. Something about you just seemed to fit. I'd never had the urge to get into a meaningful relationship with anyone else, until you.'

Rationalising her behaviour out loud was strange. But even stranger than that was the fact that Evan was still beside her, his shoulder comfortably touching hers. He hadn't run when she revealed her true self.

'I'm glad you told me, Maddie. About the other guy, I mean, and about Riley and your history. I'm sorry I pushed you away in the first place by thinking I needed to be on my own to get my head sorted.'

He pulled her to standing, towering above her. His fingers rubbed lightly against the palm of her hand, and then he reached up and let his fingers run down the side of her face, past her lips. She longed for him to lean down and kiss her. She had imagined it a thousand times, dreamt about it too. But just when she thought she was about to find out, he said, 'Come on, I know just the place to make this a perfect second date.'

'Where are we going?'

'You'll see.'

Hand in hand they ran across the footbridge that linked Flinders Street to the opposite side of the river, and moments later they had boarded a small boat and were chugging their way over to Williamstown.

The temperature of late afternoon had dropped, and Evan took out the scarf stashed in the inner pocket of his coat. He looped it over Maddie's neck, pulled her towards him and planted a firm kiss on her lips as they passed beneath the Bolte Bridge.

'What was that for?' she asked.

He leant closer and she felt his warm breath on her cheek, sweet smelling from the creamy hot chocolates. 'No reason.'

She started to speak, but his finger rested against her lips to silence her. She felt warmer than she had done all night and her lips tingled from his touch.

They sat and let the breeze float across their faces, the occasional drop of water splashing them from the river as they approached Williamstown.

'I'm looking forward to getting to know you, Maddie Kershaw.' His hand rested on her thigh and sent a jolt of electricity through her. 'These jeans are sexy. They suit you.'

'Thanks.' She giggled like a total girl. 'I do have a bit of an obsession about jeans as it happens.' His hand didn't move an inch and it felt good, comforting. 'According to my friend Ally, I buy jeans like other people buy postcards. When I went to New York, I came back with four pairs: True Religions, Dylan George, Diesel and Stitch's. When I last went home to Sydney, I bought another two pairs, both Levi's but different cuts.'

'You're addicted then, aren't you?'

'I'll let you into another secret.'

'What's that?' he asked as the boat docked and they stood to disembark.

'I would never date a guy whose bum didn't look good in a pair of jeans.'

He let out a loud laugh and turned to give her the opportunity to make her judgement. 'So, do I pass?'

'I'll let you know.'

Still laughing, he steered them in the direction of a row of shops where the scent of vinegar filled the air and the warmth of steaming hot slices of potatoes drifted out on to the footpath from a fish and chip shop. They were lured inside to make their selections beneath the bright strip lights.

Wrapped parcels in hand, they headed back to the waterside where they found a bench overlooking the water. The steam from the chips and the crisply battered flake hit Maddie with an overwhelming force when she pulled off the paper wrapping.

'I didn't think you'd be hungry after those hot chocolates,' Evan mocked as he unzipped his jacket, the warmth of the food taking away the need for extra layers.

'I'm starving,' she admitted, scraping a thick chip through the ketchup.

They looked out over the blackened water. Intermittent lights in the distance came from boats and buildings that were unidentifiable. A young couple eating ice creams walked by.

'They must be freezing,' whispered Maddie, still toasty from the warm food that lined her stomach. She licked her fingers as Evan gathered the rubbish and stuffed it into a bin nearby.

When he sat down next to her again he said, 'So without getting all emotional, and without mentioning what's going to happen to me in the next couple of weeks, do you think you'd like to go out on another date?'

'I'd really like that.'

'You're shivering,' he whispered into her hair. He lifted an arm and let it settle across her shoulders. The scent of salt and vinegar played tricks with her mind, and she was unable to distinguish who the smell was coming from, him or her.

When she turned towards him, the warmth of his lips didn't take her by surprise. It felt right. His tongue gently pushed at her own as she reached up to his neck, pulling him towards her. His hands grabbed hold of her hair that hung loose, gripping it between his fingers and holding her head so he could kiss her more deeply.

He pulled her to her feet, wrapping her in the warmth of a hug. 'That was amazing.'

She buried her face in his chest, unable to stop smiling. His heart pounded against her cheek, beating in the same crazy way as hers.

'We'd better go or we'll miss the boat.' He combed the wavy strands of hair away from her face.

They hurried back to the boat, hugging each other tightly all the way along the Yarra as darkness fell and stars winked at them knowingly. And they stayed like that as the vessel retraced its route back towards the lights of the Crown Entertainment Complex.

When they disembarked Evan pulled her to him again, his head settled on top of hers. She felt him inhale the smell of her hair.

'Can I walk you home?' he asked.

Her breath caught in her throat as though it had lost its way out. This was unlike Josh, unlike any of the men before; this was real. Any guilt about what had gone before seemed to have dissolved, and the word *cancer* was as far from both of their minds as it could be.

*

At Maddie's apartment the air filled with electricity, with longing. She felt a sudden flutter of anticipation as she watched Evan take off his coat and drape it across a stool in the kitchen. Everything seemed to be happening in slow motion, but the second he looked over at her they hit the fast forward button.

He was there, his lips clamped on hers, his hands through her hair. His body pressed entirely against her own, every inch warming her in a way that felt familiar, secure. Their kiss evolved to greater depths with an urgency she didn't recognise, and his hands moved from her neck down to her breasts and stroked them through the thin material of her top, the lace of her bra. A familiar longing flushed her entire body, and her hands froze for a moment on his upper arms as she relished the closeness.

His hands ran down past her waist, over her buttocks, and he watched her all the while. She pulled his top over his head, and when it dropped to the floor, she drew in a breath at the sight of him, at the feel of skin on skin, the definition of the toned chest covered with dark hair. She let out a soft moan.

'Is this okay?' He drew back, misreading the signals.

'Don't stop.'

He grinned, a thankful, voiceless gesture as he slid the ivory silk bra straps off of each shoulder and then traced the outline of the cups. She wondered how much more she could take, but this time she knew she wasn't using sex as an escape; this time the sex was building on something that had foundations and a future. She wasn't running from the past this time; she was being set free from it.

He reached around behind her as his eyes begged for more. He unclasped her bra, dropped it to the floor in one fluid movement. He lowered his mouth and trailed kisses from her neck to her collarbone, down to her breasts, taking each nipple in his mouth in turn, this time not pulling away when she gasped. Her head tipped back and his kisses made their way back up her neck to meet her lips again, and he fumbled with the buttons on her jeans. She tugged at his belt, and with some manoeuvring they were free of their clothes and he eased her down on to the sofa.

'You're so beautiful.' The muscles in his arms held him hovering above her.

She reached up to cup his face between her hands after he pulled on the condom. Her heart was working overtime, and when she felt his hardness against her, she wrapped her legs around his torso. They moved together. The heat in the room had reached boiling point, and when he stilled she knew he was holding back, for her. She guided his hand to touch her and his fingers worked their magic until waves of pleasure took over. She wrapped her legs even tighter around him, kissed him deeply. Her hand stilled on his buttocks; she daren't reach any further for fear of touching the lump, scared of hurting him. But the ecstasy on his face told her he wasn't even thinking about it, and she felt him come, hard. She listened to his gasps and the whisper of her name on his lips.

They lay there languidly, Evan on top of Maddie as she trailed fingernails lightly up his back. Goose

152

pimples sprung up across his skin, and he gave a shiver of satiated pleasure. He kissed the soft curve of her neck all the way along to the tip of her shoulder, setting every nerve ending alight again.

'Can I ask you a question?' said Maddie.

'Ask away.'

'Did it hurt? I mean, you know … with the lump?'

He stroked her cheek with the back of his hand. 'No, it didn't hurt. Some guys have pain, but I've been lucky, depending on how you look at it.'

'So that's a good sign, right?'

His eyes didn't leave hers for a second. 'Don't look so worried.'

'I can't help it.'

'Hey,' he said, moving his body so she couldn't avoid looking at him. 'It's not like I'm going to die … at least not yet.'

She couldn't hold back the sob.

He leapt off of her and pulled her on to his naked lap, kissing away the tears that spilled over.

'I'm sorry, Maddie. That was uncalled for. I'm a dickhead who thinks jokes will make it less serious.'

She buried her head against his shoulder. His fingers combed her hair, and she felt his long, drawn-out sigh before he spoke again.

'Let's hope that everything will be okay,' he said.

She nodded as he scooped her up in his arms and took her into the bedroom. He held her tightly and his steady breathing soothed her like a lullaby. And for the first time since Riley, she went to bed with a man and spent the entire night curled up in his arms.

*

Evan did his best to be quiet, but his belt jingled as he threaded the leather through the buckle.

'What are you doing?' Maddie sat up in bed and rubbed her eyes.

He leaned over and kissed her, smiling at the way she lay down again and snuggled into the duvet. 'It's early, go back to sleep.' He bent down to get his shoes.

'You pass, by the way,' Maddie muttered.

'Pass what?'

'The jeans test.'

He wiggled his bum at her. 'Glad to hear it.' He knelt on the bed so he could kiss her, and as her tongue probed his mouth and she pleaded 'stay' into his ear, he straddled her and she grasped his bum in her hands, pulling him towards her.

'Believe me when I say that I'd much rather stay here with you, but I have to go.' He pulled away regretfully. 'I've got to get home so that I'm in a fit state to face a class of twenty kids, none of whom would understand that I was late because of a beautiful girl who wouldn't let me get out of bed.'

His fingers stretched out to lightly caress the side of her face from her forehead down to her mouth and lingered on the lips he had just kissed.

Maddie's hand reached beneath his shirt and stroked the bare skin of his stomach. When he groaned she rubbed the dark line of hair that sneaked down below his belt buckle, ready to go further.

He stopped her hand and held it for a moment as the giddy feeling of having this hot girl between his thighs subsided just enough. 'I'll call you tonight?'

'Okay.'

He dropped one last kiss on her lips before he pulled on his jacket and closed the apartment door quietly behind him.

Back at his place he showered and thought about Maddie, lounging in bed, her sexy little body tangled between the sheets. Now that he knew about Riley, he hoped this was the beginning of something special, long lasting. She was a genuine girl and she could've easily kept quiet about the other guy and her past involvement with men, but instead she had chosen to be honest and deal with the consequences, and he admired that. If it were possible, it made him fall for her a little bit more.

He pulled the towel from the rail and wrapped it around his waist, and when his phone rang shrilly from the kitchen, he ran, expecting it to be Maddie.

'Evan Quinn, speaking,' he said when her name didn't appear on the caller display.

He knew by the formality of the voice that this was it. This was the call he had been dreading, the call that would make him go from happy to feeling miserable and downright petrified.

Chapter Sixteen

The children filed into the classroom in an orderly line, and Evan waited for them to settle at their desks. He felt sure he had walked all the way to school that morning in a daze, still reeling from the phone call.

As he tried to imagine how he was going to tell Maddie, he turned to find Carly, a doll-like girl with wide eyes and a neat, raven-coloured bob.

'Mr Quinn. Do you have a wife?'

He loved how kids had no qualms in coming out with questions. They were yet to learn appropriateness and tact, but then again, some adults couldn't manage that either.

'No, I'm not married.'

'Why?'

'I guess I haven't met the right person.' Until now, he thought.

The rest of the class were starting to settle, but Carly had more questions. 'My mummy thinks you're cute, but she already has Daddy, but she does have a friend who isn't married.'

Evan wondered whether match making was in every woman's genes. He was glad it was in Jem's or he never would've got to know Maddie. 'Well thank you, Carly, I'll bear that in mind.'

He ushered the little girl over to her desk so they could begin their reading groups. Each group had a nominated monitor who was responsible for setting up, and at the end of the session, a new monitor would be appointed for the next time. The kids loved the responsibility, and Evan saw it as a vital stepping stone to independence and responsibility.

At lunchtime Evan had playground duty, but he sneaked a moment before leaving the classroom and sent Maddie a text.

Hi beautiful. Had a great night last night, hope you did too. x

His feelings were jumbled. One minute he was relieved the operation had been scheduled and the deed would be done, the next he was absolutely terrified. When he thought about last night with Maddie his insides lit up, and he couldn't bear the thought of ripping that pleasure away from either of them, at least until after work when he could see her face-to-face.

He picked up the silver whistle and looped it around his neck as he prepared to referee lunchtime.

After lunch Evan sat all the children down in a semi-circle, cross-legged in front of him. He sat on the chair and pointed to the calendar that faced the class. 'Who was our calendar and weather person this morning?'

Brianna's hand shot up proudly. The children loved the ritual each morning whereby one lucky pupil would be chosen to come up to the front and stick the day of the week on to the magnetic board, plus the month and then the numerical date. And the good thing about Melbourne and its four-seasons-in-one-day weather was that the chosen pupil often got to change the magnetic symbol from cloudy, sunny, rainy or windy, no matter what the season.

Brianna stopped wobbling her front tooth long enough to select the right magnetic symbols, and Evan's thoughts drifted to Maddie yet again; it was hard to maintain focus on his class today when his mind was as far from Huntley Primary as it had ever been. It was going to be hard to tell her about the impending operation, to see the worry on her face, the fear that history could repeat itself and she could lose another man she cared about. As the classroom became a hive of activity in preparation for this afternoon's art session, Evan craved the simplicity of a child's life away from the responsibilities of an adult, away from the realities that could be so painful.

*

'Maddie, you look like your face is set in that position.' Ally teased. 'Come on, what's going on?'

They squeezed on to the tram with carrier bags full of ingredients for tonight's dinner. Tonight would be a girls' night in with a movie, wine and gossip.

'I could ask you the same question. You look pretty happy yourself,' said Maddie.

Ally spied a couple of spare seats at the back of the tram and they plonked themselves there, wedging the bags between their feet.

'Joel's taking me to the *Loft in the Mill* up in Olinda,' said Ally. 'Think open fire, spa bath, romantic walks …'

'That sounds wonderful.'

'It does, doesn't it? Come on then, your turn. Why are you so smiley all of a sudden? Unless …'

'Unless what?'

'That's it! You've seen Evan again, haven't you?' Maddie nodded.

'I knew it! So come on, how was it? How is he?'

'He's fine. Well, not fine obviously, but we went out yesterday. We met for hot chocolates, took a boat to Williamstown.'

'That sounds very romantic.'

'It was.'

'Oh come on, and?'

'And what?' asked Maddie, enjoying the game, enjoying her friend's desperation to know the details.

'Maddie Kershaw!'

The tram jerked to a stop outside Maddie's apartment block and, carrier bags hooked on to each arm, they stepped down on to St Kilda Road.

'He walked me home.'

'Oh, this is painful,' said Ally.

'And we slept together.'

'Well hallelujah! It's about time.'

When they dumped the carrier bags on top of the kitchen bench, Ally said, 'I'm glad that it was Evan and not Josh.'

So was Maddie, unbelievably so. Evan's feelings had been hurt when she'd told him about Josh, and she suspected he would've hated the thought of too much intimacy with someone else. Even though she and Evan weren't an item when she'd gone back to Josh's place that night, there were things that hadn't been said.

Maddie diced the chicken, coated it in a honey soy marinade and put it in the fridge. Ally took charge of the wine and poured two large glasses of red.

159

'It's a turning point, isn't it?' Ally asked, chinking her glass against Maddie's.

'You know, I really think that it is.'

'So who made the first move?'

'I think we both knew what was going to happen.' Maddie sniggered.

'What do you mean?'

'We had to stop at 7-Eleven for condoms.'

'Awkward.'

'I know. I skulked around outside while Evan went in. I'm in my thirties and I'm still embarrassed every time.'

'You should add them to your weekly shop … that way they get buried amongst the toothpaste, bread and potatoes.'

'I'll try to remember that.'

'I'm proud of you, you know?'

'Why?' Maddie passed the red onion to Ally to chop.

'Well, because it's taken a long time for you to get to the place you're at now. I think you can finally see there is still a life out there for you, and it has more to offer than you realised.'

She was right of course. Maddie could see a future with Evan.

The girls spent the evening swapping stories about the men in their lives, Ally showed Maddie pictures of where she was going for the weekend and they swooned at Josh Lucas in *Sweet Home Alabama*.

When Ally left, Maddie pulled her phone from the depths of her bag. Her tummy flipped when she saw she had four missed calls from Evan – she had forgotten to take it off silent mode when she left work. She felt a rush of excitement at the thought of Evan's body against hers, the warmth of his tongue inside her mouth. She listened to the messages with a big grin on her face; it had to be a booty call, didn't it?

The first message was a normal, upbeat Evan asking her to call him back; the second was the same. The third was a hang up but the fourth made her freeze. He told her it didn't matter what time of the night it was, he had to speak to her. And she knew what this meant. It meant the operation was scheduled; he was a step closer to learning his fate.

Her hand shook as she pressed call, but he picked up the second it connected.

'Maddie, I … I …'

Her voice shook as she spoke. 'Come over. Please, come over.'

He arrived fifteen minutes later and she fell into his arms.

'It's tomorrow, the operation is tomorrow,' he said.

'But it can't be, don't you have to see a specialist, an anaesthetist, have checks?' It was all happening too fast.

'It's classed as a minor operation.' He rolled his eyes indicating that it was anything but 'minor' for him. 'It's only a day procedure, so I just turn up in the morning. At least I won't have to stay overnight, I guess. I can be back in my own bed by the afternoon if all goes to plan.'

Maddie led him by the hand into the bedroom. They undressed perfunctorily, in comparison to the night before when they hadn't been able to get one another's clothes off quickly enough, and climbed underneath the duvet where he wrapped his body around hers as though she was the one going under the knife. He held her tightly into the night and she knew she was in deep: too deep to back out, too deep to protect her from the world of hurt that could be looming. It was like Riley all over again except in slow motion with a warning beacon. Evan was her second chance and she had fallen head over heels in love with him, and the beacon would do nothing to lessen the pain if he was taken from her.

*

Evan took a taxi to the hospital the next morning. When Maddie had woken at the sound of his alarm, he silenced her with a kiss and told her he would be in touch when it was all over.

He hadn't had anything to eat or drink since before midnight, and as the taxi pulled into the car park at Huntley hospital he felt nauseous, shaky. Terrified of what lay ahead, Evan took a few deep breaths before crossing the threshold, leaving the world outside where people went about their everyday business, entering the place that was about to forever change his world. He repeated over and over in his head that everything would be fine, this needed to happen; it was a good thing he was having the operation and he would finally know whether it was cancer or not.

He handed over his details to the receptionist, and everything felt like it was happening to someone else as he robotically completed the requisite forms and then took a seat in the waiting area. He watched a man being wheeled to the chairs set at a right angle to where he was. He was all dopey-eyed and greeted by a woman Evan presumed must be his wife. He wondered what the man had been in for. Did they do a bulk round of orchidectomies? Or was it something entirely different? Perhaps it was an appendectomy, the lucky bugger.

Evan felt the itch again on his balls, the itch that had been there on and off for the last few days. He tried to discreetly rid himself of it without the nurse sitting behind the dimly lit desk clocking him touching himself. He suspected the itch could just be his imagination playing tricks on him, cruelly reminding him that his manhood was still intact for now, but not for much longer.

Strangely enough he hadn't felt the itch when he was at Maddie's last night. It had been a weird night in comparison to the previous one where they had been hungry for one another with an urgency that made a space shuttle launch seem slow. Last night had been intimate in a different sense and it was a first for him. He wondered what his mates would think of him going to bed with an incredibly hot girl and not even making a move. He laughed inside at the irony.

A hand on his shoulder made him jump. 'Ben? What are you doing here?' He looked around expecting to see Holly and Ava too.

'Relax, mate. The girls are still tucked up in bed. Ava's come down with a cold so no kindy for her today, and Holly, well she's in bits worrying about her brother after his brief phone call to say, "By the way sis, I'm having an operation tomorrow."'

'I had to tell her that it was happening.'

'I think she wanted you to come over and spend the night, so you weren't alone.' Ben took the seat next to his brother-in-law. 'You know it took all her strength not to tell your mum last night when she called.'

'I can imagine.'

'Did she call you too?'

He nodded. 'I didn't pick up. I couldn't.' Martha had called when he was sitting beside the phone trying Maddie's number over and over, only to get her voicemail.

'You should've come over to our place last night,' said Ben.

'I don't think I could've handled the whole goodbye-and-good-luck-ceremony, like I was going off to war or something.'

'You're not wrong there.' Ben smirked. 'Holly would've done a whole big dinner, dessert, the works. And besides, there's plenty of time for you to come over once this is out of the way.'

Evan caught a waft of coffee as Ben spoke. 'Blimey, back off! I'd almost kill for a coffee right now, you know.' He mockingly wrung his brother-in-law's neck. 'Seriously, what I'd do right now for a strong, double shot. And one of those mouth-watering cinnamon muffins from the coffee shop …'

'Spoken truly by a man held in limbo; a man in pre-op non-eating, non-drinking mode.'

'Couldn't have said it better myself. So did Holly send you? Where's your suit, aren't you on the way to work?'

'Evan, I know you don't want me to get all mushy, so I won't, but Holly didn't suggest this. We've been mates from the moment I met your sister, and you're like a brother to me, so I wasn't going to let you do this on your own. I know you asked for me to be there to take you home when it's all done, but I figured you could use some support beforehand too.'

Evan sighed and sat back in his chair, his mouth dry and his stomach empty. 'I'm crapping myself, mate. I mean, an op is bad enough, but one to chop off a ball is fucking terrifying.'

'I can't pretend to understand so I won't patronise you by saying that I do,' said Ben, 'but I can *imagine* what it must be like, and that's terrifying enough for me.'

Evan looked around. 'What's taking them so long? Now I'm here I want this over with.'

The receptionist talked in hushed tones on the telephone, another patient sat three rows of chairs away, but apart from that nothing was happening, not even the sounds that you came to expect in a hospital. It was as though in this beige-toned waiting room with its pristine tiled floor, pot plants standing to attention along one wall, they were detached from the reality of it all.

Evan drummed his fingers on the metal part of the arm of his chair, and luckily the man who had taken a seat a couple of rows in front had either managed to block the sound out or he was far too polite to request that Evan stop it.

'How about we try some good old-fashioned distraction, eh?' suggested Ben. 'Tell me about Maddie. Did you ever get in touch with her again?'

'I did. We went out again for coffee and I took her to Williamstown for fish and chips.'

'You old romantic,' said Ben with a wink and a nudge.

'We'd planned to go running this morning before her shift, but instead I get to do this.'

Ben let him wallow for a minute and then Evan said, more brightly, 'I spent last night at her place.'

'You dirty stop out! No wonder you didn't want to come over to our place.'

'It wasn't like that. At least it wasn't last night. I didn't speak to her until after midnight to tell her the op was today and I think she was in shock, so I went over.'

Ben pulled a face.

'She just wanted me near.'

'Well I never.' Ben scratched his head. 'Who'd have thought? Evan Quinn, the big softie.'

'We spent the night together after Williamstown too.' Evan doubted it was difficult for Ben to fathom what had gone on that night judging by the smile on Evan's face.

'Well that's a relief. You're still the Evan we know and love.'

Evan leant forwards, his arms resting on his thighs. 'She's fantastic, Ben. And I'm not just talking about the sexy stuff – although that's pretty damn good too – but I don't think I've ever met a girl who has got me quite the way she does. Somehow we click, and it's as though we've known each other for a lot longer than we actually have.'

'How did you leave things with her?'

'I'll see her again,' he replied firmly. 'I'll get in touch when I'm out of here.'

'Evan Quinn?' A nurse with a clipboard stood at the front of the now bustling waiting room filling up with more poor bastards waiting to be operated on.

'Looks like you're up.' Ben looked at Evan. 'You okay from here?'

His heart raced at the enormity of what lay ahead. 'Bit late to be backing out now.'

'You'll be all right, mate. Now skedaddle. I'm dying to get another coffee and a doughnut from the canteen but didn't want to torture you. I've got my iPad so I'll be right here until it's time to go.'

Being alone through all of this had been one of the scariest parts for Evan, so knowing Ben had his back was reassuring.

Evan was shown to a cubicle where he removed his clothes and pulled on the hospital-issue gown. He pulled the cool, stiff sheets over his legs and lay back on the bed, sinking his head into the flimsy pillow and staring up at the stark white ceiling and the lights swallowed up by it. It seemed like forever until the nurse came and ran through his details, including the operation he was in for today, double-checking so they didn't operate on the wrong body part or remove a healthy organ by mistake, he guessed.

When the nurse wheeled him towards his fate, he felt the bed trundle beneath him. He noticed every crack in the ceiling and counted the lights at regularly spaced intervals. It felt surreal, like he was part of a television medical drama, and he silently hoped this wasn't a teaching hospital like he'd seen in *Grey's Anatomy* – Holly was a fan, and Jem – where the love lives of the doctors seemed more of a concern than the actual surgery.

167

He blocked all thoughts of that when he was faced with the masked anaesthetist who tried to make small talk. Evan muttered a response to the question about what books he liked reading, and the last thing he remembered was counting backwards from ten as the anaesthetist talked about Matthew Reilly's latest book.

Chapter Seventeen

Maddie hated to think what would've happened had she not got in touch with Evan last night after Ally left. He had held her and comforted her as they talked about inconsequential things, anything to take their minds off of what was about to happen. They had laughed about the kids in his class: yesterday one of them had let out an enormous fart and nobody had batted an eyelid, never mind admitted to being the culprit. The whole group of twenty had carried on with their painting, splashing bright colours everywhere, oblivious to the amusement of their teacher.

The thought of their conversation allowed a small smile to form on Maddie's lips, but the thought that Evan could be under the knife right now was enough to stop it in its tracks. At lunchtime she checked her phone again, although it was pointless when Evan had told her his phone would stay at home while he was in hospital. All she could do now was to wait.

*

'Evan, how are you feeling?'

Groggy and squinting beneath the lights that felt like they were burning a hole in his irises, Evan came face-to-face with a woman about the same age as his mother. For a moment he panicked, thinking he was at home, but when the nurse spoke again, the reality hit.

He fell back to sleep, and when he woke his mouth was as dry as the Sahara Desert. His groin ached – probably what had woken him – and the same nurse was at his bedside babbling about a prescription for strong painkillers. She adjusted the bed so he was no longer completely flat and handed him a cup of water. 'Small sips,' she urged. 'We need to make sure you can keep it down. Then we'll try a bit of lunch.'

The water went down fine and made him feel semi-human, but then another nurse appeared with a tray. For one tiny moment it looked like an oasis for his empty stomach as she pulled off the plastic wrap from a row of triangular sandwiches. Then, quick as any baseball player, glove ready to catch the pitch, the nurse had a bowl beneath Evan's chin before he vomited.

*

Maddie lay on the sofa, her coat in a heap on the floor. The sky was heavy with rainclouds that matched her mood and showed no signs of clearing. She had forgotten to take an umbrella today, and the smell of rain lingered in her hair, damp and matted from the wind and the downpour that had conspired against her as she ran for the tram.

Over the last few weeks, she had felt a shift in herself, as though she was on a bike, climbing uphill, and as the struggle became tougher, she realised that by shifting into a lower gear, she could make it; she could make it all the way to the top. And that was Evan's doing. His cancer scare seemed like a test, a test to see whether she could go the distance with

170

anyone else. But with lack of news from Evan's camp, it was like the chain of her bike had come off and she was rolling backwards, unable to move forwards no matter how hard she pedalled. Sometimes she felt as though she was in a hole as deep as Ground Zero, destined never to climb out.

*

'Maddie, are you there?'

Maddie sat up on the sofa, still in her work uniform. She must have fallen asleep after she curled up in a ball, mesmerised by the rain outside lashing against the window.

'This is Ben,' the voice continued. She realised it was her answer machine and the person was mid-message. Who the hell was Ben?

'I'm Evan's brother-in-law.'

She snatched up the phone, cleared her throat and hoped she didn't sound too groggy. 'Hello, Ben? How is he?'

'Hi, Maddie,' said Ben. 'The operation went smoothly. Evan's moaning away anyhow. You should've seen how grumpy he was when the nurse told him he couldn't go home unless they were satisfied that he could piss properly.'

She giggled, more in relief than anything else.

'Sorry,' said Ben. 'I must apologise for my bad language.'

'Don't be, I really appreciate the call.'

'He said to tell you that he'll be in touch when he's up to it.'

She tried not to feel too disheartened that it hadn't been Evan's voice on the phone. The main thing was that he was well and the surgery had gone smoothly. 'Do you know anything more? Was the lump cancer?'

'I'm afraid I don't know much else for now, Maddie.'

When she hung up she knew she had to stay positive. Whatever the outcome of the operation, whether the cancer had spread or not, she had to believe the past wouldn't repeat itself. It couldn't, could it? Surely meeting Evan was a sign that she needed to start pedalling up the hill again, and this time she would refuse to stop until she reached the top.

Chapter Eighteen

Five days after the operation, when the results were in on the Monday morning, Ben took Evan to see the specialist.

'I'll take it from here. I shouldn't be long.' Evan didn't want anyone else witnessing the news, good or bad. He wanted to hear it himself, take it in, process what was happening.

He didn't have to wait too long to be seen by the specialist, who shook his hand and led him to a room at the end of a long corridor.

Evan tried to read the man's expression, but he had his poker face on for sure.

'I'll get straight to the point,' he said once Evan had carefully lowered himself into a chair beside the desk. 'The operation went well, as you know, and now that we have the pathology results back, we know that your lump was cancer.'

It was as though a gong had been struck at deafening volume and was still reverberating next to his ear.

The specialist's voice pushed on through. 'The good news is that it's stage one seminoma.'

'That's the good news?'

'I know it doesn't seem that way when I use the word *cancer*, but stage one means that it hasn't spread.'

Evan tried to get his head around the complex explanation of what a seminoma was, but he couldn't process it. He felt as though the specialist was speaking a foreign language. He'd been told all this before, he'd read about it time and time again, but with all the medical jargon it was easy to be confused.

'You'll need a round of chemotherapy in four to six weeks, and from past experience that's usually enough to eradicate any cancer cells,' the specialist continued.

'Isn't that too long to wait? Shouldn't we get going with the chemo straight away?'

The specialist seemed to sense the panic in Evan's voice. 'We need the body to recover from the operation first, and with this type of cancer, it's fine to wait that short time. And, Evan, please remember the chances of making a full recovery without the recurrence of cancer are extremely high.'

'How high?'

'The single dose of chemotherapy that will be administered for you is associated with a cure rate of about ninety-seven to ninety-eight percent.'

'And what are my chances of getting the cancer in my other testicle now that I've had it in one?' Please God, don't let him lose any more of his manhood.

The specialist took a deep breath. 'There is a very small increased risk of patients with testicular cancer getting it in the other testicle. But,' he said before Evan lost the plot completely, 'it's a small risk of about two percent.'

They ran through other details – the expected timing of the chemotherapy; the annual CT scans he would need; the checks with the specialist every few months. The specialist checked the incision and declared that it was 'healing nicely'.

Evan walked out to the car park to meet Ben and climbed gingerly into the passenger seat. He knew he should be grateful that the prognosis was good, that compared to some people he was getting off lightly. But how could he possibly look on the bright side when he had been diagnosed with cancer? He wanted to crawl into a big black hole and sleep until it was all over.

He managed to relay the information to Ben, who was a hell of a lot more positive than he was, but back in the safety of his own apartment, Evan felt as though the walls were closing in on him. Last night he had stopped the seriously strong painkillers, but when he saw the packet lying there on the kitchen bench, he picked it up, roared as loudly as he could and flung it across the room. Next to go was the empty glass right next to the packet that would've been used to swallow the last dose. That went the same way as the pills and made a satisfying smash as it hit the glass sliding door. He upended the coffee table, sending an iPad, a newspaper and a coaster flying, and only when he wanted to kick the living crap out of the sofa and swung back a leg did the pain in his groin kick in along with his senses.

He slumped down beside the sofa, his eyes filled with tears. He touched a hand to the wound in his pubic area to make sure he hadn't torn open the skin during his outrage, but it was fine, just as before: a florid swelling that would disappear in time. He wondered whether mentally the damage would last a lot longer.

The painkillers had knocked him out good and proper up until now, and today was the first day he had really been able to think straight, to let his emotions try to untangle themselves, but combined with the diagnosis only an hour ago, it was a lethal combination.

He wondered what Maddie was doing right now. He'd sent her a text the first night he was home, to say he was sleeping an unhealthy amount and felt like a bear going into hibernation. They had been firing jokey words back and forth for the last couple of days too even though at times he had barely had the energy to think of anything to say. He knew she was waiting for him to tell her to come and see him, but he hadn't banked on feeling so bloody useless once he wasn't so spaced out on painkillers. And now he shied away from contacting her because he didn't want the girl whom he was trying to impress to see him as less of a man, wincing in pain when he moved or falling asleep at the drop of a hat.

Evan checked the window for damage before he picked up the larger pieces of glass from the carpet. Thankfully his momentary loss of control hadn't caused any further damage other than breaking the glass and creating a mess. He pulled the vacuum cleaner out from the laundry room at the back of the bathroom to get the tiny splinters that had embedded themselves in the thick fawn pile.

Holly had been over yesterday and filled the fridge, basing her assumptions about what he ate on most men rather than the healthier foods he enjoyed – usually it was muesli or porridge for breakfast, a plain sandwich for lunch, meat and vegetables for dinner –

but today he had reached new depths of despair, and when he finished cleaning up he took out eggs, bacon and a fistful of mushrooms. He couldn't train anyway – no running for at least six weeks – so before long the scent of a fry-up filled the apartment, and he took his plate outside to enjoy it on the balcony.

The food barely touched the sides as it went down; amazing how much of an appetite you could build-up with a cancer diagnosis and a good old-fashioned violent outburst.

When he had slept next to Maddie the other night, she'd suggested using flexible ice packs after the operation, for comfort, and so he had asked Ben to pick some up from the sports clinic in the city. He retrieved one from the freezer now, wrapped it in a tea towel, and pressed it against the wound. He knew he was lucky he hadn't ripped it open with the little stunt he pulled earlier, and his hand reached for his phone because this was one of those little things he wanted to tell Maddie. It had happened yesterday, and the day before. He couldn't remember what had been the reason now, but like today, he had stopped himself just in time, before he showed weakness, asked for her pity.

He propped up his iPad on the table – luckily it had survived its unplanned trip through the air – and skimmed through *The Age*. He flicked past stories of doom and gloom, and settled instead on the sport section to read about the build-up of footy fever now that they had hit winter. He'd only made one match this season what with everything going on.

When the phone rang Evan ignored it, pulling a fleece tighter around himself as he skimmed through

Facebook's News Feed before checking his emails. This had become his daily morning routine in the absence of being able to go for a run. His body felt tight, unused. All he wanted to do was get out there into the big wide world, taking in the city skyline with its bossy tall buildings outnumbering the smaller ones that had been there first. He looked across at one of the entrances to the Crown Entertainment Complex, barely feeling the usual buzz of this cosmopolitan city that he loved being a part of.

The phone refused to give up on him and rang again. He shut the balcony door, preferring to feel a part of the noise of the city outside. He knew it would be Holly; she'd phoned umpteen times in the last few days, and he just couldn't take any more sympathy right now. Perhaps he should be grateful to have so many people worried about him, but at the moment all his thoughts were insular.

When the phone finally stopped ringing and he felt a chill, Evan went through to the kitchen and ran hot water over his plate so the residue from the egg didn't set hard. At least he'd maintained some common sense amongst the worry that his cancer would return in his other testicle, the fear of infertility, and his obsession that he wouldn't be able to get a hard-on and have sex like he used to, ever again. He'd started to get paranoid though, which was new for him. A couple of days previously he'd developed a slight cough and had spent hours trawling the internet, concluding that the cancer must surely have spread to his lungs.

Evan flung himself on to the sofa. He was being ridiculous; a weak emotional wreck. Evan reminded himself that he'd got off lightly compared to some people with cancer, but the depression that had taken hold during his cancer journey wasn't something he had foreseen. It had crept up on him unexpectedly like a ghoul in the night, wrapping him in a cloak of darkness.

With no desire to do anything else, he picked up the remote control and prepared to lose himself again in the stupidity that was daytime television, anything to zone out and take his mind off of what was happening.

Chapter Nineteen

'Sorry I'm late.' Maddie flopped on to a seat opposite Ally in Jerimiah's. 'I was running late with a patient, and then Mum called just as I was about to leave.'

'How is she?'

'Good.' Phone calls with her parents were pleasant enough, but Maddie missed what she used to share with them, particularly her mum. Pre-Riley they had chatted for hours on the phone or in person, and Maddie knew that part of her had shut down to block out any memory of the past.

'Does this mean you're planning a visit home?' Ally asked warily.

Maddie grinned. 'I booked the flight at lunchtime. I think Mum was only calling because she's so excited.'

'It'll do you good to see them after everything that's happened recently.'

Maddie knew she was talking about Evan. She smiled and pulled out the band from her hair to free it from her work-typical pony tail. She sucked the straw in her glass hard to get the strawberry smoothie moving.

'How's Evan doing?'

'Okay. I think.'

'You think? Haven't you been in contact with him? It's been three weeks since his surgery.'

'We've been texting, but I haven't actually spoken to him. I don't even know his results yet.'

'Do you think that means it's bad news?'

Maddie shrugged. 'I have no idea.'

'Men.' Ally shook her head. 'I'm sure he'll be in touch eventually. It must be one hell of a journey for him, regardless of the diagnosis, and the way I see it, he wouldn't have come over the night before the operation and he wouldn't have texted you afterwards if he never wanted to see you again. It's not like you're a member of his family who he *has* to humour.'

'True.' She always could trust Ally to put a smile on her face. 'I did think about baking a funny cake for him and taking it over as a surprise.'

'Please tell me you're not going to replicate the penis and testicles, because I think under the circumstances that would be pretty sick.'

'I'm not that insensitive. I was thinking more of a naughty cake, something to put a smile on his face.'

'Are you sure it's a good idea?'

'I gave him space last time and it was him who ended up getting in touch with me. Maybe it should be me this time. I don't want to screw this up, Ally. I finally feel as though I'm starting to move on. I can't let that chance slip away.'

When Maddie got home she frantically pulled out ingredients, determined this was the right thing to do, determined he was pushing her away for some reason that had nothing to do with how much he wanted or needed her. And again, she lost herself in the world of baking as she made the cake she hoped Evan would appreciate.

*

The next evening after work, Maddie iced the cake, excited at the prospect of seeing Evan again. She paused in the middle of sifting the icing sugar. What if he really didn't want her? What if after the operation he had realised everything was going to be fine and he could carry on with his life pre-Maddie, without a care in the world?

She shook away that thought along with the rest of the icing sugar. Coping alone was something she had tried to do for far too long after Riley, and it had got her nowhere. She recognised the signs of Evan doing the same and she couldn't let him deal with this on his own. And if he told her to get lost, well then, she would just have to accept it.

Determined that this would all work out, she made the finishing touches to Evan's cake and drove over to his apartment, the cake safely inside a plastic cake carrier box and sitting in the passenger footwell wedged with towels on either side to prevent it from sliding when she turned corners. She thought back to Riley's exams and when he had failed the most important one at the end of his first year at University. He'd been crushed. Maddie had baked him a set of assorted cupcakes decorated with boobs, penises and pert female bottoms. It had worked like a charm.

After she pulled up outside Evan's apartment block, Maddie battled the wintry air that blasted her cheeks as she carried the cake box up the steps to the building's main entrance. She balanced it on one knee and buzzed Evan's apartment, her heart thumping as she waited to hear his voice for the first time since the night before the operation. Surely this gesture could go some way to bridging the gap between them. She didn't want it to widen any further than it already had, like a crevice she could slip through if she wasn't careful.

She buzzed again, hoping that after the first buzz he hadn't taken one look at the video intercom, seen her face and decided not to let her in.

His voice sounded over the intercom. 'Maddie, come on up, I'm on the eighth floor.'

She blushed as she looked at the monitor, knowing he could see her yet she couldn't see him.

When she stepped out of the lift he emerged from a doorway towards the end of a long, carpeted hallway with soft lighting, not too dissimilar from her own apartment building.

'This is a nice surprise.' He leaned in to kiss her on the cheek when she reached him.

The greeting and the kiss were a good sign, weren't they? You didn't say or do that when you wanted the person to get lost.

Inside, she slid the cake box on to the kitchen bench and, noting the fawn carpet, pulled off her knee-high boots.

'This place is great, it's so central.' Nerves were making her babble. 'You don't find it too noisy?'

'Nah, I'm too young for noise to bother me. Give it another five years, though, and I'll probably be desperate to migrate to the suburbs.' He took her coat.

'I know what you mean. My place is pretty quiet, but the odd party or being woken up by the dinging of the trams sometimes makes me think about living further out.'

She looked around at the bachelor pad that felt strangely non-lad-like. There were two identical black leather couches set at right angles to each other – okay, so pretty bachelor-like – and a tall lamp cast a soft glow across the room. A chocolate-brown rug on top of which sat a glass coffee table was positioned in front of the couches and matched the colour of two side tables. Even the walls held a couple of paintings and she paused to look at them.

'That one's Huntley High Street,' he said from behind her right shoulder.

His proximity sent goose pimples up her arms. 'I know. I recognise it. And what's that one? I recognise that too, but I can't place it.'

'That one's Brighton beach – I gave Jem a similar one for her birthday with those bright, colourful bathing boxes. She loves it.'

Her insides melted at his demeanour when he mentioned his family. It made him all the more attractive when she could see beyond the tall, dark-haired man with melting-pot eyes to someone who was caring and considerate too.

She had done the right thing in coming; she was sure of it now.

With her coat still draped over one arm, he took it over to an old-fashioned coat stand behind the door.

'That's pretty stylish.' She put a hand out to feel the wooden, carved piece.

'It belonged to my dad. He was a stickler for us hanging up our coats and now it's a habit that I've never been able to shake off.'

'It's beautiful.'

She moved along to another picture. 'This is you,' she said, focusing on the photograph of a younger Evan running across a finishing line with a black number on a white background pinned to his chest.

'That was the London Marathon,' he said.

'I'm impressed. And this one of the London skyline is great.'

'London at night. Impressive, isn't it?' She caught her breath when his arm reached from behind her, across her shoulder as she stood in front of the painting. 'There's Big Ben, the Houses of Parliament, Westminster Bridge and, of course, the Millennium Wheel.'

'Who took the picture of you crossing the finish line?'

'That was Jem.' When he moved away she felt able to breathe again. 'She made the trek across the seas with Mum. She was almost ninety.'

'I'd love to go.'

'You could sign up for the London Marathon.'

'Steady on. I was thinking more like a visit someday to see my sister, perhaps shop on Oxford Street, lunch in Covent Garden.'

'Females.' He shook his head, and then as though suddenly remembering the cake box, he pointed to it. 'What's this?'

At once she felt embarrassed at what lay inside. She paused, her hands on the box, ready for the big reveal. 'It's something I thought may cheer you up. Now I don't know you well enough to know whether you're a breast, leg or arse man, so I went for the most likely.' She didn't admit that the time they'd laid naked together and he had lingered over her breasts had given her the biggest clue as to his preference. She wiggled the lid off the box and said, 'Ta-da!'

A wide grin spread across his face. 'Come here you.' He pulled her into him and she drowned in his long, lingering kiss, the unkempt stubble on his face softer than usual now that it had grown.

'She must've had a boob job.' He looked admiringly at the cake.

The breasts Maddie had made didn't have a person attached, but they were two generous sized cakes piled with buttercream over vanilla sponge.

'Those are some crazy looking nipples.' Evan's arms lay relaxed, draped across Maddie's shoulders.

She looked down at the two chocolate discs with multicoloured sprinkles. 'I made it on a whim. I didn't have much else to use, so I had to make do with chocolate speckles.'

'So multicoloured nipples it is, then.' He kissed the top of her head. 'You're really talented, you know.'

'I can make tasteful cakes too, but these get a better reaction.'

'Can I get you a drink?' He pulled away and Maddie wondered again whether she had done the right thing in coming here tonight. She was scared of making everything so wrong by trying to make it so right.

He filled a glass of water for her and pulled out a couple of plates, and it was then that Maddie got a glimpse of the same Evan who had captured her attention in the first place. They laughed over which boob to slice up first, over who would get the chocolate nipples covered in multicoloured hundreds and thousands.

'It's the patient's prerogative,' Maddie concluded. 'You can choose.'

He cut two slices off the right cake and stole the speckle from the other so they each had one.

'Thank you.' Maddie sat on the sofa. 'How are you feeling?' She stopped herself from adding, 'What's the diagnosis? What the hell is happening?'

'Good.' He bit into the cake, halting the conversation in its tracks. It was as though the Evan she had been smitten by was playing peek-a-boo; one minute he was there and the next he was hiding again.

'So have all the follow-up checks gone well?' Her words came out staccato as she grappled to balance compassion with phrases that wouldn't make him feel as though she was prying.

'So far, so good.' He popped the chocolate speckle into his mouth. 'This cake is fantastic.' He paused before his next bite. 'It was definitely cancer, by the way. Stage one seminoma, if that means anything.'

He made his announcement with as much emotion as he had when he told her she'd baked a good cake.

'Apparently it's not a bad diagnosis, considering,' he continued. 'And if the cancer was going to spread it would have most likely have been to the abdomen, lungs and the lymph nodes in the chest, even the brain or bones in some cases. But there's no sign of any of that at this stage. I'll still need to be monitored, but they say with chemo to kill off any cancer cells that may have spread prior to the operation, the relapse rate is down to about five per cent.'

187

He took another bite of cake, unaware that as he ate, Maddie sat beside him reminding herself to breathe in and out. The sweet cake mixture felt too sickly in her mouth as she finished the last piece.

'When will the chemo start?' she asked.

He pushed his empty plate on to the coffee table. 'The fun starts in a couple of weeks.'

The game of peek-a-boo had suddenly come to an end. He finally let his guard down. 'I don't know how I'm supposed to feel, Maddie.' She let him reach out and pull her hand into his own. It rested, with his, on top of his thigh as they sat side by side on the sofa.

Evan had so much to deal with, a fight to go through. But then so did she. It was happening all over again; the man she loved could be taken away from her and it was beyond her control.

'You're tired. I should probably leave you to it.' Maddie wanted to run from the apartment. She wanted the icy wind outside to take hold of her and push her far, far away from reality.

When she stood, his hand tugged her own. 'Don't go, Maddie. Would you stay, just for a while?'

Helplessly, her eyes met his and she lowered herself back down and settled against the leather sofa. He lifted her hand to his lips and brushed it with a kiss, sending tingles snaking through her body as she remembered what it felt like to be with him, to make love to him.

'Stay, watch a movie with me maybe.'

It seemed so easy now if she just let herself be in the moment; no future, no past, just the two of them alone in a room. And she had to do it for him; that was the reason she had come, wasn't it?

'I will, on one condition,' she said.

'What's that?'

'It's not an action flick.'

'Hey, patient's prerogative, remember. What about a compromise?' He held up the DVD case of *Armegeddon.*

She nodded. It could be *Bambi* or *Die Hard* for all she cared. She had to focus on fighting the urge to run, to protect herself from more hurt.

'Is your neck okay?' She noticed his hand on his shoulder as he sat next to her, his head tilted to one side as though trying to stretch away a knot.

'Just a bit stiff, probably slept funny.'

'Well, it looks as though I can use both of my professions tonight, then.'

His eyes flittered dangerously, flirtatiously, and she felt her cheeks colour. That giddy feeling of something new took over and she relaxed. She indicated for him to sit on the floor and she sat on the sofa, putting her legs on either side of him.

Massage of the neck was something she did frequently at work, but never before had her hands shaken like this, had she been so mesmerised by her patient's skin beneath her own. She could feel the knots in the left side of his shoulder in particular, and as the film began she worked away to release the tension.

'Wow, that's good. If you end up leaving the physio business, don't ever give up the massage talent, will you?'

After a while she let her fingers lightly graze the skin on the back of his neck and felt him shudder. He moved back to the sofa and held Maddie's hand as they watched the movie, his body stretched out and his head tilted on to her shoulder.

It wasn't until the movie reached its climax that she realised how heavy Evan's head had become. He was sound asleep.

She looked down at his faded blue tracksuit pants and the grey T-shirt with a stain at the bottom. With the stubble that would need to be cut before it turned into a full-on beard, he had never looked so sexy. This big, strong man was just as vulnerable as she was.

As the final credits began to roll, they woke Evan. 'Are you crying?' He looked up at Maddie before rubbing his hands across his face to wake himself up.

'Guilty.' She pulled a tissue from her pocket. She didn't tell him the ending of the film was only part of the reason she had turned into a blubbering wreck. Her yo-yo of emotions hadn't given up and as she had watched him, so peaceful, lolling around with her as though they were the only two people in existence and nothing else mattered, she had realised that this was actually real. She was falling in love for the second time in her life.

'I'd better go.' She stood suddenly. 'You need to rest.'

She kissed him gently, her lips hovering on his before she pulled away. 'Goodbye, Evan.'

'Maddie.' He caught her arm before she managed to push it into her coat sleeve. 'What's wrong?'

'Nothing, I just need to go.'

'I know I'm not the best company at the moment, and that's why I hadn't invited you over before.'

'You don't need to explain. I'm sorry I put you on the spot.'

'I'm glad you did, really glad.' He reached up and cupped her cheek. 'I need to work through this at my own pace, but I still want you.'

'I shouldn't have come.' And with that she let the door click shut behind her and fled down the fire escape just in case he opened the door to his apartment and tried to stop her from getting in the lift.

Chapter Twenty

Sydney often outshone Melbourne in the weather stakes, and it was the perfect weekend to showcase the Northern Beaches with their never ending golden sands, swirling oceans that went on for miles, and towering palm trees that lined the walkways and surrounding green space.

Maddie hadn't been in Sydney since Christmas, and with everything that had happened with Evan and the fact she had left his place in such a panic the other night, she felt she needed this distance. She smiled as she drove the hire car from Kingsford Smith Airport all the way up to Palm Beach, the northernmost suburb of Sydney. The drive was breathtaking, with surrounding bushland and glimpses of the unspoiled blue waters of the Pacific Ocean along the way. The breeze drifted through the open windows, grazing her neck, and the hair of her ponytail lifted and danced freely. It felt good to be free from everyday life, and although her thoughts followed her, a change in location was a welcome escape.

'Maddie, you're here!' When she arrived her mum was first out of the door to meet her. Dressed in a floaty violet cotton dress with her hair in a neat grey bob, sunglasses nestled above the fringe, she looked as though Palm Beach had been her home her entire life.

'Hi, Mum.' Maddie hugged her. It felt unexpectedly settling to be back in the warm embrace of her family, and she blinked away the tears that took her by surprise.

'You found the place okay, then?'

'It was easy thanks to your directions, and there's a Sat Nav in the hire car anyway.'

'Oh, you don't need one of those things,' her mum dismissed the notion with a wave of her hand. 'We still have our Sydways and have no intention of modernising any time soon.

'So how have you been?'

'I'm fine. It's great to finally see the new place, and I'd forgotten how fabulous it is up here.'

Maddie's father had worked his way up the ranks and ended up as the Chief Executive Officer of a successful software company that had resisted the recent economic downturn. Growing up, Maddie and her sister, Jennifer, had been lucky enough to enjoy a grand house in the suburbs complete with a pool, trampoline, a sand pit, swing set and climbing bars. It had been nothing short of a child's paradise and they had always been a close family. It was exactly how Maddie had envisioned her future with Riley – not the wealth, but the importance of family being at their very core.

Maddie walked up the worn steps to the renovated townhouse washed in ivory. 'Where's Dad?'

'He's popped out for some lunch.'

Maddie inspected the place from the granite bench tops in the kitchen area to the view beyond the wide balcony that stretched the width of the house. She was instantly drawn outside to see the ocean: boats bobbed drunkenly on the surface; the cries of gulls sounded as they organised each other in the sky. Back inside she found newly renovated bathrooms with gleaming accessories and her mum's homely touches, including a basket of travel-sized toiletries with everything from mini Clinique soaps to miniature shaving kits – her mum had travelled frequently with her husband on business, and they always came back with more freebies than they needed from hotels and flights.

Maddie passed into the guest bedroom. The shutters opened back and the ocean refused to be ignored again.

'This place is perfect.' She left her weekend bag in the room and followed her mum into the kitchen. She took a breadstick from a plate and ran it through the tzatziki dip. 'You must've been so pleased to get this place.'

'We were very lucky.' Her mum fanned out julienned carrot sticks on to the plate. 'Our house in Cammeray went for far more than we hoped.' She pulled a continental cucumber from the fridge and chopped it the same way before adding the pieces to the collection. 'And there's that beautiful spare room, so no excuses not to come and visit.'

When Riley died, Maddie's parents had lost him too. He was like a son to Diane and Peter Kershaw. At the time Maddie had only been able to think of her own pain, and as a consequence she had kept herself to herself, and her visits home had become less and less frequent. She just hoped Evan wouldn't make the same mistakes she had; she knew he hadn't told his mum about the operation, and possibly the single biggest mistake Maddie had made after losing Riley was to hold those she loved at bay.

Her dad bounded through the door and Maddie moved to his open arms.

'Dad, it's lovely to see you.'

'It's great to have you here, Maddie.' He grinned at his daughter as he pulled out plastic containers, small and large, and a French stick which brought the scent of the local bakery to the kitchen with its freshness.

'Did one of you make this?' Maddie picked up a small, round pottery bowl glazed in navy blue with white sea-shells that she hadn't seen before.

Her dad raised his hand. 'Guilty.'

'Dad, I'm impressed.'

'It's awful, I need more practice.'

'Nonsense. Just for that I'm going to put this in it.' Maddie emptied out the Quinoa salad with red onion, spinach and sunny peppers.

The family chatted over bold tomatoes stuffed with tuna, and slices of golden quiche. Maddie made a show of spooning out the Quinoa salad from her dad's creation, and her mum poured out glasses of homemade lemonade, a childhood favourite of Maddie's and one that never ceased to appeal all through adulthood. They talked about her work; they talked about Palm Beach and the difference it made to their lives to be out of the busier suburbs.

'I've even taken up golf.' Her mum tucked her hair behind her ears. Her hair was cut short but slightly longer on top and the graduated lengths coming down in a fringe sat above wide-set hazel eyes. She had gone grey but added shades at regular hairdresser appointments made her look good for her sixty-nine years. Pale skin that had been looked after by vigilant use of sunscreen and the wearing of a hat over the years helped too.

'I never thought I'd see you take up golf, Mum. Whenever Dad watched it on TV or went off to play you couldn't have been less interested. What was it you used to call it?'

'A sport for gossips and middle-aged men,' her dad chuckled, spooning out more salad and adding an extra helping of butter to his bread.

'That was it!'

Her mum's cheeks flushed in exactly the same way Maddie's did so often. 'We're both ready to enjoy our retirement now, so I'm entitled to saunter along with the other women and discuss whatever we like.'

'Husbands,' said her dad, jolting Maddie's arm.

'Maybe you two could go touring around Australia visiting all the different golf courses,' Maddie suggested.

'Ah, that's right. Riley's father was into golf in a big way wasn't he? Didn't he do that once?'

Now it was Maddie's turn to flush at the name so easily dropped into conversation. It had happened so effortlessly, so naturally, yet it felt like she had been caught on barbed wire. It had been a long time since Maddie had let her guard down in front of her parents, and she didn't miss the look that passed between them as she focused on slicing through the tomato on her plate.

'We're here for you, love,' said her dad before they continued with lunch, and the conversation moved to Ally and how her time at University was going.

After she helped to clear away the lunch plates, Maddie went for a walk. The beach was close to the new house, a tiny slice of paradise, and as soon as she got there she trailed a stick in the sand, tempted to write her name like she had done when she was a child. Both she and Jennifer had written their names along firm, wet sand on every beach holiday and then the game was to sit and wait for the tide to come in and wash the letters away. Of course, it didn't always work. Sometimes the tide didn't come in far enough, sometimes they had to leave early, and other times they just got it plain wrong and the water would never touch their writing.

Palm Beach sat at the end of a long peninsula. On one side, the surf reached lofty heights, but on the other was Snapperman Beach Reserve, where Maddie found the tranquillity of calmer waters. She made her way along the cool, wet sand, her Birkenstocks dangling from her fingertips as she watched the water gently lap against the shore. She'd spent a lot of time at this spot after Riley died. Whenever she felt hemmed in by the suburbs she would jump in her car and drive the picturesque route through the Northern Beaches and up as far as she could go as though running from everything that had happened.

The squidgy sand beneath her feet covered the tops of her toes with deep, golden mud, and she walked it off on the grass when she retreated to a place overlooking the pier. She sat down and watched as a seaplane came in to land.

'Mind if I sit down?' A voice came from behind her.

Her mum sat down on the grass and they both gazed out at the pier, and then on the three children frolicking waist deep in the water a bit further along Snapperman Beach.

'You didn't think I was going to let you come up to visit for a weekend and then go off on your own did you?' Her mum took a deep breath of the salty air. 'You used to spend a lot of time here.'

Maddie brushed the sand from between her toes as it dried.

'You can fly from here to Sydney Harbour, you know,' said her mum, watching the seaplane bobbing about on the water now. 'It's pricey, but maybe next time you come up we could treat ourselves.'

'I'd really like that.' Her insides yearned for the in-depth chats they used to share, but she had surrendered those for fear of the painful reminders of a past that once was.

Her mum's gaze was transfixed on the three kids now. 'You and Jennifer always loved the beach.' The kids had emerged from the water, and the beginnings of a sandcastle were being produced from the first filled bucket of packed sand.

'I know. I still do, just in a different way.' She may not build sandcastles any longer, but the ocean and its freedom had a magic that nothing else could compare to. Just closing her eyes and listening to the water lapping against the shore had the ability to make Maddie believe everything would be all right in the end.

'How are you really, Maddie?'

'I have my good days and my bad.'

'It's been a long time … since Riley.' Her mum seemed to be choosing her words carefully.

'Why do I get the feeling that there's something you're not telling me?'

Her mum's shoulders sagged. 'There's no keeping anything from you is there?'

'What is it? Is something wrong with you, with Dad?'

'No, no, it's nothing like that.'

'So what is it, then?'

'It's about Caitlin.'

Riley's mum's name jolted her. It was the last thing she had expected to hear. 'What about her?' She brushed the dry sand from the arch of her foot. Her mum knew Caitlin had cut Maddie out of her life, but not the brutal way in which she had ended their contact.

'She called me.'

Maddie froze.

'She wants to get in touch with you.'

Maddie's toes jammed into the grass. Her jaw tensed as she took a deep breath in. 'Why? Why after all this time?'

'She said that she has something, of Riley's, and it's important that you have it.'

What was it? Was it a watch, a chain? Something of his that had been found after he'd been killed? Maddie racked her brain to think what it could be.

'When she called I didn't know what to say.' Her mum's arm remained on Maddie's as though she was worried her daughter would take off again, back to Melbourne before they had a chance to resurrect the relationship they'd always had. 'I almost put the phone straight back down again to shut her out in the same way she did to you.'

Maddie plucked a blade of grass and ran it through her fingers. Her mum didn't know the half of it and it was then, as she looked out at the gentle ripples of the water, that Maddie realised how much it could've helped her if she'd shared the burden.

'I'm a mother, Maddie. I can't even begin to imagine what it has been like for her.'

'Are you saying that she was right to drive me away?'

'I'm not saying anything of the sort. All I'm saying is that I feel for her. Life is too short to push people out, and I think her call was her reaching out to us, to you. Oh, I know that doesn't make it right, what she did, but I couldn't be angry at her after everything she's been through.'

'What about what I've been through?'

'You've been through too much, I know.'

'I didn't tell you the whole story, Mum.'

'What do you mean?'

'I didn't tell you what Caitlin said to me that day at the memorial.'

'It sounded as though she didn't say much.'

'Oh, she said something all right. She said that I would replace Riley soon enough with someone else. She said that I had no right to grieve as heavily as she was, because I had no idea what it was like for her. She said that my pain was nothing in comparison.'

Her mum let the words hang in the air for a moment.

'She was hurting, Maddie. She wouldn't have meant it.'

'No? She looked me in the eyes, didn't blink when she said those words to me. When she said that I would get married, I would have a family of my own one day, and then the only way I could ever understand her pain would be if something happened to one of my own children. She said it as though she wanted the same to happen to me so that I would know my pain over Riley was nothing; it was invalid compared to hers.'

Her mum pulled her daughter close as they turned their eyes back to the water. 'Just words, Maddie; they're just words. And remember, I knew Caitlin once upon a time. She's not the sort of woman who would wish harm to come to anybody else's child so that they could know how hard it is for her. No mother would wish that.'

'Those words have haunted me ever since,' Maddie blubbed. 'I've never been able to date men like Ally has, never been able to enjoy the company of a man without the shadow of those words hanging over me and every decision I've made. I couldn't even tell anyone what she said to me that day, because I know there was some truth in it.'

'Now that's nonsense.'

'You said it yourself. You said that you're a mother and you can understand the pain that she is in.'

'Oh, Maddie, that doesn't mean I don't understand the pain you went through too.' Her voice caught when she said, 'Riley wasn't my child, he wasn't my boyfriend, but just because he wasn't either of those things doesn't mean that your father and I didn't grieve when he died. Everyone hurts when someone they love and respect is taken away from them, and Caitlin had no right to question that. She had no right to leave you with those words. I suspect that, rather than her words, it's your own feelings that have made you shy away from other men.'

'What do you mean?'

'I know you so well, Maddie. You're a good person, a beautiful person. You loved Riley with all your heart and you can't bear to think of erasing the memory of him.'

Maddie's shoulders shuddered as sobs left her body. 'I sometimes take out his photo and look at it, talk to him even.'

'There's nothing wrong with that.'

'You don't think it's a tiny bit crazy?'

'No, I don't. Can I ask you, Maddie, have you pulled away from us – me and your dad – because you didn't want to remember Riley and what might have been?'

Maddie nodded through more tears. 'Part of me loves thinking about what it was like, but I know as soon as that stops, I'm faced with the reality that it's over. I should have moved on by now, and I didn't want to talk about it with you because I feel like such a failure, such a no-hoper that I'm still stuck in the past.'

Her mum pulled her in tighter. 'I wish you could've told me what Caitlin said and I could've talked some sense into you.'

'I didn't feel that I could question the love between a mother and a child.'

Maddie sat huddled in her mother's arms wishing she could've let her secret go before now.

'I bet Caitlin's words have haunted her almost as much as they have haunted you,' said her mum. 'I heard a lot of regret in her voice when she called, and now I know exactly why. It's taken a long time, but perhaps now she sees how wrong she was.'

Maddie pulled a tissue from her pocket. 'The trouble is, Mum, how do I move on from that and ever forgive her for what she said?'

Her mum sighed, a deep sigh laced with thought. 'I think that our happiness lies in the future, Maddie, not in the past. But sometimes we need to deal with that past if we are to ever move forwards. It takes a strong person to reach the stage of forgiveness, and you have to want to forgive, you have to want to move forwards.'

'I wonder what she wants to give me.'

'I've no idea, but for what it's worth, the woman sounds as though she's been in her own private hell.'

They sat, soothed by the rocking of the sea plane, the sounds of innocent voices playing in the sand, the sun caressing their skin, and by a sharing of the past that brought them together in the present, as close as ever.

Without saying a word they walked silently back home. Her mum linked an arm through Maddie's, just as she had when she was a kid, much to the chagrin of her dad, who joked that he was always an outsider in a house full of women.

Back at the house they opened up the balcony doors and took a jug of homemade lemonade outside and set it on the table between the two chairs.

'Where's Dad?' Maddie lifted both arms of the chair so the footrest and back opened out, stretching with her on the lazy afternoon as though it too had released a burden that had been weighing it down for too long.

'He left a note to say he's playing golf.' Her mum reclined in her chair too. 'I think he sensed we need some girl time. And I'm glad we had it.' She reached over and ruffled her daughter's hair as though she were still six years old.

Maddie looked out at the canopies of the Cabbage Tree Palms that lined the shore as she gulped down the long glass of lemonade and crunched the ice cubes at the end. She closed her eyes and lay back to enjoy the breeze on her face.

'Has there been anyone else since Riley? I know you said you chased other men away, but it's been a long time.'

Maddie opened her eyes and fixed her gaze on the thin lines of white foam from the waves in the distance. 'There wasn't anyone special, until recently.'

Her mum turned in her chair to face her daughter.

'You look like a teenager ready to gossip.' Maddie giggled. 'His name's Evan.' And then she sank deeper and deeper into the story about the man who had managed to capture her heart.

'The first date sounded promising. And the trip to Williamstown, that sounds very romantic.'

'I haven't told you the whole story yet.'

'Go on, we've got all day, after all.'

Maddie was glad they had started to repair their relationship. It reminded her of how they used to sit and gossip when she first met Riley. She couldn't look at her mum but heard the gasp of disbelief when she said, 'He has cancer.'

'That poor boy. Well, he must think a lot of you to have told you that.'

'Do you think so?'

'I know so. That's not the sort of thing you just share with anyone. That sort of admission, especially if it wasn't conclusive at that stage, isn't something you share unless you trust a person.'

'But he couldn't have trusted me after one date.'

'Strange things happen when you fall in love.'

Maddie's cheeks reddened.

'Do you love him?'

'Mum!'

'Well?'

Maddie nodded. 'I think I do.'

Her mum handed her a woollen blanket as the late afternoon air brought a chill with it. She sipped her drink thoughtfully.

'It sounds as though this Evan has a lot going on.'

'I panicked when I last saw him, Mum.'

'Panicked?'

'I didn't think I'd ever want a future with anyone when Riley died. And now, it feels as though it's happening all over again. I'm scared of letting myself love Evan in case I lose him. I don't think I'm strong enough to go through it again. I went to see him at his apartment, and I ran away.'

Her mum held her arm open and beckoned her daughter over to her chair. They perched on the end hugging one another. 'Never be afraid to give your heart to someone else, Maddie,' she said, lightly rocking her daughter. 'It was broken once, but that doesn't mean it can't be fixed. After all this time you deserve to be happy.'

Maddie knew she deserved to be happy – didn't everybody? But whether that happiness featured Evan, she wasn't so sure, and for now Caitlin and whatever it was she had to give her dominated her thoughts and she had no idea what to do.

'Grief is maddening, Maddie. It's like you're drowning, and I think that's what happened with Caitlin. At the time I was so angry with her for deserting you, but now I realise she had to face the battle in her own way, just like you have.'

'You think I should call her, don't you?'

'You do what you think is best. But you never know, it could help you too. See what she has to say. You're a beautiful young woman, Maddie. You don't turn people away when they're reaching out, not really.'

They sat wrapped in each other's arms right up until Maddie's dad came home.

*

Saying goodbye to her parents was done with a heavy heart. Maddie still wasn't sure what to do about Caitlin, but talking it over, and talking about Evan as well, had been exactly what she needed this weekend. She felt as though, regardless of whether she contacted Caitlin, regardless of what happened with Evan, she had got back on the bike again and was keeping the pace uphill to the very top.

Chapter Twenty-One

Ben's voice on the answer machine told Evan he would have to get up sharpish if they were to make the chemotherapy appointment that morning. It was ten o'clock already and, again, Evan had been in bed for more hours than he had been out of it. Since the operation more than a month ago, he felt useless, like a spare part. And since Maddie had been over that night with the cake and had left so abruptly, he had never felt so low. Perhaps her departure had been for the best though, because if she hadn't pitied him then, she sure would once the chemo started.

The weather did little to help his spirits: cold and wet, and one look out of the window couldn't entice him on to the balcony most days. So he literally got out of bed, had whatever meal he was already late for, and then went back to his pit. He didn't always sleep either. Sometimes he would toss and turn as dreams plagued him; other times he would lie and look at the closed venetian blinds or the ceiling, as though his brain had run out of power to do much else.

Today's chemotherapy session was to kill any cancer cells that could have spread prior to the orchidectomy, and his doctor had assured him that he shouldn't experience any significant hair loss. Hopefully he wouldn't be vomiting all over the place either, although there could be some nausea for a while.

Everything *down there* was in good working order too – he'd tried it out himself, tentatively – and the fact that his manhood was still intact had been a huge relief. At first the prosthesis had felt as though he had nabbed one of King Kong's balls to stick between his legs, but now that the swelling had subsided and the bruising had all but disappeared it didn't feel so absurdly out of place.

Physically, Evan was as strong as he ever was. But emotionally he felt like a seven-stone weakling as he and Ben set off for the hospital that day.

*

Following her shift Maddie waited at the tram stop with the biting wind whipping around her as she looked up at a sky dusted with stars and a crescent moon as their protector. She wrapped her coat tightly around herself and pulled a beanie down over her loose hair so that she was as snug as a tea pot beneath an old-fashioned tea cosy.

The last couple of weeks had dragged by slowly. Since she had taken the cake to Evan, and since her weekend in Sydney, the familiar dank and low feeling of winter had taken over. She still hadn't called Caitlin, and as time went on it became easier not to get in touch with Evan either. On evenings like this, when it was dark and miserable and the tram crept slowly along St Kilda Road towards home, she often found herself wondering if Evan was thinking about her, whether he had been tempted to chase her the night she left his apartment. Or had he given up on her altogether? Then she would scold herself for being so self-obsessed. The guy had cancer, bigger things to think about than her.

She made a quick pit stop at home, and then the wintry temperature propelled her around the Tan Track in record time. After a shower and change, she was back out again into the cold and bundled up in her thick, cream coat, heading back into the city to Chinatown where she met Ally at their favourite restaurant.

They ordered the Peking duck, requesting to assemble their own pancakes. Maddie spread a generous helping of plum sauce across the surface of the pancake, added a small amount of duck and a decent sprinkling of the cucumber, but no spring onions.

'I can't believe you never told me what Caitlin said to you that day.' Ally spread a more modest helping of plum sauce around a fresh pancake. She tore some duck apart on the centre plate and arranged it on top, added a few slivers of spring onion and cucumber.

As soon as Maddie returned from Sydney, she had confided in her best friend. Saying the words out loud had diluted them in a way, and she couldn't believe it had taken her so long to see them for what they really were – just words.

'I know that now, Ally. I should've told the people I love most in the world and saved myself a whole lot of pain.'

'I'm still worried about you, Maddie.' Ally tore away some more duck and positioned it on the pancake. 'Is Evan off the scene for good?'

Maddie finished her mouthful and licked away the plum sauce that had oozed down one finger, giving her a chance to cast her mind back to that time alone with him in his apartment.

'I haven't heard from him,' she answered honestly, rolling another pancake into a perfect cigar shape, all its contents safely tucked inside.

Ally topped up both glasses of wine and changed tack. 'Have you decided what to do about Caitlin?'

She shook her head. Caitlin's number was programmed into her phone, but that was as far as she'd got.

A bowl of steaming egg fried rice appeared in the centre of the table, along with a sticky offering of sweet and sour pork that Maddie began to spoon into rice bowls.

Ally armed herself with a set of chopsticks. 'You know how every year I try to take you away from the 9/11 hype?'

'It's only July, Ally.'

'I know.' Her friend shrugged. 'Call this an early getaway, then.'

Maddie thought back to Ally's attempts over the years. 'Let me see: last year it was the Blue Mountains, the year before was Olinda, the year before that was Noosa.'

'Okay, okay. It's just that Joel has been offered a holiday apartment up on Hamilton Island in the Whitsundays for the first weekend in August. It's a three-bedroom place, and Josh said he's up for a weekend away, Todd too. It'll be about a few friends getting away from the cold and warming up for a while, at no cost apart from the flight. I think it could really do you good.'

'I'm not sure.' Maddie hadn't seen Josh since the night she went home with him, and she still felt guilty for the way she'd led him on.

'Don't worry about Josh. He knows you're invited and he's totally cool with that.'

'I'm not sure I could get time off work,' she teased.

'I'll ring your boss myself – tell him it's essential for mental health!' She pointed her chopsticks at Maddie.

'There's no need you daft cow. I'm in.'

'You are?' Ally's chopsticks went flying in her excitement and a waiter nearby scuttled over with a fresh set.

'Just try and stop me.'

Chapter Twenty-Two

The chemotherapy session wiped Evan out even more than he had expected, but he would take the tiredness and the nausea anytime over hair loss and constant vomiting that he had assumed would be part and parcel of the affair.

Ben had waited with him for the two-hour session and they had played cards to take his mind off the needle going into his arm and the drip leaking poison into his body. Evan had seen others coming and going for their own treatment, surprised at an atmosphere less tinged with stress and fear than he had expected.

He knew he should be happy, happy that he wasn't one of those poor bastards who had already signed up for relentless chemo sessions day after day, week after week – longer sometimes. A pale, drawn-out man had passed by just after Evan started his own session with the IV drip, and Evan was shocked that he couldn't even begin to guess the man's approximate age: with no hair and skin that looked as delicate as the thin film that sat beneath chicken skin, it was impossible.

How on earth did people go through it time after time? How on earth did they manage to keep going? He shared his doctor's hope that his experience with chemo would be a very short-lived one.

Evan had chatted briefly with one of the jolliest women he had ever met just as he was about to leave the hospital room. Lorraine had bantered on about her selection of fluro headscarves she had at home, used to hide her bald head – fluro green was today's choice – and she had told him that this wretched chemo wasn't going to cure her, but it would buy her some time with her kids. It would let her see her youngest daughter get married in a few weeks, and then she intended to stop prolonging the inevitable.

After Lorraine shuffled off to her treatment session, Evan had gone into the men's and cried, sick to the pit of his stomach that life could be so cruel. He and Ben had driven home from the hospital in silence, and Ben had taken some convincing to leave him alone in his apartment.

*

In the days following his chemo, Evan lapsed back into the same gloominess he had seen following his operation. The words of the doctor still rang in his ears: 'Attitude can make a huge difference to recovery time.' Yeah, well, that was easy for him to say. Evan alternated between sleeping and moping on the sofa. He sat outside on the balcony if the weather allowed, for fear that he would forget what fresh air felt like; that or become severely vitamin D deficient. With another couple of weeks of scheduled sick leave to go, and with a ban on running for the time being, Evan felt grotty, grim and unable to climb his way out of the hole he was in. Apparently these feelings were quite normal with a cancer diagnosis, but it didn't make the everyday dealing with them any easier to handle. Some days he felt determined – determined that he wouldn't let the wretched disease get one up on him again – but on other days he could barely recite that positivity in his head, let alone be strong enough to tackle it.

Evan pulled himself to a sitting position on the sofa, not even sure of what day it was now. He ran a hand through his hair, tugging from the roots, paranoid that clumps would come off in his hand even though the doctor had said it would be highly unlikely with such a short burst of this sort of chemo. He was right; the only hair loss came from the strands he had managed to pull out himself with the strength of his sheer frustration.

When the phone rang he waited until the answer machine clicked in, in case it was Holly, Jem or Ben – they had all phoned eager to join the pity party. He hoped it wasn't Maddie either. She'd been on his mind a lot, but the thought of her seeing him like this, helpless and weak, was almost too much to bear.

When he realised that it wasn't any of them, he snatched up the phone. 'Jack, it's great to hear from you!' The different name thrown into the mix felt like a tonic, and Evan was alert, happy to talk to one of his best mates who knew nothing about the shit he was dealing with.

They swapped greetings, bantered about The Demons and the approaching footy Grand Final in September, but Evan's sudden rosy outlook soon took on another shade, and this time it was a whole different kind of red when Jack said, 'I heard about the cancer.'

*

214

'What the fuck gives you the right to go telling people?' After his conversation with Jack, Evan's temper had propelled him out of his apartment for the first time in days and he had driven in a rage over to Port Melbourne. When he arrived Ben dragged him outside so they didn't have the fight in front of Ava.

'You need people around you, Evan.'

'I've got people around me!' He wiped his mouth as saliva landed on his chin. 'I've got so many people calling me, fussing around me that I feel claustrophobic. You're all on at me: "Get out of bed, Evan"; "Have something to eat, Evan"; "Maybe a shower will make you feel better, Evan"; "Maybe it's time to rest, Evan." I'm going insane with you lot being in my face all the time!'

When Evan's roar subsided he leaned back against the cold bricks of the house. His T-shirt was damp with sweat, and his body began to shiver from the cold and the anger inside of him.

Ben took up position leaning on the wall next to him. 'I know you're having one hell of a time right now, but don't push us away. Jack has been your friend since high school, and I can't imagine why you wouldn't want him to know. That's why I told him. You'd never mentioned that it was a secret.'

Suddenly, Evan was exhausted. The surge of adrenalin had used every ounce of energy that he had left, and when he realised he was shaking, he didn't know whether he was cold, about to pass out or just plain frightened.

'Wait there,' said Ben. He ducked inside, and Evan heard him murmur, presumably to Holly, and he reappeared with a fleece.

215

'Thanks.' Evan pulled it over his head. He waited a while, watched the tiny grey clouds as his breath met the air when he exhaled. 'I guess I wanted there to be some people who didn't know about the cancer. I know that you all mean well when you ask after me, encourage me to do things, but I need some people around who aren't looking at me with pity.'

'We don't pity you,' said Ben.

'Maybe not intentionally, but that's what it feels like, and all it does is remind me of everything that's bad right now. When my father died I remember those same looks, those same soft voices. People would pass us in the street and you knew that they were thinking, "Those poor Quinn children."'

Ben didn't speak, he just listened.

'I remember flying over to Perth on holiday not long after Dad died and Mum bumped into a lady she used to work with. She had two kids, a boy and a girl about our age, and for some reason Mum decided that we wouldn't tell them about Dad. I went along with her game and she told these people that our dad wasn't around.' He raked his hand through his hair before pushing his head back against the wall as though it gave him the strength to stand up. 'She made it sound as though we were on the run. It was quite an adventure. But it didn't hurt that Mum wasn't being honest. I totally got why she did it.'

Ben stayed in position next to Evan on the wall but rubbed his hands briskly together and blew into them for warmth.

'We hung out with the lady, Beth, and her kids for the whole week, and it was the best time that Holly and I had had since Dad died. There were no

216

sympathetic looks, no informal counselling by someone who wanted to help. We came back from that holiday a hell of a lot more positive than we had been in the days since the funeral, and from that moment whenever we were sad Mum would bundle us both into the car, load up the buckets and spades, and whether it was winter or summer she didn't care; off we would go to the beach.'

'That sounds like the crazy sort of thing Holly would do. Like mother like daughter, eh.'

Evan sighed deeply. 'Now do you see why I didn't want to broadcast my cancer?'

'I'm sorry, mate, I really am. I shouldn't have opened my big mouth without talking to you first. But for what it's worth, telling Jack will make it easier in the long run. You may think we look at you with pity, but I can assure you we don't. We look at you as a man who has a fight on his hands, that's all, and that doesn't make you weak.'

Evan suspected that his anger was misplaced. Perhaps the person he was most angry at was himself – for being so down since the operation and the chemo, and for letting Maddie slip through his fingers because of the wall he had built up. She had told him she had been hurt badly before when Riley died. He wished he had been strong enough to support her, to know that this wasn't easy for her either. He wished he was man enough to do that, at least.

'You can make it up to me by rustling me up some dinner. I'm starving.' Evan grinned, all the fight gone out of him for now.

'You're on,' said Ben as he pushed open the front door. 'Mission accomplished at any rate.'

'How do you work that out?'

'I got you out of your apartment, didn't I?'

Holly emerged from the kitchen and hugged Evan. Ava ran at him full throttle, and he knew in that instant that he was in the right place. In minutes Holly had thrown together sausages, eggs, beans and thick-cut chips. She reprimanded him for being so aloof and made him swear that he would make the effort to at least check-in with them more often.

'Right, then.' Ben stood up as they finished eating. 'There's no time like the present.'

'I'll clear all this up,' said Holly. 'You have a great time.' She hugged her husband and gave him a kiss on the lips.

'They're in love!' Ava giggled into Evan's chest. 'Where are you going, Daddy?'

Ben leafed through his wallet. 'I'm taking Uncle Evan out for the evening.' He held a hand up to stop any protest. 'My main mission was to get you out of the house, but part two is to get you out with all your mates. Jack and the others will meet us there in half an hour, I texted him. And before you say anything, he hasn't passed on your news yet. It's been what, a grand total of seven hours since I told him, you came round to knock my block off, and I told him to keep quiet. Gossip doesn't run quite the same race with men as it does with women.' He ducked as Holly flicked a tea towel at his backside.

Evan knew his first move had got him this far so he may as well go along with the rest. And besides, he was looking forward to seeing his mates. He hadn't seen these guys in almost six months, their jobs and lives, girlfriends and families all getting in the way, not to mention his own personal battle.

*

'You need to get back into the swing of things,' said Ben as they parked up in the city. They crossed the road and headed towards the agreed pub for tonight. 'If you can't handle a night with your mates, how the hell do you expect to handle a pack of kids screaming at you to tie their laces, yelling at you to wipe their snotty noses when you go back to work a week Wednesday?'

'Fair point, but I wouldn't go near their snotty noses even if the government paid me an extra hundred grand a year.'

'Glad to hear you haven't gone completely soft.' Ben gave him a friendly punch on the arm as they approached the Irish pub.

'Evan.' A voice stopped them before they opened the door. It was Jack. 'Good to see you, mate.' Jack pulled him into a typical man hug: distance and back slaps. 'I haven't mentioned anything to the others.'

'Thanks, mate.' Evan felt almost ashamed that he had kept this huge secret now.

'Oh, and I don't pity you at all if that's what you're worried about.'

'I should hope not.' Evan grinned.

'I haven't cooked you any dinners or counselled you over the telephone—'

'Yeah, you've been pretty crap!' Evan ran a hand across a stubbly jaw as they entered the pub. He had given in and had a shave a few days ago after Holly kissed him hello at his place and claimed that his

219

beard was beginning to smell not too dissimilar to the guinea pig hutch at home.

'You know they'll wonder why you're not getting on it tonight,' continued Jack when Evan told him that he wouldn't be drinking. He could have a beer, maybe two, but the chemo hadn't left him with much of a taste for it. Whether that was the chemo itself or his emotions wreaking havoc, he had no idea. 'I'll cope, even if it means you have to drink mine for me.'

'Happy to help,' said Ben, 'although in that case you'll have to drive us home.'

'No worries.'

They found Simon and Will hogging the wooden table towards the back in the dimly lit bar. They looked as though they were into their first beers and man hugs ensued as well as exclamations at how long it had been since they had all been out together. Talk inevitably turned to sport and which teams were most likely to be battling in the AFL Grand Final this year.

'You want to support a real team.' Simon deliberately tried to provoke Evan, which was typical and not always one-sided.

He didn't rise to the bait. 'I stand by my team. Go Demons! I've always barracked for Melbourne. I'm a Melbourne boy through and through.'

Ben had been right to get him out tonight for drinks. He felt more human by the second; one of the guys as much as any of the others, with or without both balls.

Will knocked on the table in the absence of something to tap against his glass. 'I've got a bit of an announcement to make,' he said sheepishly.

'You've decided to shave your hair off and get rid of that receding hair line?' put in Jack.

'If you could all be quiet for one second, I'd tell you that it's nothing to do with my hair, or any other part of my anatomy. It's Ginny.' He paused for effect. 'She's pregnant. We're having a baby!'

A raucous cheer went up that Evan felt detached from. He could hear himself making the appropriate noise, he could see his glass raised in the air, chinking into the others and then slurping the amber liquid of his light beer along with his mates. But the normality of a few seconds ago had come crashing down, and all too quickly his mate's journey into fatherhood made him feel as though he had stood on the prongs of a garden rake and the shaft had shot straight up and smacked him in the face. What if the doctors were wrong? What if one testicle wasn't enough to give him the chance to father children? What if the cancer had spread undetected and, while he stood here in this pub, was already ravaging other parts of his anatomy?

'Can you believe Will's gonna be a dad?' Jack battled into Evan's thoughts as they stood at the bar and placed their order for snacks and another round.

'It's fantastic. It looks like they're up for a big celebration tonight.'

'Hang on a minute, mate.' Jack pulled him back before he could go back and join them. He felt like a member of his class caught doing something untoward. 'You're not fooling me.'

'What do you mean?' Now Evan knew that his wide, innocent eyes gave away his inability to act convincing.

221

'This is why I really think you should tell them what's been going on,' said Jack. 'They can't be tactful unless you do – hell, they probably can't manage tact anyway, but why don't you give them the benefit of the doubt?'

Evan looked over at Will who, along with Ben, was building some kind of origami-stack with whatever beer mats he could get his hands on. 'I don't think now's the time.'

'It won't ever be the right time, but they're your mates.'

'You're sounding like a girl. Maybe I'll have a word with Shelley, get her to give you the pants back?'

'Don't try and joke it all away like it's no big deal. It is a big deal when you've lost one of your bloody balls!'

'Tell the world, why don't you?' Evan hissed and led the way back to the others.

Will put an arm across Evan's shoulders, a move most men didn't try until they were three-quarters of the way to being comatose from alcohol. 'So come on, mate, good looking guy like you, when you going to make some lucky woman happy?'

'One day, mate, one day.' He pulled clear of the man hug and exchanged a look with Ben.

Evan thought back to the last time they had been in this very pub and realised it was when Jack's third baby, a daughter, was born. They had come to 'wet the baby's head', although with their two other kids to look after, his girlfriend had texted him and told him that she could use a hand at home. Evan hadn't envied their relationship then, but that tight family unit seemed so out of reach now. His mates' voices echoed around him as they debated the merits of having girls versus boys, teen horror stories, home footy teams, being looked after in your old age.

A bowl of steaming hot fries arrived and the conversation about kids lulled, although Evan couldn't stop thinking about fatherhood. He wanted children of his own, and he wanted them to have two parents present in their lives until they left home and formed families of their own. When his own dad died, he had felt as though a piece of him were missing. He had seen friends and their dads going to the cricket, the AFL, even heading to the pub for a drink and a chat. He wasn't asking for the world, he was asking for something that many people took for granted; he wanted a future with a family in it. Somehow, over the years Evan had become a one man band, wanting to do everything independently, but that wasn't what he wanted anymore.

'How's work, Evan?' Simon's question pulled him back to the present. 'You'd be an expert on kids after spending a whole day with them, wouldn't you? Maybe you could teach Will here a few pointers.'

'I'm not sure how much help I'd be. I get all the nice bits, or so I'm told. I get to teach them all the cool new things and their parents get the tired-out kids when they get home.'

'So do you reckon you'll have them? Kids, I mean?' Simon unwittingly put his size twelves right in it.

'I hope so, mate,' said Evan truthfully.

'Make the most of it before you do,' said Ben. 'Because once you have them, you'll be sex starved like the rest of us.'

Evan couldn't keep it to himself any longer; this was excruciating. He should be able to talk about anything with these guys, and goodness knows he needed to.

'I've got a bit of an announcement myself. I've been in hospital, for an operation.' No point trying to put it delicately; he knew that he needed to get to the point. 'I had testicular cancer.' He wasn't sure whether past tense was the correct terminology. Maybe it was wishful thinking.

Simon and Will sat in stunned silence, Jack and Ben sipped their beers thoughtfully. But once the questions started, Evan couldn't hold any of them back.

'How did you find the lump?' Will asked. 'Were you, you know?'

'Trust you, Will. No, I wasn't touching myself – not in the way you think – I found it when I was in the shower.'

'Did it hurt?' asked Jack.

'Not really. I think once I knew that it was there, it kind of just irritated me.'

'Was the chemo horrendous?' Jack sipped his beer. He stretched a hand up and stroked Evan's dark, thick hair. 'You still have your luscious locks,' he teased.

'Okay, easy tiger, no need to touch me like a big girl. The chemo wasn't as bad as I thought, but I was lucky. I only had one round – some people have it for weeks, months on end. It all depends on how serious the cancer is. I know now how grateful I should be that I found the lump when I did, that the cancer hadn't spread.

'Go on, Simon, ask.' He noticed the hesitation on his mate's face.

'Have you been with a girl since? I mean, did it affect anything down there? Can you still get a hard-on?'

'Bit personal!' declared Ben.

'It's all right. You'll be pleased to know that everything is still in prime working order.'

'So is it just saggy skin left where your bollock was?' Simon asked.

'No, I had the prosthesis put in.'

'Does it feel the same?' Will asked. 'Does it look the same?'

'Jeez, Will, you'll be asking him to unzip his pants in a minute,' Jack scolded.

'What about Maddie? What does she think of the fake one versus the real one?' said Simon.

Her name in the air took Evan by surprise.

'That's right, men can gossip as well as women,' admitted Simon. 'I bumped into Ben in the city one day, mentioned I hadn't seen you in a while, and he told me you were loved up with this girl, Maddie. So what's happening with her, is she hot?'

'Too hot for you to handle,' quipped Evan.

How did Maddie feel about his fake ball? That was a good question. In fact, how did Maddie feel about anything, how did she feel about him? She practically ran from his apartment that night. They'd had a nice evening, even though he spent most of it dozing on her shoulder, and he had no idea why she left so suddenly.

'So what's the next step?' asked Will, and Simon's question about Maddie was forgotten already.

Evan took a deep breath, puffed out his cheeks. 'Now we wait. Fingers crossed the chemo did its job and I won't have to go back for more. The cancer looked contained and we got to it early, so the odds are in my favour. I'll be on a surveillance program for around three years, so every four months or thereabouts I'll have bloods taken, chest X-rays, CT scans.'

The men sat in silence; he'd scared the lot of them.

'That's it, I'm going home for a good feel tonight,' said Simon, his face so comical with its lines of worry that they all burst out laughing.

'I'll try not to think about that too much, mate,' said Evan. 'But I think it's a good idea, and for the rest of you guys too. Before all of this I never checked myself. I never felt around for lumps, I guess I never really thought about it. I mean, there's so much publicity about women checking their breasts, but for blokes, cancer of the balls isn't exactly shouted from the rooftops, is it?'

Anxious to steer the conversation on to something else, Evan turned to Jack. 'Any plans since you proposed to Shelley?'

'Actually, there are. And I need to ask you a favour. Would you be my best man?'

'I—I don't know what to say.' Evan sniffed, feigning tears and patting at his eyes.

'Say yes, you pansy!'

'Of course I will.' He'd been through school with Jack, and he couldn't be more honoured.

'Charming,' Will said. 'Just because he's had cancer, he gets the sympathy vote?'

'Get stuffed, Will,' laughed Evan. He turned to Jack. 'So when's the big day?'

'Three weeks.'

'That's close, isn't it?'

'Now this is the best part. Neither of us wants a great time lag so that our families start to interfere, so we're heading up to the Whitsundays to do it. Hamilton Island.'

'Nice, seriously nice,' they all choroused.

'After the debacle of my sister Lori's wedding, we don't want the same happening at ours. So that's why the short notice, and that's why we're heading away from Melbourne. Most of the extended family will be too stingy to pay for the flights let alone the accommodation. I've already booked some rooms at a hotel for you guys, though, so no excuses.'

Evan had gone along to Jack's sister's wedding for moral support, and it was chaos from start to finish: hats with a life of their own, drunken speeches that didn't even border on funny, a wasted uncle who stripped down to a leopard skin posing pouch. It was no wonder Jack didn't want a repeat performance.

Evan left the pub that night feeling like a changed man. He had started the day in a pit of despair and now he felt amongst friends, ready to deal with life again. The only thing missing now was the girl he had fallen for: Maddie.

Chapter Twenty-Three

Despite the expected tiredness, Evan's professional life picked up where it had left off when he returned to work two weeks later. He felt like Arnold Schwarzenegger in *Kindergarten Cop*, minus the loud whistle, when the kids all rushed at him on the first day, brandishing handmade cards and drowning him with their questions. Even paperwork at the end of the week felt like a reward for good behaviour, and he was glad to finally be using his brain again instead of flicking through mindless TV programmes, feeling sorry for himself.

Evan and his mates had made a pact to meet up at least once every month too, vowing never to leave it as long next time. He suspected that wives and girlfriends had been placated when they were told about his cancer, but he hadn't minded. He was just glad he had realised how much he needed to be around people rather than burying himself in misery and the four walls of his apartment. Since the chemotherapy session the cancer, so far, hadn't dared to rear its ugly head again, and Evan had even made a return to running, completing the Tan Track in a half decent time twice that week.

On Friday morning, his mind had already escaped up the east coast of Australia to the Whitsundays even before the sun had battled its way to the uppermost rungs in the sky, and with the feeling of freedom that came with that, he ran around Albert Park Lake and decided that it was time he got in touch with Maddie.

Back at his apartment he tried her phone, but there was no answer. He tried once more, after school that day, before he hopped into the cab to go to the airport, then again just before he boarded the plane. He hoped this didn't mean she was ignoring his calls; he at least wanted the chance to talk to her to explain why he hadn't been in touch, to let her explain why she had left him so abruptly that night.

He relaxed back in his seat as the plane taxied down the runway and hoped that when he finally got in touch with Maddie again, she would still want to talk to him.

*

Maddie looked amongst the collection of suitcases that had been unloaded from the flight and set down in the allocated area outside Hamilton Island's tiny airport. It didn't take long to spot hers with its red and white polka dot bow wound around the handle, and Ally's did the absolute opposite of blending in: it was fluro pink and in a league of its own.

'Welcome to paradise.' Ally breathed in the island air layered with warmth as they were ushered on to an awaiting minibus that would take them to their apartment. 'The boys got here yesterday, so I hope they haven't trashed the place already.'

They found two seats across the aisle from each other and Maddie couldn't tear her gaze away from the window as the bus bumped its way up hills and down the other side, turning left, right, like a ball falling about on a crazy golf course. Thin roads were surrounded by the lush green of a tropical paradise, and the heat seeped through the glass. Local palm trees swayed gently in the breeze, the late-afternoon sun danced off the leaves, and as they made their way around the small island towards the accommodation, Maddie watched golf buggies zip to and fro in place of cars that weren't permitted on this small, approximately five kilometre squared island.

'This place is beautiful,' said Maddie.

'Sure is.' Ally smiled over at her friend. 'I'm so glad you came.'

Joel was already waiting when the minibus swung round a corner and stopped outside the apartment complex. Ally yelped with excitement and rushed for him, leaving Maddie to wheel both suitcases.

'Here, let me help you with those,' Joel apologised on behalf of his girlfriend.

'Sorry, I'm a bit excited,' Ally said sheepishly.

'You're allowed to be.' Maddie didn't mind really. Already she could feel the sun soaking into her skin, and she didn't want the kiss of paradise to end when they drifted into the shade outside the front door and into the open-plan kitchen and lounge. She felt her heart surge when she looked out to the balcony and Josh raised his hand in greeting. She hoped that he wouldn't make this too uncomfortable.

'You're in the end room,' said Ally, taking charge of the luggage this time. 'I'll put your suitcase in there.'

'Thanks.'

'Hey, Maddie, it's good to see you again.' Josh pulled open the sliding balcony door and picked up the T-shirt that had been draped across the back of a chair in the kitchen, pulling it over his tanned torso.

'It's good to see you too, Josh.'

'You'd think they hadn't seen each other for months, wouldn't you?' He nodded towards Ally and Joel, who couldn't leave each other alone. 'Can I get you a drink?'

'That'd be great.'

'We've got red, white, beer, or non-alcoholic drinks.' He pulled open a few cupboard doors until he found the glasses.

'I'll have a white wine spritzer please.' Her request met with a look of confusion. 'Half a glass of wine and then top it up with lemonade.' There didn't seem to be any animosity between them and Maddie was glad.

He passed her the drink, and they headed outside to the balcony where Todd was soaking up the rays as though he had never heard the *slip, slop, slap* slogan. He looked up briefly to say hello and then laid his head back down again.

'That's an amazing pool.' Maddie leaned against the balcony railings next to Josh. Below was a kidney-bean-shaped pool for the sole use of the eight apartments in this block, and with the beach a short buggy ride away it was like having nirvana at their fingertips.

'Have you two been in yet?' she asked.

'We sure have. The water's beautiful. We could head down there now if you like?'

Maddie took a long sip of the spritzer and watched two cockatoos bravely edging their way along the balcony railings, beaks clattering against the metal, claws doing the same. Their yellow tufts stood tall in the wind as they dipped their heads to see if this apartment's occupants had been careless enough to drop any food.

'Isn't this place great?' Ally squealed as she reappeared. 'How about we leave these guys to it and go explore?'

Grateful to be rescued from Josh's invitation, Maddie made a quick exit to her bedroom and rummaged through her case to find swimmers. She pulled on a navy and white tankini and then a navy and white striped dress so that she was ready for every eventuality.

By the time she was ready, Ally was already waiting in the driver's seat of the buggy, shades pulled down. Her blonde bob swung gently as she giggled at the horrendous stop-start jerking of the buggy when she pulled away, and then again every time she had to negotiate a junction.

'I love the way everyone waves at each other.' Ally raised her hand at yet another person as she approached the brow of the hill, sliding backwards before she managed to accelerate enough.

Maddie felt at Ally's mercy in this thing. 'Concentrate!'

'Back seat driver,' Ally retorted.

They drove past the school, past the little white chapel, where they paused to speculate how beautiful it would be to get married there. They made their way down to the marina and the main shopping strip on Front Street. Buggies were parked in allocated spaces, just as cars would be in a regular car park, and the mode of transport iconic to the island symbolised the freedom and fun that Maddie could already feel.

'Joel mentioned Popeye's.' Ally indicated a fish and chip shop. They journeyed on past a convenience store, a chemist, a collection of restaurants and then turned up another steep hill taking them in another direction. They pulled into a parking spot outside some of the larger hotels for guests who preferred the convenience of serviced rooms, food laid on, and without the independence of having their own place. From there they wandered down to the beach. A winding bushy path led them to an unexpected pool area with smooth rocks leading over to the calm aqua waters and pale golden sands of Catseye Beach.

'Look at that,' said Ally, pulling out her iPhone. 'Photo opportunity, come on Maddie.' They stood with their backs to the beach and, flipping the camera on the phone round and holding the device at arm's length, Ally snapped a picture of them both with the sparkling sea behind them framed between lofty palm trees.

Both girls kicked their thongs from their feet and stepped on to the sugar-soft sands. They watched a handful of brave swimmers bobbing around in the freedom of the sea, the sun caressing their skin when they let it show above the water.

'Let's warm up before we even think about that.' Ally pointed at the two men in the sea.

'It can't be that bad, they're in up to their necks and they look like they're enjoying themselves.'

Maddie pulled one of the plastic sun loungers out of the shade and towards the sun, lay down and pulled out a book, but it rested spine up on her chest as she looked down past her fuchsia-coloured toenails and out to the Coral Sea. Beyond the hot pink and lemon windsurf sails in the distance sat other land masses which she couldn't identify, and she shut her eyes and let the sun lick her entire body, glad to be away from everything that was so familiar at times it was suffocating.

'It's nice to get away from it all, isn't it?' said Ally. 'Uni is full-on at the moment. I needed this.'

Maddie was so relaxed she knew she could doze off at any second. She hadn't realised how much she'd needed this time away until now. She'd even left her phone at home, so great was the need to escape. There would be no staring at Caitlin's number, her fingers asking her whether she should call or not.

'Are you going to give me the silent treatment all afternoon?' asked Ally.

'I'm trying to.'

The next minute Maddie felt warm, tiny pin pricks across her legs. 'Hey!' She opened her eyes to find Ally drizzling sand over her from between her fingers.

'You're lucky I'm too blissed out to go down to the sea and get some cold water,' Ally warned. 'Aren't you reading your book?'

'All in good time, all in good time.'

'You know it's great to see you so relaxed for a change.'

This time Maddie didn't even grunt an 'Mmm'.

'Have you given any thought to getting in touch with Caitlin?'

'No,' she said flatly. 'And I'd rather not talk about her if that's all the same with you.'

'I wonder what she has that's so important she needs to give it to you after all this time.'

'Didn't you hear what I said?'

'Ah, I chose to ignore it.'

'You're too nosey.'

'Or maybe I *do* have the energy to get a little water from down there.' Ally nodded towards the sea. 'Look, that toddler has a bucket. I'm sure she wouldn't mind me borrowing it.'

'Ally, you're a giant pain in my arse sometimes.'

The truth was Maddie was itching to know what it was that Caitlin wanted to give her after all this time, but more than that, she wanted to know whether Caitlin felt any remorse about what she'd said. Or, had she forgotten her words in the same way she had forgotten Maddie, the girl who had been her son's world before he died?

Recently Maddie had felt as though she had seen a light at the end of a very long, dark tunnel that she had been burrowing around in for years. There had been cracks along the way, but nothing had ever brought her out safely at the other end. Did she really want to revisit the past?

She pulled down her sunnies and lay back to enjoy the light breeze from the palms standing like soldiers in a row behind her, the laughter carrying down from the busier end of the beach where it was water sports central.

The peace ended half an hour later when the boys made an appearance.

'There you are,' said Joel.

Maddie propped herself up on her elbows. 'Did you get bored without us?'

'Of course,' he said as he bent down to give Ally a hello kiss. 'Have you been in the water yet?'

'You must be joking,' said Ally. 'It's too cold in winter.'

'Rubbish.' Joel pulled off his cap as he waved to Josh and Todd, who were by now making their way towards them along the beach.

'It's a holiday.' Ally lay back smugly. 'You do what you want to do and we'll do what we want to do.'

Maddie sniggered because she knew exactly what was going through Joel's mind even before he scooped Ally off her sunbed and charged down to the water's edge, ignoring the squealing and shrieks of 'don't you dare!' as he chucked her into the water.

Josh was first to reach Maddie and perched on the end of the now vacant sunbed. 'Ooh … she's gonna be annoyed at that,' he smirked. 'It's not exactly warm in there until you've swum around for a bit.'

Despite her friend's protests, Maddie could see that Ally was now happily ensconced in Joel's arms and they were dunking each other and play fighting in the water.

'You going in?' asked Josh. 'Relax,' he said when Maddie tensed and got ready for the fight. 'I won't chuck you in.'

She looked out at the sea, the waves gently breaking against the shore and leaving behind frilly lines of white foam, sizzling as the water retreated again.

'Come on,' Josh urged.

'Okay,' she grinned.

She followed him down to the water, and when the ocean reached her knees the chill kicked in.

Josh beckoned, already chest-deep in the water.

This time away on the island was all about getting away from it all. But the taking it oh-so-slowly, bit by bit, was too painful. Maybe that had been her problem for years. And with that thought in mind, Maddie took a deep breath and dived forwards into the waves.

She came up next to Josh, squinting in the sun.

'Not that bad, is it?' he asked.

'It's freezing!'

'If you swim around a bit, you'll be fine.'

He was right. Once she got used to it the water was absolute bliss. It surrounded you like nothing else could, bobbed you about as though rocking you into relaxation.

When they emerged from the ocean, droplets of water dripping from their hair and bodies, Josh nodded out towards a couple in the Coral Sea being pulled along in an inflatable rubber ring in the shape of a doughnut. 'Fancy giving that a go?'

Maddie listened to whoops of joy as the speedboat propelled the couple through the water, their inflatable attached to a long rope. 'Maybe tomorrow. I think I'll lay back and read, just relax today.'

'I'll hold you to that.' Josh smiled. 'Wait up!' he called to Todd. 'I'll catch you later, Maddie.' And with that, off he went to try out the water sports with his mate, leaving Maddie wishing she could fall for someone as nice and as uncomplicated as him.

*

By the time they left the beach, clouds up above had formed a clique and were threatening to spill over at any second. The group decided that a barbecue on the sheltered end of the balcony would be perfect, and with Todd having gone AWOL with two Nordic blondes, it looked set to be a cosy foursome for the night.

Maddie and Ally did most of the food preparation and left the boys to the 'men's work' as they put it. Before long the sizzling sounds of the barbecue filled the air, and the scent snaked across the balcony mingling with the smell of the rain and carried off, thanks to the wind direction.

'The veggie kebabs are great, girls,' said Josh. 'What's the cheese?'

'Haloumi. It doesn't melt.' Maddie answered.

'That's good to know. That way I don't make a prize berk out of myself and use cheddar and have it melt over everything else.'

'Now that would be funny,' she said.

'Er, not for the person cleaning the barbecue.' Joel was already scraping at the cast iron surface and directing the gunk towards the hole at the front.

'Did you remember to get ice cream?' Ally asked as she finished up a satay skewer.

The men groaned, too full for anything other than alcohol, which was a rite of passage on a holiday with friends.

'Men: beer …' Josh began in a mock deeper-than-deep voice. 'Women: ice cream.'

'I can't believe we don't have any,' Ally moaned. 'I really want some and we've all had too much to drink to drive the buggy.'

'We've got chips and dips and a few slabs of chocolate.' Josh leant inside the sliding door and pulled out a carrier bag.

'It's not the same.'

'I could take a walk down there, get you some. I could use the exercise,' said Josh, patting his stomach. 'What flavour?'

Ally chopped and changed her mind several times about what flavours would be the most enticing, and with Ally cosily tucked up on Joel's lap, Maddie offered to go with Josh rather than act as the gooseberry for the evening.

Armed with a golf umbrella, they set off into the hilly streets that were lit in some places, pitch black in others. They chatted about the island, their jobs, about Ally and Joel, and when they felt a few drops of rain, they launched the umbrella and walked side by side down the steep hill with the marina to the left, until they reached the ice cream parlour.

Josh joined the queue – the storm that was brewing hadn't deterred people from making the most of the island. Maddie took a seat just inside the doors and watched the lights from boats twinkling like stars as the water lapped around them and they held tight to their moorings.

'What's this?' Maddie asked when Josh pushed a takeaway cup in front of her. She sniffed the top, instantly warmed through by the smell of chocolate.

'I thought we deserved a treat seeing as we're out to get Ally's fix.'

'I think you could be right.' She caught the froth that had escaped through the small spout in the takeaway cup, and they looked out to the blackened water.

'Actually, I wanted to talk to you. I wanted to ask you about that night, when you left my apartment so suddenly.' Josh wrapped both hands around his takeaway cup.

She gulped. 'Josh, this is going to sound terribly cliché, but …'

'Let me guess: "It's not you, it's me"?'

She grappled for the right words. 'I hate to say it, but that phrase really sums it up.' She paused before adding, 'You're fun, you're kind, you're gorgeous with a great body—'

'Been looking, have we?'

She blushed. She hadn't meant to be quite so honest.

'What I mean is that you're what we would call a "catch" in a lot of ways.'

'But not for you?'

'Let's just say that it would be far easier to knock you back if you were a nasty person with poor hygiene and bad manners.'

'Ally told me about Riley, and that there's been someone else since, but it didn't work out.'

For once Maddie didn't mind that someone new in her life knew all about Riley. But the thought of him knowing about Evan made her uncomfortable.

'Relax, Ally didn't go into detail. All she said was that you had some things you needed to sort through before you could get into another relationship.'

It was the truth, and at least this time she was pining after a living person; it didn't feel quite so sad, so hopeless. She felt a certain amount of satisfaction that even though she hadn't fully moved on, she was getting started.

'We'd better get back before the ice cream melts and Ally sends us down here again,' she said.

They took their takeaway drinks with them and when Maddie offered to carry the shopping, Josh wouldn't hear of it.

'I hope we can at least be good friends, Maddie.'

'You can count on it.'

When they got back to the apartment, Todd was off with the Nordic beauties still, and as Josh and Joel fell into footy conversation, Ally and Maddie dished out the ice cream. When they joined the boys on the balcony, Maddie watched Josh. She wondered why the emotional Catherine wheel of fireworks couldn't pick up pace and whirl faster when she was with him. How could some men make that happen and not others?

Chapter Twenty-Four

Evan started his morning with a run. He had
requested a trail map as soon as he had arrived on the
island, but this morning he passed it up in favour of
running on the regular roads. They provided
challenge enough with their steep inclines and they
were so quiet with only buggies to dodge instead of
cars. He was also able to savour some spectacular
views, and when he ran up to One Tree Hill, he took
the opportunity to lean against the white wooden
gazebo and look out over the Coral Sea. He stretched
out his calves as he watched the shimmer from the
winter sun dance across the water and felt the peace
of this early hour before many people on the island
had even surfaced.

The gentle tap-tapping of his runners took him
back to the hotel where he helped himself to the
buffet breakfast of cereal, a fresh fruit salad of
pineapple and three kinds of melon, plus a yogurt
plucked out of the pyramid arrangement. Now that he
was almost back to his former self, he had bypassed
the fat-laden hot food options even though the smell
of bacon and sausages was tempting.

Following breakfast a sleep was non-negotiable;
tiredness still caught him out, particularly now that he
was running again. He had tried Maddie's number
several times since he arrived on the island, but with

no answer when he tried yet again after he woke, he showered, shaved and kicked back on the balcony for a while.

Evan ordered room service for lunch, preferring the solitude of the hotel room to take it easy before the wedding that afternoon, and when he was dressed he headed down to the entrance of the hotel to meet Jack.

'Hey, mate.' Evan shook his friend's hand, patted him on his opposite shoulder. Dressed in their black morning suits with a three-quarter-length jacket, a silver waistcoat and a lilac cravat, both men were ready for the off.

'Penny for them,' said Jack as they climbed into the parked buggy.

Evan took the driver's seat as today's chauffeur. He felt like a big kid taking a brand new go-kart for a spin as he started up the buggy. 'Couldn't be better, mate. I was just thinking about the stag do,' he lied.

'Yeah, that pole dancer was something else.' Jack launched into a recount of his send-off into married life that had involved copious amounts of alcohol and landed them in a seedy place that Evan had been glad to escape from.

Evan looked up at the sky and then reversed out of the parking space. The air was still fresh with a faint whiff of the rain that had hammered the hotel last night, the trees gleamed with moisture, and the black clouds had been scared away by big, puffy white balls which dared to pass slowly across the cobalt sky.

Jack waved at Will and Simon, both of whom looked equally as well-groomed, sitting in another buggy waiting to follow Evan.

As he drove along, Evan still felt out of sorts, but he put it down to tiredness that still hadn't fully abated with all the cancer crap that had been going on. It could be lingering after-effects from the physical strain of the op; perhaps it was being a human pin cushion with constant syringes being plunged into his arms at check-ups; it could just be the emotional imbalance at losing a ball.

'You know we've all checked ourselves,' Jack said quietly, even though the only company they had were the trees lining both sides of the road. 'I don't think any of us could say we'd ever done that before, at least not properly.'

'I'm glad I could be of some help.' Now that his mates all knew about the cancer, it was amazing the change that Evan could see within himself. Before, he would have cringed at talking about it; now it felt normal.

Evan let Jack direct him to the chapel. Despite the size of the island, one hill looked much like another today.

'Take a left up here,' Jack instructed. Once Evan had made the turn he asked, 'Do you worry that the cancer could come back?'

'Yes, all the time,' he said without hesitation. 'Now drop it. This is your day, remember.'

They pulled up outside the white wooden wedding chapel that sat on top of a hill overlooking Catseye Bay.

'It'd be good to see you down at the oval sometime for a friendly kick about,' said Jack, 'even if it's to tell the rest of us that we play worse than a bunch of primary school kids.'

'Do you really need me there to tell you that?' Evan asked as they made their way inside the chapel.

The chapel was about as picturesque a venue as you could get for your big day, with its whitewash exterior, the bell tower and its traditional stained glass windows. Once inside, Evan allowed his eyes to adjust from the bright sunshine to the subtle interior tones. Rows of classical wooden pews sat on either side of the aisle, and tied to the end of each was a bouquet of white roses. The place smelt woody and warm, mixed with the floral notes you came to expect of a wedding.

'You look nervous,' Evan told Jack when they reached the altar. He was fiddling with his cravat as though the thing was trying to strangle him. He looked just like some of the kids at school on their first day when they were forced to wear the unfamiliar uniform. Still, Evan felt it was a good sign. Jack had been with Shelley for years and they had three kids together, so marriage was practically a done deal. Yet their love for each other still had the power to make his burly mate, who stood a good two inches taller than him, as nervous as a footy player in the AFL Grand Final about to kick the goal that could give his team victory.

Guests filled the front rows of the chapel first. Shelley and Jack had invited close family and friends, but looking around it had to be close to fifty people. Still, it was set to be the relaxed affair they wanted. Evan watched on as more and more couples began to fill the place, and he realised that, while not having a significant other hadn't bothered him before, since he had met Maddie, it did.

'You do have the rings don't you?' asked Jack.

'Relax, mate. They're in here, safe and sound.' He patted his breast pocket. 'This is it, Jack.' Evan nodded towards the doorway of the chapel where the sun dappled bride had begun to make her entrance.

The guests gradually fell silent, and the sounds of a string quartet playing *Ave Maria* accompanied Shelley on her slow, deliberate walk down the aisle. Her three children followed: two holding the train, and the third gripping tightly to three boxes of rose petals ready for the aftermath.

Evan's eyes brimmed with tears when, instead of Shelley making her way towards his friend, he envisioned Maddie, the brown shades of her hair dancing in the sunlight as she passed through the church entrance, walking towards him. And as Shelley locked eyes with Jack, he imagined looking into Maddie's eyes, taking her hand in his, feeling her soft skin against his own.

Evan tried to focus on the ceremony. If someone had told him six months ago that he would be standing at the altar of his best mate's wedding wishing it was his turn, he would have laughed in their face. How quickly things change. These days he saw the little things that mattered, the more delicate moments in time that often went unnoticed and the importance of family and friends in your life.

'Evan, the rings,' Jack said.

Evan realised he hadn't heard him the first time. He gave Shelley an apologetic smile and produced two rings. This time he tried to listen to what was being said and share their moment rather than thinking about his own wants. But when Jack kissed his bride, there was Maddie again. She was in his head, and he wondered now how he could have ever thought she would leave it. He wanted to get on a plane now, land in Melbourne and head straight for her apartment. He had been stupid to let her run away that night, stupid to let his own fear of showing weakness hold her at bay. There was no way he was going to let cancer beat him in any way, shape or form.

The wedding party congregated for photos at the front of the chapel before the happy couple were whisked away for shots on the beach. Then it was time for the reception which was to be held down at the main pool on the island. A sumptuous seafood buffet dinner greeted the guests, and the men passed out cigars banded with 'Jack & Shelley'; it was one of the few extravagances Jack had insisted on and even the non-smokers, including Evan, lit up to bathe in the aroma and the ambience as Jack basked in the glory that, finally, he was a married man.

When the reception was over and the guests waved Jack and Shelley away as they set off for three nights, child-free, at the luxury qualia resort on the island, Evan decided to take the long way back to the hotel. He left Will and Simon puffing away on their cigars and started to walk. He could thank this morning's power nap for recharging his energy levels, and the spike of adrenalin caused by thinking about Maddie had left him buzzing.

It was a clear evening and the last before he headed back home, back to reality and back to another check up with the doctor. This holiday had been a turning point, and rather than constantly worrying himself stupid about the cancer coming back, he knew he had to take each day as it came. This trip to Hamilton Island had helped him to haul himself out of the worst of his nightmare, and better than that, it had helped him to realise what he really wanted.

He wanted Maddie; he wanted a future.

Evan made his way past the now-closed designer shops with hideously escalated prices that were par for the course on an island like this. He tried Maddie's number again, but there was no answer. He rounded the bend past the real estate agents and stopped to look at some of the photographs in the window. They depicted amazing views, the climate, and the laid-back island lifestyle that most city dwellers daren't even imagine. He crossed over Front Street to the wooden picnic tables, brushed a few crumbs from a seat and sat down. The overpowering waft of vinegar and salt spread from Popeye's fish and chip shop opposite, and he watched people come and go clutching their cardboard boxes containing their meal for the night. The smell evoked memories of that night in Williamstown with Maddie, and if it were possible, it made him miss her all the more: her smile and her laugh, her unbelievably sexy figure and the way her hips swayed when she walked.

He looked out to sea and watched the boats peacefully bobbing up and down in the water until his gaze once again settled on Popeye's. He noticed a girl with hair similar to Maddie's, although in the dark he couldn't quite make out the colours. He remembered how Maddie's hair had smelt too; something fruity and fresh, although he never had worked out quite what it was.

He puffed out his cheeks. He'd never had it this bad for any girl before, daydreaming about her and imagining that she was right there in front of him.

He stood up to leave and continue along Front Street to do a big loop before heading back to his hotel, but as he glanced left and then right to check for golf buggies, he heard the same girl laugh.

God, not only was he thinking about Maddie constantly and seeing her everywhere, but now he was hearing her. She was well and truly under his skin.

When the girl laughed again her head titled back, and this time he saw her eyes, sparkling away in the mesmerising way that he remembered.

A buggy tooted and Evan jumped out of the way, apologising to its driver for his freezing in the road like a bunny caught out in headlights. He stood back in the darkness behind a parked buggy, his heart pounding. It was as though his thoughts had conjured her up for real. Maddie was here, on the island.

He moved to cross the road again. He couldn't wait to hold her in his arms, tell her that he had been a fool to not get in touch sooner, ask her why she hadn't contacted him either. His body pulled towards her, but when he was just a few feet away his legs stopped moving.

She wasn't alone.

He fell back into the shadows and watched her with a man about her age, good-looking and obviously keen as he sat trying to feed her a chip out of the opened cardboard box in front of them.

Evan yanked a hand through his hair and swore under his breath before he turned and dragged his feet back to his hotel, shoes angrily kicking any stone that crossed his path.

He should've never let her go, and now he was too late.

Chapter Twenty-Five

Maddie, Ally and the boys were at the beach nice and early, making the most of their weekend away from it all.

'Come on, Maddie, you did say you would,' Josh insisted.

She groaned. 'I guess I did. Okay.' She lifted her arms in the air to stretch languorously. 'Race you!'

Maddie sped off along the beach before Josh could reply, but she had forgotten how hard it was to run on sand and soon he was powering past her, grinning from ear to ear as he ran backwards.

'Keep up, slowcoach!' he called, looking back at her.

Josh beat her to the water sports area at the other end of the beach where they watched two teenage boys being towed back in on the inflatables.

Maddie climbed into the first inflatable ring, and just as Josh was about to climb into the other, a man grabbed his arm and yanked him back.

'Evan!' shouted Maddie.

'I think this seat's taken,' he said to Josh, who was too stunned to react quickly enough before Evan launched himself into the inflatable next to Maddie.

The speedboat driver seemed oblivious to Josh's protests and he headed out to sea. Maddie felt the tug as the rope lost its slack. Evan hadn't said a word since he'd climbed in next to her, and she was so surprised to see him that she hadn't said anything either.

At first they bobbed along at a pleasant pace, lightly bouncing along the surface, but then the speedboat's driver upped the ante until they were flying across the water. The inflatable skimmed across the waves and every time it landed it thumped on her bum. Despite the situation, she couldn't help but laugh her head off, as much at Josh's face and Evan's out-of-character bolshiness as the thrilling ride.

They were whipped left, whipped right. And when the speedboat pulled them into a straight line again Maddie turned to Evan, opened her mouth to speak, but nothing came out.

'Hold on!' Evan called from his inflatable.

Maddie looked up to see that the speedboat had changed direction suddenly, and she knew what that meant. She tightened her grip, unable to stop smiling, and the inflatables flew across the water side by side, whacking the water every time they made contact.

When the speedboat slowed and pulled them back towards the shore, Maddie tried to sort out her hair that hung in clumps around her face, full of the salty sea. Her heart pounding, she daren't even look at Evan.

Maddie climbed out of her inflatable first, and Josh handed her the rash vest and sunglasses that she had left on the shore.

'What the fuck did you think you were doing?' Josh gave Evan a powerful shove in the chest the moment he stepped out of the other inflatable.

Evan held his hands up. 'I don't want a fight, mate.'

'Well you're going to get one!'

'Josh!' Maddie stepped in between both of them. She faced Josh but could feel the warmth of Evan's chest against the bare skin on her back, his chest hammering as he tried to get his breath back.

'Josh, this is Evan,' Maddie explained. 'He's the guy I was seeing.'

Josh's face softened when she met his eyes. 'Yeah, well it was still poor form.'

Evan still stood so close behind her that she felt his breath in her hair when he spoke. 'You're right. I was an arsehole to do it. I just wanted to get close to Maddie.'

He still wanted her, and the feeling was mutual. This time she didn't want to run from the past, she wanted to confront it.

Josh only left when he was sure he could trust Evan with Maddie.

'That was really out of order, you know,' said Maddie as she wandered along the shoreline with Evan. She tugged the rash vest on over her bikini, suddenly self-conscious.

'I know. I don't usually behave like such a caveman. Usually I'm your average calm and collected primary school teacher. But when I saw you with him again, I just—'

'Were you jealous?'

She heard him sigh and he stopped walking, stared out into the ocean. She could see jealousy leaking out of his every pore. She'd seen it on his face, heard it in the tone of his voice.

'How have you been?' she asked.

'Not bad. I had the chemo.'

'How did it go?'

'It wasn't pleasant, but it also wasn't as bad as all that. I was lucky compared to some.'

Maddie stepped ankle-deep into the water and rinsed the pearly shell that had stuck underfoot. She held it in her hand, admiring the grooved outside, the smooth inside.

'Why are you in Hamilton Island, Evan?' She wondered if he could possibly have known that she would be there, but that was crazy.

'A good friend of mine got married.'

'In the white chapel on the hill?' she asked.

'Have you seen it?'

'Yes, it's beautiful.'

They walked on, their feet just touching the ocean.

Evan cleared his throat. 'So was that the same guy as before?'

'That was Josh, yes. But we're not together, Evan. I'm here with my friend Ally and a few others, him included. I promise you.'

Had she imagined his body relax?

'Are you interested in him?' he asked.

'No.'

'Why? I bet he's uncomplicated, and you seem happy in his company.'

'Evan.' She felt her cheeks colour. They had been intimate with each other, but the way he was looking at her in broad daylight sent goose pimples racing up and down her arms as though anticipating the feel of his touch. She wanted to say, 'Because of you;

because I'm head over heels in love with you', but in her head it sounded crazy, let alone out loud.

His hand wrapped around one of hers as he pulled her to a stop. 'I'm sorry I didn't contact you sooner, Maddie. After all the shit I had to deal with, I know that I didn't behave very well. But I've been trying to call you for the last couple of days.'

'I left my phone back in Melbourne, Evan. And I was the one who left your apartment that night, remember?' She watched her toes sink into the sand as the tide moved out. 'I could've called you, but I didn't.'

'And why was that? You were happy when you brought the cake over. You seemed to want to keep trying with us. Was it because I told you that I definitely had cancer?'

She couldn't take her stare away from his hand that drowned hers within it. 'I know that it shouldn't have been a shock. I thought I was prepared for it, but I panicked. And I shouldn't have barged into your apartment that night in the first place being a do-gooder with my cake, thinking a naughty sponge could fix everything.'

His hand reached up, and she felt his fingers against her skin as he moved a clump of hair away from her face.

'You know, after you came to see me that night I convinced myself your leaving was for the best. I didn't want you to see me having treatment for cancer, I didn't want you to see me feeling sorry for myself and I couldn't bare you thinking less of me.'

'I would never have thought less of you, Evan.' She wanted to believe they both had the strength to

255

start this relationship and carry it forwards. 'I should have explained about Josh before now, too.'

'You have already.'

'No, I apologised for what happened, but I didn't elaborate on why I had gone back to his place that day.'

'I think that going on one date with a guy and being told he has cancer would send anyone into a blind panic.'

'Your cancer was a huge shock, but it was more than that.' She took her time to find the words. 'When you told me, all I could think about was dying.'

He made a face. 'That's encouraging.'

'Sorry, that didn't come out right. I meant that immediately I thought of Riley, how he died, and how I've never really come to terms with losing him. You see, Riley wasn't just my boyfriend of the moment, he was the man I wanted to spend the rest of my life with.'

'You never told me what happened to him.' Evan followed Maddie as she moved further up the beach away from the water and sat down on the dry sand.

Linking Riley's death with the events of 9/11 was what Maddie did her utmost to avoid. She hated letting that one day in history define who she was now, who Riley had been. It was as though her life was a newspaper and 9/11 made front page news no matter what the date; no matter what had come before, what had come afterwards. But if she wanted any hope of having a relationship with Evan, then it was time to tell him everything.

'Oh, Maddie, please tell me he didn't die of cancer.'

She knew that her eyes had glazed over, but she needed the tears to hold back this time. 'It was nothing like that, no.

'Riley spent some time working in New York – it was his dream and he thrived on it.' She let herself wallow in memories for a moment as she raked the sand and let the granules fall through her fingers. She remembered Riley's face, elated at the prospect of going to live in the States, living in the city that never sleeps.

'Riley was killed in the September 11th attacks.' She watched the speedboat in the distance have its fun with another couple braving the doughnuts.

'Maddie, you should've told me.' Evan's voice fell on her like a blanket around her shoulders.

'Every year, in September, I still avoid newspapers, the radio, internet, the television. I've never been able to watch the coverage of the 9/11 attacks and I'm not sure that I ever will. Linking Riley's death to 9/11 feels to me as though I'm sensationalising it. I know that sounds ludicrous to other people, but to me that's how it feels.'

'It sounds perfectly logical to me.' Evan nudged her arm. 'But how on earth do you avoid the coverage? It pops up all over the place in this day and age with the internet and media everywhere.'

'It's tough, but somehow I manage it.' She looked out across the ocean. 'It's a self-preservation thing. And I don't need to see the footage over and over again to remember it from the first time round. I don't need to see the photo of a man freefalling from the towers preferring to die that way than wait to be engulfed in debris and smoke. I don't want to think of how Riley died, how he would've suffered. Some people say that it's therapeutic to see a united front.'

'But you don't see it that way?' Evan picked up the shell Maddie had discarded.

'I remember the counsellor telling me that some people look at anniversary events as a chance to stop the forward focus and feel the pain of the past and the loss. But I've always avoided it. It seemed like the right thing for me to do.'

Evan left the shell on the sand and sat forwards, his arms hugging his knees. 'My dad died years ago now, but I couldn't imagine having those reminders year after year, sometimes when you least expect it. I'm not surprised you find it hard to cope with.'

He briefly leant his hand on his forearms, shook it side to side. 'No bloody wonder you freaked out when I told you about my cancer. You must've thought, "Here we go again, someone else who will end up hurting me, intentionally or not". God, you don't deserve a bloody hopeless case like me.'

'You're far from hopeless, Evan.' She smiled at him, moved her hand closer to his in the sand. Now that she'd started to talk, she couldn't stop herself.

'There was no lead-up to Riley's death, no time to say goodbye. One minute he was there, as part of my world, and the next minute he wasn't. They never even found a body.' She looked up to the sky, her head tipped back to enjoy the feel of the warm sun on her skin; the simple pleasure that Riley and too many others had been robbed of forever on that day.

'Tell me about him. Tell me about Riley.' The tip of Evan's little finger touched hers in the sand.

Nobody had ever come out and asked her to do that before, and she didn't know how she would have reacted if they had. But sharing with Evan felt different in so many ways.

'He was charming, fun to be around and always had the ability to see the good in people. He had a passion for travel – I didn't really share that – and more energy than you can imagine.'

'Did he ask you to go to New York with him? I'm sorry, you don't need to tell me that if you don't want to.'

'I don't mind you asking. It's nice to remember all the good things that we shared rather than just that one awful day in history. I realise that now. I never did before.

'Riley did ask me to go with him, but I was busy here, had a job that I was happy with. I lacked the travel urge, and so we agreed that I would visit on holiday, he would go and get the experience, and then we would settle down back in Australia.'

'Get married you mean?'

It was endearing to hear a note of jealousy as Evan spoke. 'Yes, we would've got married and bought a place down by the beach, had kids, the whole package. I think Riley would've had me barefoot and pregnant in New York if he could, but he knew how much I wanted to stay in Australia. We were in our early twenties; marriage and babies were way, way into the future.'

'Do you still want all that? With someone else, I mean.'

'For a long time, I didn't. It was Riley or nobody as far as I was concerned.'

'That was your grief talking. You know that, don't you?'

'I do now.' She wanted to reach for his hand or for him to make the first move, but no matter how hard she stared, both hands stayed where they were in the sand.

'Please don't think I'm a bunny boiler, Evan, when I say that I saw a future with you from the night of our first date. My problem was that I had settled into a pattern of life on my own. I felt safe in my own cocoon, protecting myself again, from ever losing another man that I loved, and when you came along you upset the equilibrium I had found. You made me feel things I haven't felt in a long time and part of me was scared. I kept telling myself not to let you slip away from me, and that's why I came over to you that night with the cake. But when you told me your diagnosis, I didn't have the strength to stand back and let it happen all over again. That's why I ran. I was a coward and I'm sorry.'

When Evan's hand lifted and covered her own, grasping it reassuringly, she realised this was the moment that would open the floodgates and let the tears flow; the moment when she realised her world hadn't stopped when Riley had died. Her world had been on pause, and maybe she had finally found the play button again.

'It wasn't cowardly. After what you went through with Riley, I get it now.'

A tear popped out of the corner of Maddie's eye and began its slow journey down her cheek, but Evan wiped it away with his thumb.

'It wasn't just about me getting hurt again though, Evan. I didn't want you to have to hold me up as well as yourself. I didn't want you to have to deal with an emotional wreck, a girl who constantly panics that she's going to lose you.'

'The doctors are pretty positive that I'll be fine,' he assured her. 'Hell, even I'm positive that I'll be fine, and believe me, it took a while for me to see that.'

She swiped a tear that had come from the other eye now as though racing the first one.

'All the scans and all the tests tell us that the cancer hasn't popped up anywhere else either,' he said. 'But it's bloody scary. Cancer doesn't discriminate. One minute it isn't there, the next minute it is. You can do everything right – exercise, eat right, don't smoke – and still it can get you.'

'I've thought about you a lot recently,' said Maddie. 'I went up to Sydney for a weekend and saw my parents, and when I realised how much I'd pushed them away and how it made things so much worse for me, I hoped that you wouldn't do the same.'

'Don't worry,' said Evan, shuffling closer and looping an arm around her waist. 'I tried to push everyone away, but they refused to let me: Jem, Holly, Ben, Jack. The lot of them. Persistent buggers, they were.'

'I'm glad.' She grinned. 'Mum told me that Riley's mum wants to get in touch with me.'

'How do you feel about that?'

'I haven't seen her since Riley's memorial. I'd probably be okay if our relationship had merely fizzled over the years, but it didn't happen quite like that. Caitlin, his mum, said some pretty awful things to me at the memorial. She basically told me that I couldn't be hurting as much as she was because she had lost a child. She told me that I'd move on, get over it and be happy again. She told me that I'd replace Riley someday.'

'That must've been awful. Wait a minute. Don't tell me that you believed it?'

'I did for a long time. And I think that's also why I panicked when you told me about the cancer. Part of me was scared to go through more pain of losing someone I cared about, the other part of me pushed away because I didn't feel that I should be happy with someone else because it would prove Caitlin right.'

'You know that's nonsense though, don't you?'

'I do now, yes. It's taken a long time, but I can finally hope those words were uttered under the influence of intense grief. She wants to see me apparently, has something to give to me.'

'Oh.'

'Exactly: "Oh."'

'And do you want to see her?'

Her voice went up an octave. 'I'm angry with her, Evan. I don't see why I should make it easy for her after the way she treated me.' Her fists balled into little parcels of fury.

'Okay, okay.' He tightened the arm around her and his hand stroked the bare skin of her forearm. 'I'm not saying you should forget everything that happened, but the point is that she's reaching out to you now. I lost my dad when I was eight years old and it was incredibly painful. Mum dealt with it in her way, sometimes pretending she was divorced rather than widowed. Holly cried, a lot. Me, I cried in private and I used to go quiet at the strangest of times. Once I was playing cricket for school and the team were shrieking at me to run, but I was frozen on the spot. I'd spotted a dad in the crowd who was the spitting image of my dad and it got to me.'

Maddie leaned into him as they watched a jet ski take to the water.

'Ever done that?' Evan asked, nodding towards the sea.

She shook her head. 'I don't go on the water nearly enough anymore. Riley was always big into water sports and we rowed a few times, I tried water skiing, and now doughnuts of course.' She grinned.

'Do you mind me talking about him?' She kept her head on Evan's shoulder, their hands sandwiched together.

'Not at all, he's part of your past.' They watched another jet ski join the first. 'I think that different people deal with grief in different ways, Maddie. Grief is an individual journey. You'll face yours in your way. Caitlin will face it in hers. There's no one-size-fits-all and there's no time limit.'

'Are you sure you're a primary school teacher and not a shrink?' She lifted her head to look into his eyes, their faces closer now. The smell of the salt on his skin was intoxicating, and she couldn't help it when her gaze drifted to the golden sand clinging to his tanned chest. He really was a beautiful man.

She pulled herself back to the moment. 'For such a long time after Riley died, I couldn't smile.'

'Now I can't imagine that.' He tilted her chin upwards so that she had to face him again, and she couldn't help but smile right on cue.

'I felt as though I had no right to smile, because I felt guilty.'

His lips close, he asked, 'Why?'

'Because I didn't feel like I should be happy. Riley was dead, gone, and he was everything to me. How do you pick up the pieces and carry on after that?'

'People can, and do, every day, Maddie.' This time he leant in and touched her lips with his own.

She closed her eyes and savoured the salt of the sea mixed with the warmth of the sun, and when she opened her eyes, he said, 'I'm not saying it's easy. What I'm saying is that you have to believe in the ability to move on before you ever can. Otherwise it's just one step forwards and two steps back.'

She swallowed. The kiss had thrown her off course.

'I tried counselling after it first happened,' she said. 'I talked to Ally non-stop and searched the web for support groups. I guess I was looking for a magical cure for my grief.'

'Can I offer you a bit of advice?'

'If I say no, will you keep quiet?'

'Probably not,' he teased. 'Look, I know it's not the same: you lost Riley; I just lost a ball.' She appreciated the attempt at humour. 'But Maddie, I think that with any major change in our lives you have to get on the emotional rollercoaster and take the ride. It's a crazy ride and you don't always know where it'll take you.'

'You should write a children's book with that imagination.'

'Don't take the piss.' He poked her gently in the ribs. 'I think it'd be good to speak with Riley's mum.

I think it could help you to get some closure, you know?'

Her lips twisted as she thought. Nobody should ever have to lose a child, and she wondered whether becoming a mother one day would make her realise just how much pain Caitlin must have been in that day and still must be in now. She wondered how any mother had the strength to carry on after something like that.

'I always fall apart around about the same time every year,' said Maddie. 'When the winter sets in come July, that's when I remember. It's not like I forget the rest of the year, but around this time it all becomes so real. There's the smell of winter – the air that bites the minute I leave the apartment, even the warmth of my face buried in my scarf. The bleakness of winter became what I associated with the way I felt back then. This was the first time that Ally successfully persuaded me to go away somewhere, to try and get some distance.'

'And has it worked?'

'It was working until you showed up.' She grinned, scraped her bottom lip with her top teeth and then remembered something he had said to her when they first stepped off the inflatable. 'When you apologised for being a caveman, you said that you hated seeing me with Josh "again". What did you mean?'

'I saw you outside the fish and chip shop last night.'

She gasped and a hand flew to her lips. No wonder he had been so angry over by the doughnuts when he saw her with Josh.

'I heard your laugh before I saw you. It got right under my skin.'

'We're just friends.'

'I know that now.' He rested his arms on the tops of his knees and looked out at the catamaran that had taken to the water.

Maddie reached up and ran a hand through his hair. It was still soft despite the salt from the sea, but it was dry now and she watched the sun catch the sprinkle of greys that hid amongst the dark.

'What made me different from the other guys, Maddie?'

She pulled her hand back and fiddled with the shell that had fallen between them. 'I knew you were different from the moment I saw you – even before our first date.'

He looked at her now.

'It was when I saw you dancing with your niece, Ava, at Jem's party. Her world stopped with you in it, and both of you were in this magical place where nobody else got a look in.'

'She's a pretty special little girl.' He stood up and his mood seemed to shift down a gear when he pulled Maddie to her feet.

They stood watching each other, hands dangling by their sides, neither sure of whether to reach out for the other.

'Do you want kids, Maddie?'

She looked up at him earnestly; it was no time to shy away from anything but the truth. 'Yes, I do. Does that scare you?'

He didn't answer.

'I want a family, Evan. I've always wanted that traditional part of life. I can't imagine a life without it.'

He stared at her, stroked her cheek with the back of his hand, but he wasn't smiling.

'What's wrong? I didn't scare you, did I?'

He softened. 'No, no it's nothing you've done wrong, I swear.'

'Then what is it?' He had that same look of apprehension that she knew she'd had on her own face that night at his apartment.

'Maddie, I think I should go.'

'Evan, I don't understand. Why?' She could feel her heart pounding, ready to sink like a helium balloon drained of all its gas. She moved towards him to close the gap, to reach out to him, but his body was rigid, his head a sudden weight on his shoulders. She hadn't missed the watery sheen in his eyes, either, and she felt sick to the stomach.

Finally he spoke, but they weren't words that Maddie wanted to hear.

'I can't give you what you want.' He stepped forwards, bent down and kissed her on the lips, lingering as though trying to imprint the taste and feel of her on his mind forever. 'You've been through enough. You deserve the world, Maddie, and you should never settle for anything less.'

'Evan, you're not making sense.'

His arms hung hopelessly by his sides, and he had a pained expression on his face. Right here on Catseye Beach they had both shared their pasts, their hopes for the future, and from the way Evan had looked into her eyes, Maddie had known they'd both

267

found what they were looking for. What had changed
so suddenly?

She wasn't sure how they had missed the bruised
sky that passed overhead. A few spots of rain served
as a warning that the heavens weren't far from
opening, but Maddie didn't move an inch when she
felt a drop land on her eyelash and noticed another
land on Evan's cheek.

When he said goodbye and turned and walked
away from her, a knot formed in her belly, growing
more and more as he moved further and further away.
And as she stood beneath the blackened clouds, hair
in clumps around her face and rain dripping from her
cheeks, she knew that he had gone, gone from her
life.

Chapter Twenty-Six

As the minibus trundled its way up and down the hills towards the airport and the sun unleashed its full glare, it was as though the storms of yesterday had never happened.

'You know what we should do next time?' Ally asked.

'What?' Maddie assumed the smile that she had used so many times before to hide that anything was wrong. Last night she had hidden in a warm shower, cried all the tears she needed to before she faced the others for dinner and drinks on the balcony.

'We should do lunch on Whitehaven Beach on those pristine white sands,' said Ally.

Maddie nodded. 'You're on.'

'Goodbye, palm trees,' said Josh reluctantly when the minibus pulled up outside the airport.

Josh had corned Maddie when she emerged from the bathroom last night, handed her a large glass of red and told her that he was there if she needed to talk. He hadn't told the others about their encounter with Evan, and Maddie thanked him for that. It was one of those situations that she wanted to work through in her own mind before she shared it with anyone else.

Once they were inside the airport, Maddie watched the luggage while Ally went off to see what they had in the shop, and the boys headed over to the café to buy pies and coffees to cure their hangovers.

'I wouldn't want to be stranded here for hours.' Ally turned her nose up as she returned from the dinky shop in the one-roomed airport. 'I was going to buy a book but they've got about five, all ridiculously expensive and all crap.'

'I thought you'd brought your Kindle?'

'I forgot. I can see it right there on my bed waiting to be shoved in my hand luggage.'

Maddie leafed through the remaining pages of her own book. 'I've got less than fifty pages left of this one, so you can have it when I'm finished.' She knew that it could take a while though, her mind preoccupied with Evan and what had happened yesterday. Last night she'd slept more soundly than she had expected, probably from the run back to the apartments, from the emotions of the day, but this morning her thoughts were all jumbled up again, screaming for attention.

Ally sidled up to her friend. 'What's going on, Maddie? You've been quiet ever since you came home from the beach yesterday.'

'Nothing's going on. I've had a lovely time, I'm just tired.'

Ally wasn't convinced. 'Are you thinking about Evan?'

'What makes you say that?' Her head whipped round to look at her friend.

'No reason. So what happened with Josh, anyway? You two have spent a fair bit of time together this weekend: in the water, buying ice cream, at the fish and chip shop, riding the doughnuts.'

Maddie coloured at the thought of the doughnut ride.

'Josh is just a friend, always will be.' That she was sure of.

'Josh is also gorgeous – don't tell me you haven't noticed.'

'I had noticed.' She smiled. 'But I'm not feeling the thing.'

'What thing?'

'You know.'

'No, I don't.'

'That giddy, head-over-heels feeling that you get when you like someone. You get goose pimples every time they accidentally brush past you, and even when you're with them you just can't get enough. Like you and Joel.' Just like her and Evan yesterday until he left her so suddenly. It felt like payback for walking out of his apartment that night when she'd taken the boob cake to him.

When they boarded the plane, Maddie took the seat next to Josh. 'Do you mind?' she asked. 'Ally wants to sit with Joel.'

'No worries.'

She tightened the strap on the seatbelt and fastened it across her lap. She was glad that they could be friends, civilised. It could so easily have gone the other way.

'Are you okay?' he asked.

'I'm fine, really.'

'What's that?' Josh pointed to the trashy magazine perched on Maddie's lap.

'I swapped it with Ally for the book that I've just finished.' She had pretended to finish it, anxious to avoid questions about the day before.

'I doubt she'll be reading a lot of your book with Joel sitting next to her.' He nodded in their direction.

'As long as they don't *do it* on my book, I'll be happy.'

People started to fidget as they were already past their departure time waiting for three remaining passengers, but then came the announcement that the cabin doors should be armed and the flight attendants passed through the cabin to check seatbelts, overhead lockers and prepare for their safety speeches.

Josh leaned closer to Maddie. 'I'd hate to have to do the walk of shame past all the passengers tut-tutting because you've held up the flight.'

A flight attendant made her way down the aisle to show the guilty-as-charged latecomers to their seats.

'Jeez, it's a long walk of shame. You'd want to be sitting at the front wouldn't you?' said Josh.

Maddie couldn't help but let a snigger escape. Josh's arm rested against hers in the confines of economy class and as she looked up she met with the chocolate eyes of the first guilty passenger and her mouth fell open.

She knew that Josh had seen him too, but she noticed both men nod at one another as though they had a mutual understanding.

When Evan moved on past without stopping, Maddie almost reached for the paper bag in the seat pocket in front of her. The tumble drier of emotions churned over and over, and with it she fought the urge to be sick: sick that she had lost him and didn't really know why, sick that she'd run away that night in the first place, sick that she hadn't chased him yesterday at the beach and asked him to spell it out to her.

Josh's hand squeezed her arm.

'I'm fine, really.' She closed her eyes as the plane taxied down the runway, and she was determined not to open them until they landed back in Melbourne.

*

Will and Simon had been on a total bender last night and waking them this morning was a nightmare. As a result they were late to the airport and could count themselves lucky that the plane hadn't taken off without them.

But that had been nothing to the giant kick in the guts Evan had felt when he saw Maddie just now, and yesterday on the beach. Yesterday he'd been headed for a cool off in the surf after his run and spotted her – her hair blowing in the wind was a dead giveaway – waiting for a turn on the doughnuts. She was with the same guy whom he had seen her with outside the fish and chip shop and something inside him snapped. He hadn't lost both balls; he was still man enough to fight for what he wanted, and what he wanted was Maddie. What he hadn't accounted for was the story she shared with him on the beach, the story of Riley. He'd known that her boyfriend had died, but what he hadn't known was how long she'd been carrying that grief around with her, how much it still affected her every day. And when she mentioned marriage, kids, the whole package, he realised that he had to walk away or risk hurting her all over again. She didn't deserve that.

He sat rigid, his eyes glued to the back of her seat – probably the only advantage of being tall on an airplane was that he could see over other people – and his insides clenched when he spotted her slender wrist stretch up to adjust the overhead air vent and twizzle it her way.

'Can I interest you in a tea or coffee, sir?' The flight attendant passed by Will and Simon, who both had their heads back, mouths wide open.

He shook his head. Without anyone to chat to he decided that the best thing would be to close his eyes firmly for the rest of the flight so that he couldn't look in Maddie's direction. He hoped that he wouldn't hear the giggle that could warm him all the way through like a whiskey on a cold night, and he hoped that she would forgive him for this and move on.

Chapter Twenty-Seven

Evan's appointment with the doctor was encouraging.
All the latest tests indicated no signs of the cancer
occurring anywhere else – for now. Hooray for the
removal of a ball and the blessed chemo.

Evan walked into Huntley Primary School and past
the open doors of the assembly hall. He loved his job,
and in times like this it was his saviour, his way of
operating within the realms of what he knew rather
than venturing into the unknown.

Rows of children sat straight-backed, eyes glued to
the front as the Principal presented the birthday
awards for that week. The piano chords sounded to
announce the start of the birthday song and Evan
sneaked past on the way to his classroom, willing
himself not to think about Maddie and what might
have been, and what a prize bastard he was for
walking away two days ago. She would be wrong if
she thought that her talk of marriage and kids had
scared him off. On the contrary, it was exactly what
he wanted too. But it would be selfish of him to stay
with her. He had seen the pain of her past loss still
swimming in her soft, brown eyes; he had seen the
passion in her eyes at the family she needed to have
someday. How could he deny her that?

Since his diagnosis, and even in the early days
when he thought that it was a harmless lump, Evan

had done enough surfing on the internet and stalking of online forums to know how much of a mess testicular cancer could cause: some guys found that their remaining testicle wasn't producing enough sperm anyway, so their chance of fatherhood had gone; others had a recurrence in the remaining testicle and therefore were rendered infertile. Some men talked about how the stress of having cancer had taken its toll on their relationship and their girlfriend/wife/partner had left them.

Well, he wouldn't put Maddie through that.

Evan used his time wisely before the kids descended on him once again, and in the stock cupboard he pulled out a roll of butchers paper and a bag labelled 'decorative bits', ready for an art session later that day.

'So how was the doctor's appointment?' His colleague Mike took the roll of paper from Evan before it slipped out from under his arm.

'It's all good,' said Evan as they took everything into the classroom. 'Chemo seems to have done the job so far and the chances of recurrence are low.'

'That's good to hear.'

Evan heaped the art supplies on to the cabinet closest to the window and looked up at the darkening sky. It reminded him of the afternoon he left Maddie down at the beach.

'A little bird tells me that you're running again,' said Mike, reminding Evan that he was still there.

'I'm getting there. Not quite back to the same fitness as before, but more or less.' His body was certainly coping, which was more than could be said for his mind.

'Can I count on you for the school fun run? It's nothing major. A run around Albert Park Lake if you're interested. We thought we'd raise money for Blue September.'

'What's Blue September?'

'It's all about raising funds and awareness about the cancers that can affect men. You may not know this, but my brother died – it would've been before you came to teach at Huntley Primary – of prostate cancer. Last year my daughter's swim club held a Blue September event and she swam with a blue wristband with her uncle's name on it. They raised a considerable amount too.'

Evan felt a jolt at how easily it could've been him who died, ashamed almost at the level of self-pity he had indulged in.

'I'm sorry to hear about your brother, Mike.'

'Thank you. I'd been thinking about arranging an event this year but hadn't got around to it, and when we heard your news there were a few shakes of the head around the staffroom, a few comments that cancer in men isn't widely thought about. Nobody else seemed to have heard of Blue September, but around about the time you went into hospital we got talking over lunchtime and decided to do something about that.'

'It's a good idea.' Evan rolled a pencil beneath his fingers on the table and then sharply released his hold so that it shot all the way to the back and toppled on to the floor.

'Are you sure you're okay?' Mike bent down and picked up the pencil.

Of course he wasn't. How could he be when he couldn't pursue the very thing that he wanted more than anything? What he wanted more than all those marathons he had put himself through. What he wanted more than the career he had fought his way into despite the constant flak.

'Forward me the email, I'd love to join in.'

The rain held off that afternoon, and the winter sun shone as Evan took his class outside for sports. He returned to his childhood, kicking a soccer ball, twirling hula hoops and balancing on stilts. He showed his prowess at skipping with a single rope to the envy of some of the girls. He didn't let on that Holly had always wanted a sister, and when Evan was born the fact that he was a boy didn't stop her from putting pretty things in his hair, making him participate in tea parties with her dollies and getting him to play skipping games. It was a wonder he had been able to keep a single masculine bone in his body.

When he left that day, one of the kids in his class, Billy Turner, waved at him across the playground. The boy could be a pest, but he had a kind heart and Evan had faith that all his kinks and knots would be ironed out over the next few years. He looked on as Billy ran to his parents waiting at the school gate. Billy hugged his mum as every boy should and then his dad lifted him up and over his head and settled him on his shoulders.

Evan's heart broke at the sight of that family unit: the father he hadn't known for long enough; the father he may never get to be. He knew then that he was right to walk away from Maddie. He needed to give her a chance to have it all.

Chapter Twenty-Eight

When Evan walked away, Maddie couldn't deny that it had hurt. It was as though a bone inside her body had snapped beyond repair. But meeting him had also taught her that she could heal eventually; she could love again. And she realised now, more than ever, how important it was to confront the past rather than run from it.

Those feelings had prompted her to pick up the telephone and call Caitlin, and now here she was, making her way across the lawns at the Royal Botanic Gardens to at last deal with the woman whose words had held her in limbo for so many years.

'Thank you for agreeing to meet with me.' Caitlin stood from the bench beside the Ornamental Lake as Maddie reached her.

Maddie sat down and Caitlin followed suit. They both looked out over the serene water. The rain had dissipated, but the smell lingered in the air and the power of the sun had dried the bench almost as if it had done so especially for them. Hopeful flowerbeds had already started to sprout their colours as though they were backstage and getting ready for their spring performance.

Caitlin clasped and unclasped her hands and Maddie gazed at the water so hard that she wondered whether her stare could be powerful enough to see to the bottom. Meeting here had been Maddie's idea. It had felt easier than in the confines of a coffee shop with a table to separate them, not knowing where to look or what to say. She had hoped that this calm location would lift their spirits if they felt them sag with the weight of their history together.

'I didn't think you ever wanted to lay eyes on me again.' Maddie knew her voice sounded colder than she had intended, but she wasn't entirely sorry.

Caitlin waited a while before she spoke. 'I can't even begin to tell you how much I regret what I said to you at the memorial, Maddie.'

Maddie wanted to make her suffer like she had for more than a decade, but her heart had never been that hard, and instead, she found herself thinking about the feelings behind the words as opposed to the actual words themselves. Maybe that's what she should've done all along, but she had never been strong enough until now.

'Did you mean what you said?' Maddie kept her gaze firmly fixed ahead.

'No, of course I didn't. It was like all the pain inside of me was building and building behind a dam and then … well, then the dam burst its banks and the water flooded out in those mean, spiteful words. I hate myself for doing that to you. I despise the way I acted, the way I couldn't even summon the strength to pick up the phone and call you to tell you how much I was hurting.'

Maddie sniffed. 'I've carried those words with me for years and they've haunted me ever since that day. I started to believe that what you said was true, and so

I haven't allowed myself to move on. I've never been truly happy.'

She heard Caitlin crying now and she wanted to comfort her, but she couldn't, not yet.

'Maddie, I'm so sorry for how I acted. Richard has always been upset that we lost touch, and I know that I was very wrong to push you out of our lives. I truly meant to get in touch and apologise, take back what I'd said—'

'You can't ever take that back.' Maddie thought of how close she was with Richard, Riley's dad, and felt glad to hear that he had been more on her side.

'I know I can't do that. But I'm hoping I can help you to understand that the words came out of a black place in my heart that didn't know how else to heal.'

Maddie had waited a long time to hear this apology. She watched a caterpillar edge its way along the bench next to her, arching its back, laying itself flat, repeating the process. She gently let it hook on to her finger and then she set it free on the grass out of harm's way.

Caitlin pulled something from her pocket. 'Here, I remember how Riley used to buy these for you.'

Maddie looked down at the clear, cellophane packet full of the Haigh's dark chocolate peppermint frogs that she loved. 'You do know that Riley used to eat at least half of them,' she said, accepting the chocolates. 'It was never all me.'

When Caitlin smiled, the deeper lines on her face were reminiscent of how long it had been since they had seen one another, each of those lines filled with pain and remorse for what had happened.

'Do you remember Riley's chocolate milkshake obsession?' Caitlin asked.

Maddie's body relaxed on to the bench as the sun warmed her and the conversation lightened to memories about the man they both remembered. 'I'd almost forgotten about those. He used to whip them up at home all the time.' She flexed her feet inside her runners as she thought of what to say next. 'Mum told me that you had something to give to me.'

Caitlin reached inside her chocolate-brown wool coat that was at odds with some of the spring blooms that had already popped up around them. She passed Maddie a small, velvet covered box.

Maddie took the box and placed it on her lap, her fingers resting on top of it as she stared at it, unopened.

'I shut down after Riley died, Maddie. And it wasn't fair to you, to Richard, to anyone. But most of all it wasn't fair to Riley. He would've been so disappointed in me.' Her voice caught.

Maddie put her hand on Caitlin's arm; an involuntary reaction that reminded her of how close they had once been. 'Riley would never be disappointed in his mum.' She saw a tear drop from the woman who had held her head high for so long.

'You're a beautiful person, Maddie.'

Maddie's hand stroked the velvet of the box, scared to venture inside.

'Richard and I decided that it was time to downsize when he retired.' Caitlin fixed her gaze on the lake. 'He said that I'd kept Riley's bedroom as a shrine all these years. I didn't move anything, even though most of his possessions had gone with him to

New York anyway. It almost caused us to split up about five years ago.'

Maddie paled at the thought. They were such a strong couple, one to admire and a couple whom she and Riley had hoped to emulate one day. 'Are you okay now?' she asked.

'We went through a lot of counselling – marriage and grief. I sorted through a lot of Riley's things, but the boxes from New York had been shoved to the back of the enormous walk in wardrobe and I left them. They were sealed, and I couldn't imagine ever opening them without him.

'A few months ago Richard and I opened those boxes together. I think it was one of those defining moments which let us know that we had reached a different place to the one we were in before.'

The light breeze lifted Caitlin's hair from her face, emphasising the sadness that would always be there. 'Richard and I packed those boxes ourselves when we went over to New York to clear Riley's apartment.'

'I could've helped with that.'

'I know, Maddie. It was unforgiveable of me to shut you out, but that's why I had to see you now.'

Maddie still didn't open the box.

'I think we were in so much of a trance those few days that even we were surprised at what we had packed. There was no filtering of what was meaningful, what was a part of Riley. Going through those boxes I found that I'd packed a CD that had been snapped in two, an empty cellophane bag that had had Haigh's chocolate in it. We even found old tickets for the subway. When we opened another box it was much the same.

'You know, Maddie, we'd gone into his old bedroom as two lost parents, but we ended up smiling as we went through his belongings and remembered event after event with our son, everything from when he took his first steps and hit his head on the corner of the coffee table, to when he failed to catch his mortar board at graduation and ended up with one whacking him in the face.'

Caitlin's giggle started big but ended up wavering. Maddie knew that she was crying.

'I never wanted to hurt you, Maddie. I'm so sorry for everything that I've done. You were like family to us and I realise now that I didn't only lose a son, I lost a daughter.'

Maddie let her own tears flow as she pulled Caitlin closer. They sat there on the bench overlooking the lake; the silence meant more than any words ever could. And the words that Caitlin had spoken at the memorial? Well, Maddie let them fall one by one into that lake and sink to the bottom for good. It was time.

Caitlin pointed at the box on Maddie's lap. 'We found that lurking right at the bottom of one of the boxes that had silk ties and a few work shirts. It must have been bundled in with those as it's the sort of thing you'd hide in a clothes drawer, I guess. I knew what it was the moment I saw it.'

Maddie fingers stroked the surface of the velvet box because she knew what was in it now.

'When I found it, I looked at Richard and without a word between us, we knew what had to be done. We knew that we had kept you out of our lives for long enough, Maddie. It was time to try and fix that.'

The box was tough to open but the small hinge at the back obliged and Maddie looked down to see a platinum ring with a pear-shaped diamond. She clamped her hand over her mouth as the sun rebounded off the jewel.

'Do you remember me having you try on my old rings one day, because I had a couple to give away that I no longer wore?' Caitlin asked.

Maddie nodded; she couldn't speak. And then the realisation hit. 'You did that for Riley didn't you?'

'He'd been working so hard out there, and after you holidayed with him, he knew that he couldn't wait to start his life back in Australia with you. I told him the size of the ring that fit you the best. He must have bought that ring just days before he died. He planned to propose on Christmas Eve.'

The hand that wasn't holding the box lay across Maddie's heart. She jumped when a butterfly dotted with gold and white specks landed on her knee before its antennae twitched and it fluttered off again.

'When I saw that ring, it was the one single thing that clarified what I had to do. It was the single item that made me realise exactly who Riley was – he was the man who loved you, the man who wanted to share his life with you, raise a family of his own.' She stretched out a hand and touched the back of it to Maddie's face to stop her tears that were free-falling now.

Maddie took the ring out and pushed it on to her engagement finger. 'It's beautiful.' She stared at it as though her past had a hold of her once again, and she moved her hand so that the diamond caught the sun's rays.

And then slowly she wiggled it off and carefully pushed it back into its box. 'Riley would've been proud of you today, Caitlin.' She watched as a bird with a white chin, red head and a yellow belly hovered at the edge of the water, contemplating which way to fly next.

'I think he would've been proud of us both.'

The bird took flight as they talked about Riley, about Richard's retirement, about Maddie's career and her baking hobby that was growing more and more by the day. Maddie pulled open the packet of chocolate frogs that Caitlin had brought with her and they both savoured a couple as they reminisced: Riley cooking dinner for Maddie and nearly burning the house down by leaving the pan of oil unattended; Riley getting his fingers bloody on thorns from the roses he tried to pick for Maddie on their first Valentine's Day; Riley taking the bins out in his underwear and bumping into their neighbour Mrs Urquart.

'Her face was a picture!' Maddie creased up with laughter. 'I'm not sure she'd ever seen a partially naked man in all her life.'

'I think you could be right.' Caitlin declined Maddie's offer of another chocolate frog. 'Can I ask if there is another man in your life now, Maddie? It's okay, I want to know.'

Maddie pushed the ring box into the pocket of her cardigan as though holding it and talking about Evan at the same time were at odds with each other. 'There have been guys, since Riley, but nobody ever got me like Riley did. That all changed when I met Evan.'

'Evan?' Caitlin sat forwards. 'Maddie, I mean it when I say I want to know. Don't hold back because of what I said all those years ago, please.'

Maddie took a deep breath and then said, 'Evan is the first man who made me feel that zip of magic since Riley. I don't just mean the excitement when you find someone attractive – that can happen to anyone at any time. What I mean is that pull that tugs at your heart when you look into their eyes, that leap in your tummy when they speak to you.'

Maddie pulled her cardigan more tightly around herself as the wind picked up to remind them that winter hadn't quite passed yet. The sun was still out but had started to descend, and the clouds were forming a blanket overhead, ready to tuck it away until morning. She recounted the story of Jem's party, the mix-up with the location, the huge faux-pas with the penis cake.

'So what happened to Evan?'

'What do you mean?'

'You seem to be talking about him in the past tense. Didn't it work out?'

Maddie shook her head, and that was when she fell back into the role of surrogate daughter and told Caitlin everything: their first date, their second, Hamilton Island, the near-fight with Josh over the doughnuts.

'And you've no idea why he walked away?' Caitlin asked.

'I've dissected that day, over and over, and I can't work out how he went from pushing Josh off the scene and wanting me to walking away for good.'

'Oh, Maddie, perhaps it isn't for good.'

Maddie let out a long sigh. 'I really don't know. He was the first man since Riley to put the thought of the future in my mind, and now …'

'You know, I never imagined for one second that you'd have trouble finding another man to love.' Caitlin pulled an old-fashioned handkerchief from her bag and dabbed at her eyes. 'I hate myself for what I did to you.'

'Don't be daft. I'm responsible for myself. I'm a big girl now and I should've known that you didn't mean what you said. You didn't even get to bury your son, and I hope to God I never ever find out what that's like.'

'Maddie, I—'

'Just words, Caitlin. I know they were just words, and I know that you would never wish for that either.'

Maddie's eyes followed the turquoise embroidery around the edge of the handkerchief that Caitlin was holding. 'You still have it.'

Caitlin looked down at the delicate flowers scattered across the material. 'It reminds me of you. I remember you bought it for me that first Christmas after you started to date Riley. Oh, your face was a picture that Christmas Eve. You were so nervous that I wouldn't like my present, or that we wouldn't like you – Riley told me – but you couldn't have been more wrong.'

'I thought you would've got rid of that long ago though. I don't think I know anyone who uses hankies anymore.'

'It's only for the tears.' Caitlin pulled out a Kleenex from her handbag and blew her nose. 'And it's in my bag for the memory. I thought of you often over the years, wondering where you were, who you were with, wanting to see the girl who was like a daughter to me.'

It was Maddie's turn to ask questions that had been buried in her mind for years. 'Do you find the anniversary events and coverage of 9/11 year after year hard to deal with?'

'Funnily enough I don't. I mean, the first one was horrendous, of course.' She paused for a moment, discarded the soiled tissue and toyed with the embroidered handkerchief instead. 'But after that first year, it was a comfort to know that other people had been through the same thing, still had the same pain. I knew how I would feel every year, it wasn't like a big shock to hear the news or hear victims talk on television. The videos of the planes hitting the towers, the carnage in the streets … those pictures are etched in technicolour on my mind. The television makes little difference to pre-existing images, and my grief doesn't pour out on that one day year after year. My grief gets me when I least expect it, and it gets me in different ways.

'It took me a while,' Caitlin continued, 'but I have nice moments now too. Last week in the Haigh's shop I must have looked like a crazy lady because I found myself thinking about buying Easter chocolate with Riley when he was little. His eyes were like saucers, as though he had just stepped into *Willy Wonka's* Chocolate Factory, and when he got a taster at the till he looked as though he'd hit the jackpot.'

'Riley was all about the tasters.'

They fell silent for a while, both lost in thought. Caitlin was the first to speak. 'When the grief hits, it's like a tsunami.'

The powerful word made Maddie swallow, hard.

'About a month ago I was in Myer when a lady ran past the lingerie section, her face stricken with fear. I could see she had a stroller with her but no child. She was frantic, calling for her boy, calling for 'Riley'. For a moment I froze at the name and it felt as though the ground was coming up to meet me. But then my mind snapped into gear. I went to her; I knew how I'd felt when I lost my boy. We got out a description on the loudspeaker and he was found quickly enough.

'I watched that woman hold her Riley to her chest so tightly.' Caitlin bunched up her fists against her chest to show how firm a hold that woman must have had, how tightly she missed holding her own son. 'I watched her tears of joy, listened to her cries of relief. I walked out of that shop in a daze and I just kept on walking. I'm not sure even now if I could tell you where I went exactly, but I walked until my feet hurt and until I phoned Richard to come and get me. When I got home I vomited and I cried and cried and cried. I slept solidly after that for almost twenty-four hours.'

Maddie didn't think she had any more tears left, but her eyes watered as Caitlin continued.

'So you see, Maddie, the coverage every year isn't when I grieve necessarily, but I do find some solace in watching people paying their respects to loved ones. It's their bravery that gets me every time, and the way they can hold their heads up, hold their limbs up when back then they could've collapsed with the shock of it all. Wives, husbands, children, parents: we all suffered tragic loss and the coverage to me says that life goes on, and that when we all pull together, we can become stronger, help each other. I know now that's what I should've done for you.

'I thought that it would be so easy for you to find happiness with someone else after Riley, and I guess I was angry because I had no idea how to move on with my own life. If I hadn't had Richard, I'm not sure I would've wanted to go on.'

'You don't mean—'

'I don't think I would've taken my own life, not really, but there were times when the pain was that unbearable.' She turned to face Maddie. 'We went to Ground Zero.'

The skin on Maddie's arms tingled. 'What was it like?'

'It was incredible. Painful, but nowhere near as painful as I thought it would be. It helped to see how many people were struggling to cope in the same way that I was, and still am. I felt so selfish, thinking I was the only one. It hit me just after the readings of every name of every single victim. I cried as I heard Riley's name, I barely heard any of the others, but almost three thousand people died, and looking around at the sea of faces I knew I was wrong to think that other people couldn't possibly be in as much pain as I was. And that includes you, Maddie.'

Maddie smiled.

'Riley loved New York, didn't he?' said Maddie after a moment of reflection for both women.

'He did. He'd always wanted to go and see the big wide world, right from when he was a toddler and we bought him a bright red pedal go-kart with the number 7 on its bonnet, like a racing car. He wanted to know whether pedalling hard enough would help him reach Canada. I think he wanted to see the snow more than anything, but the next day it was America, then it was Scotland. He always did have that sense of adventure.'

'That's one of the things I loved about him.' Maddie's face lit up. 'Not the passion about travel and his need for adventure, but his sense of fun about what the future could hold. We used to talk about the usual things, but he always had this twinkle in his eye, this look that showed part of him wanted to let life unfold and take him to the unknown.

'I saw that go-kart in your garage.' Maddie grinned. 'Richard once told me that Riley had refused to put it on eBay because he wanted to someday give it to his own child. I never knew the Canada story though.'

'Oh, it wasn't just other countries he wanted to go to,' said Caitlin. 'He loved reading *The Famous Five* and *The Secret Seven* too, and he'd go off on adventures in that thing, making up all kinds of worlds.' She put a hand over her mouth as though he could hear her. 'He would've strangled me if he knew I told you that story.'

'I bet he would've told his own son or daughter himself, in time.'

They sat in silence, both lost in the cherished memories of the life cut short too soon.

'I met many other mothers, daughters, sons, friends, girlfriends at Ground Zero.' Now that Caitlin had started talking it was as though she couldn't stop. 'I really connected with one lady who had lost her daughter and not only because we had both lost a child. We gelled as mothers but also as ourselves.'

Maddie listened to Caitlin talk about the friend she had made, the emotions she'd felt standing at Ground Zero. And while she listened Maddie fiddled with the ring box, her fingers edging nervously around the opening. She thought of how excited Riley must have been buying it, and wondered if he'd been nervous too; she imagined he would've been and the thought warmed her right through.

'Beth, the lady I met,' said Caitlin, 'stood with me on the deck of the Empire State Building and that was when we stopped chatting. A silence fell over us and we both stood looking out over the city that had captured our children's hearts and spirits. That day Richard had made his own way around the city: the Metropolitan Museum of Art, the Statue of Liberty; all the places that Riley had raved about to him.'

As the temperature of the afternoon fell, Caitlin shivered. 'Shall we walk? I promised I'd meet Richard in the city. Perhaps we could sort out another day for you to see him too?'

'I'd like that.'

They made their way across the Northern Lawn towards the Yarra River. Unconsciously, Maddie double-checked her pocket for the ring box that was safely ensconced inside. She cupped it with her hand to be doubly sure.

'One of the things that I found the hardest,' said Caitlin, 'was not being able to bury my son. When someone dies you have a body, right? But we had nothing. It took me a hell of a long time to come to terms with that, and for years I thought that if they found him … even part of him … then that would make me better.'

'I'm not sure it's as simple as that.'

'No, it's not.' Her eyes glistened over, but she kept the same smile, warm and genuine. 'I've made peace with it over the years and I'm not sure how much good it would do now to know that 'bits' of my son had been found. I think I'd rather remember him how he was: my son, rowing down the Yarra River, or my son arguing with me because I told him he had to clear his junk out of the garage before moving day. My son bringing home the girl with whom he saw his future.'

'Your son shouting at me when I pranged his car against the gate post,' Maddie added.

'Golly, I'd forgotten about that!'

When the laughter stopped, Caitlin looked at Maddie. 'You know that if you were my daughter then I'd be telling you not to give up on this young man, Evan.'

'Where did that come from?'

'I'm a woman, I multitask. Just because that wasn't the topic of conversation, doesn't mean that I'm not turning it over and over in my head.'

From memory, Caitlin had always been the queen of multitasking, whether it was baking a Sunday roast while filling out a tax return, or booking an overseas trip as she sorted through piles of washing.

'I didn't want to give up on him, Caitlin, but I can't chase someone who doesn't want to be found.'

'You know, one of the things I always admired about you was your strength and your ability to see the good in people, even when there isn't a lot to see.'

Caitlin's words came from personal experience. 'Life takes us in unexpected directions and they're not all bad. Take it from someone who buried their head in the sand hoping that it would all go away.'

As they reached the road, Caitlin pulled Maddie into a hug and stroked her hair in the same way that her own mum would when she was upset. 'I have to go, but we'll stay in touch.'

'I'd like that,' Maddie replied.

Maddie waved Caitlin off as she walked towards the city. The elastic band of their relationship had been stretched beyond measure, but today it had gone slack and settled right back where it should have always been. Meeting with Caitlin had helped Maddie to sort through her own grief, and as the clouds parted above it was as though they were showing her that the path was finally clear to move on towards the future. She just wished she knew whether that future could include Evan.

Chapter Twenty-Nine

'Thanks, Maddie.' Ally took the cake, shaped like a clock, with chocolate mice that had been rolled in crushed Maltesers. 'My niece will love this.'

'It's my pleasure.'

'Do you want to come in?'

'No thanks, I'm off for a run next,' said Maddie.

'Are you okay? You know, today I mean.'

The question was expected. Maddie always took the day off work on September 11th and this year was no different in that respect, yet it had changed in so many other ways.

'I did what I said I'd do; I put on the TV this morning.' Maddie took a deep breath. 'For the first time in thirteen years, Ally, I finally put on the TV. When I thought about what Caitlin said about how watching the coverage had helped her, I thought I'd see if it could do the same for me. But you know what?'

Ally shook her head as she stood at the front door, Maddie out on the path in the sunshine.

'I'm not avoiding the coverage any longer, but at the same time, it didn't capture me quite how I expected. Caitlin was right about one thing: our grief doesn't always plan when it'll strike. The media can't inflict any more pain than what I experience already, and for some people it goes a long way to help. But it's not for me.'

With the time difference between Australia and the States, there was plenty more coverage to come, but for Maddie, what she had seen so far had been enough. She would no longer live in fear of the reminders. Instead, she would embrace her own memories and try to reflect on the good times but also allow herself to have quiet moments when she would still grieve for Riley in her own way.

'Today is the start of a new beginning,' said Ally.

'It certainly is.'

On a clear day without a cloud in the sky, Maddie started to run the second she shut the front gate to Ally's sister's place. Her heart beat in time with her footsteps, the air was still and she felt as free as the rainbow infused hot air balloon that sailed above the treetops and far into the sky. Every step she took felt like a step in a new direction, a fresh start, a change of pace.

When she reached Albert Park Lake, she ignored the unusual crowds that were gathered near the barbecue area and ran past the throng of school kids who must be out on an excursion. There were dozens of adults too – possibly teachers and parents – and it was then that Maddie realised she was right in the epicentre of a charity fun run. She diverted around the crowd and turned back towards the main barbecue area so that she could take the road rather than the track and head back to her apartment, but the second she did, she stopped dead. Her chest moved up and down as her breathing failed to come to a stop along with her body.

Evan stood a few metres away clad in running gear beneath a blue banner. The banner flapped in the wind and she couldn't make out the words, but he turned as he balanced on one leg to stretch his quads. His surprise matched hers as he let his leg drop to the ground, and he stared back at her.

She wondered whether to walk away before he had the chance to do just that; the chance to leave her again.

'It's a charity run for Blue September,' he explained, closing the gap between them. She noticed the hint of a five o'clock shadow starting to appear across his jaw and his chin.

'Blue September?' Her belly fluttered now that he was so close.

'I'll explain later.' He nodded behind her and she turned to meet Jem, who enveloped her in a hug.

'It's lovely to see you, Maddie.'

'How are you, Jem?' Maddie hugged her back and took in the velour marl grey tracksuit, the blue cap pulled down over her grey curls. 'How's the wrist?'

'Absolutely fine now, no problem at all,' she said.

Maddie and Evan exchanged a sly grin.

With a comforting squeeze of Maddie's arm, Jem moved over to where Holly and Ava and another man, whom she assumed must be Ben, were waiting beneath the shade of a palm tree.

'How are you?' Evan asked.

'I'm good, really good. But listen, I'll get out of the way before the run starts. It looks like you've got a lot of competitors today.'

His eyes refused to leave hers. 'Maddie, I'm sorry about Hamilton Island.'

'You've obviously got a lot going on.'

'I have, but I still feel bad about the way I left things.'

He looked over at his family doing their best to look inconspicuous as they watched them both. 'Can we go somewhere and talk, just over to the car park, away from prying eyes?'

She'd forgotten what the sound of his voice did to her insides, setting off the fireworks that were only fuelled more when she agreed, and he put his hand in the small of her back in the gesture that she had grown to love, as they walked over to his car.

'Can I?' she asked, pointing to the bonnet she was about to rest against.

His laugh released some of the tension of the moment. 'I'm not that anal.'

No, you're gorgeous, kind, funny. But you don't want me like I want you. Before he had the chance to launch into another breakup speech, she said, 'I saw Caitlin.' She wanted him to know; after all, he was part of the reason she had finally done it and she would always be grateful.

'How did it go?'

'Better than expected. She apologised and more importantly, I could tell how sorry she was. I think that every day since the memorial she has regretted what she said and it made her grief so much worse.'

She scuffed at the gravel with her runners. 'I wanted to say thank you, Evan.'

'Thank you? Why?' He was genuinely surprised.

'You talked so candidly about the reasons why I should get in touch with her. Mum did too, but I needed to hear it from someone who didn't know

Caitlin, who didn't know Riley. Does that make sense?'

He nodded. His feet scuffed the dirt too, and seeing him mimic what she was doing made her smile.

'She gave me something too,' said Maddie.

'Ah, you found out what it was?'

'It was a ring.' She turned to look at Evan. 'It was an engagement ring that Riley bought before he died. They only found it recently, amongst his belongings that had been boxed up.'

'And how do you feel about that?'

She didn't read jealousy on his face, only concern. 'I couldn't look at it for ages, but when I did, I felt content. I felt content that he was so happy right up until the end. And even though I'll never wear it, I've kept it.'

He turned his gaze back to the dirt beneath his feet. 'I'm really pleased that you've made peace with the past. I think that it'll help you to move forwards.'

Move forwards where? She wanted to yell.

'Listen, Maddie—'

'Look, Evan. I know what you're going to say, and there's really no need. I—'

'Why do women always talk before us men get a chance to say anything?'

'Sorry.' She watched the rise and fall of his chest beside her. It was agonising not to be able to reach out and hold him, have him hold her.

'I need to explain myself, explain what happened up in Hamilton Island.' When his eyes settled on her, his pupils were large and hungry. 'I thought that walking away was for the best, but seeing you now, I know that you deserve to know why.'

She wasn't sure that she really wanted to know. She wanted him more than ever, and his proximity to her was more painful than she could have ever imagined.

'When you told me everything about Riley, I fell for you that little bit more, but I realised how much you had been hurt in the past, how you had been let down, and I realised that I couldn't let that happen to you all over again.'

His lips twisted as though with each word, it gave him more pain. 'From the moment I got my diagnosis it was as though everything I could have flashed in front of my eyes. I took for granted that I would meet someone, get married, the whole shebang, when I was ready, and as soon as that ideal was threatened it opened my eyes to the fact that nothing in this life is a given. Everything is so precious. Everything is a risk. It also made me want the dream more than ever.'

The black paintwork of his car felt hot beneath her hands.

'Maddie, you told me how much you want marriage, kids, the whole works.'

'I knew it. I frightened you off. I—'

He put a finger to her lips just as he had on the boat over to Williamstown that evening.

'When you told me about Riley, I saw the pain in your eyes. When you told me that you wanted a family of your own, I shared that dream, but when I saw the joy in your face, the hopefulness at achieving that one day, I had to walk away.' His finger left her lips this time, at the same time that his eyes left her face.

'Why? I don't understand.'

A bright pink football rolled up to them and Evan crouched down beside the little girl who came running up to retrieve it. He told her to take it over to the grass area, away from the cars. Maddie felt a twang in her heart watching him interact with a child; it was the same feeling she'd had that day he'd danced with Ava at Jem's party.

Evan sat on the bonnet of the car, his fingers millimetres from her own. 'When you talked about having a family, all I could think about was how I could let you down, how I could hurt you all over again. I want those things as much as you do, but I couldn't be selfish.'

The tendons in his arms strained as he wrestled with the right words. 'I've known from the start of all this that one testicle is all it takes to father a child. But there's safety in numbers I guess, and with one already gone it means that should there be a problem with the other then I lose my chance to be a dad. The doctors assure me that there's only a low risk of getting cancer in my other testicle and there's every chance my fertility is fine, but what if it's not? What if the cancer comes back?'

'Evan, I feel so stupid. I should've realised that was the reason.' She couldn't believe she hadn't seen it before.

'Why? I wasn't exactly giving the information away for free.'

The teasing in his voice made her smile. 'And you let me prattle on about kids, marriage, how I wanted all those things. Why didn't you tell me then?'

'Honestly? Because I know enough about you, Maddie Kershaw, to know that you're a good person, you don't push people away when they need you, and my male pride also got in the way and I told myself that I couldn't bear to have your pity. I wanted you to want me for me.'

Her heart went out to him. She wanted to kick herself at her own insensitivity. She'd been so preoccupied by her own battle that she hadn't been able to see how scared he was that he couldn't live up to her expectations.

'Evan, do you remember that day on the beach when you told me everyone follows their own journey with grief?'

'Those sound like wise words.' His lips tugged at the corners.

'They were common sense words and they were the words that convinced me to call Caitlin.'

'I'm glad to be of service.'

'I think that it's the same with cancer.' Maddie tried to ignore the hope whirling in her body as his fingers lightly touched against hers across the bonnet. 'Every journey with the wretched disease will be different, every person reacts in a different way emotionally and physically.

'Perhaps it's time for you to realise that you can't predict the future, you can't run away from it because of what happened in the past.'

'Have you turned sensible all of a sudden?'

She fiddled with the strap of her watch. 'You know it's too late, don't you?'

'I know it's too late for us.' His voice was barely a whisper. He stood up, closed his eyes and took a deep breath.

She left the warmth of the car bonnet too. 'No, I mean it's too late for me to back away, too late to protect myself in case I don't get my perfect idea of what the future should be.' She put a hand against the black running shirt as his heart beat beneath her palm. 'It's too late because I've already fallen for you.'

He looked heavenward. 'What if one testicle isn't enough to father children, Maddie? What if I can never be a dad?'

'Do you seriously think that I wouldn't want you because you couldn't give me children?'

His face said it all.

She stood on tiptoes and hooked her arm around the back of his neck, tilting his head down towards hers. She looked deep into his eyes, and their lips touched so softly that she wasn't sure whether she had imagined it.

'Firstly, not being able to have children wouldn't stop me from wanting you. Secondly, having children isn't about being able to provide the sperm.'

'Ouch! That hurt,' he said.

'What I mean is that anyone can make a baby, but it's a whole different game becoming a father, being there for that child unconditionally, giving them the best world in which to grow up.'

She linked her fingers through his as he gazed down at her. 'What I'm saying is that, yes, I do want a family one day. But if it turned out that you couldn't have kids, then we can look at other options. There's adoption, fostering, surrogacy …'

'Steady on.' He pulled back and looked at her. 'You're talking about having kids with me … we're not even dating, are we?' His lips formed a grin that reached his eyes as he teased her, but then he turned serious again. 'I want to give you everything, Maddie. I want to give you the world. What if my cancer comes back? I could die like Riley did. Do you really want to go through that again?' He reached out and grazed her cheek lightly with the back of his hand before he pulled away like he'd been caught doing something that he shouldn't.

'You're right,' she said matter-of-factly. 'In fact'—she pointed over to a silver four-wheel-drive reversing out of the car park at the other end—'I might be running one day and some moron runs me over in a huge car.' She pointed to the apartments in the distance. 'I could be in a building, in a lift, and that lift could plummet to the ground.' She pointed upwards, shielding her eyes from the sun. 'I could fly back to Sydney for a weekend and the plane could drop out of the sky.' She took a breath and turned again. 'I could—'

He silenced her with a kiss, and then, 'I think I get it.'

'I spent a long time avoiding being really happy, Evan, because I was always in fear that I would lose someone close to me again. I was afraid to let go of the past, but now I realise that it's no way to live. Living is about more than breathing in and out each day – it's about savouring every moment and filling your life with people who love you and with whom you can share a future.'

Her insides clenched as his lips twitched in that familiar way. She steadied her voice and said, 'Are you still going to say that you don't want me in case life doesn't go exactly the way you planned?'

His arms wrapped around her waist and pulled her into him until their bodies met. 'I was going to say that I love you.'

She ran her hands around his neck, pulled his face close to hers and they leant their foreheads together.

He pulled back. 'Why are you crying? I was hoping for a better response than that.'

'They're happy tears, because I love you too.'

He kissed the tear running down her cheek, then her lips, her neck, her collar bone. He buried his face in her hair as they stood holding each other. She felt his heart beat strongly, steadily, dependably. And with every inhale and exhale, she knew they had both been brave enough to let themselves into this new world that was their future. She held him tight, breathed in his warm, manly, woody smell that she knew she wouldn't want to live without again. Their relationship was one built on a strong foundation, and as she felt the stubble of Evan's chin brush across her lips before he kissed her, she knew she had found 'the one' after 'the one'.

'Promise me something, Maddie.'

'Anything,' she whispered.

'Promise me you won't back away, no matter what life throws at us. We're in this together, for keeps.'

'No backing out,' she agreed. She took his face in her hands now. 'And that goes for you too. No more pushing me away, even if you think it's for my own good.'

'No chance.' He grinned. 'You're stuck with me.'

And then he kissed her with the same urgency that she had felt building up inside of her since that day on the beach in Hamilton Island. She looped her arms around his neck, stood on tiptoes, hardly daring to believe that they were finally together and this time it was for ever.

His hands rubbed the skin on her upper arms, ran down the sides of her body to her waist, sending shivers all the way down her spine. 'Run with me?' He nodded over to the start line where people were milling, ready for the off, and as they walked over, hand in hand, he said, 'I don't suppose you'd like to come back to my place afterwards?'

They jostled for a good start position amongst the other runners underneath the Blue September banners, and Maddie couldn't tear her eyes away from the sexy grin that spread across Evan's jaw.

'Sounds like a plan. Now stop talking. It's time to man up and run the race,' she said.

Right before the start gun fired, he bent down and whispered in her ear, 'Oh, you'll find out how much of a man I am.'

Maddie knew then that she was about to run the best race of her life.

Epilogue
One Year Later

Huntley Primary had such success with their fundraising for Blue September that they decided to do it again the following year, and the first month of spring cooperated with a cloudless blue sky and steady breeze that blew across Albert Park Lake, leaving palm trees and ferns no choice but to bow slightly.

'Do you think you can keep up with me?' Evan teased.

Maddie ignored the ribbing as they limbered up at the start line. It had been a whirlwind year in so many ways. Jem had marked her 101st birthday with another knees-up, this time including a tasteful cake of Maddie's design: a square, rainbow-checked sponge covered in blue icing depicting the sky, and covered on the sides and the top with all of nature's loves from butterflies, bumblebees and ladybirds, to intricate flowers that had taken Maddie forever to get right when she was still suffering from morning sickness at six months along.

Maddie waved over at the stroller positioned in front of Jem. In it sat their little guy, three-month-old Sam, waving a giant blue rattle in the air and kicking his legs wildly to keep himself entertained.

Following last year's race, Evan and Maddie had headed back to her apartment where Evan had done exactly what he'd promised – proven how much of a man he still was – while Maddie had proven that she was ready to take a chance on love again.

A month later Evan had arrived at Maddie's place all set to go out on a run, but instead Maddie had sat him down and presented the stick showing two thin pink lines. It had taken a few moments for the reality to sink in, but when it did his eyes welled with tears.

Sam Riley Quinn was born in May of this year. And now Maddie had two new men in her life to love unconditionally and unreservedly, and in return they would do the same for her. Maddie's parents were doting grandparents visiting from Sydney as much as they could, and both Caitlin and Richard had been overjoyed when little Sam was born, and they had been honoured to attend his naming ceremony.

When Jem agreed to go and live with her daughter, Martha, Maddie and Evan moved into Jem's old place in Albert Park. They gave it a fresh lick of paint, a little bit of tender loving care, and of course the wisteria stayed exactly where it was. Jem's wooden chair had been replaced by a picnic table with a bench on either side, but whenever Jem came to visit, she made sure she sat right beside those lavender flowers, inhaling the scent of the past and appreciating what had gone before as well as what was still to come.

Maddie had come to realise that to remain frozen in grief would interfere with her capacity to remember the best of Riley. She had had the engagement ring made into a necklace and that necklace, with its pear-shaped diamond, now sat in a box in the chest of drawers in her bedroom. The box containing Riley's photograph and other keepsakes had been taped up – she wasn't sure whether she would ever get rid of it, just like she didn't know whether she would ever wear the necklace. But both were a part of the man who had held her past. The box sat up in the attic these days, along with the doll's house her dad made her as a child – maybe Sam would enjoy it someday, or maybe they would have a daughter next and she could get as much pleasure out of it as Maddie once had.

A single diamond solitaire sat on the third finger of Maddie's left hand as a symbol of Evan, the man who held her future. The cancer was still running scared these days, and if ever Maddie felt her throat closing, her fear bubbling up at what the future may or may not hold, she told herself how lucky she was to have been very much in love, twice.

Since Maddie had taken maternity leave from her job as a physiotherapist, her reputation as a baker had spread – largely by word of mouth – and she'd spent any free time she may have had making cakes: Ally's engagement party cake, a friend's baby shower cake, and, of course, designing her own wedding cake for when she tied the knot with Evan next March. Business was really taking off, and as soon as she'd had the business cards made up and she started distributing them more readily, she found she was thriving on the demand. It was hard to juggle the business with Sam around, but she and Evan made it work.

'Good luck!' Martha shouted from the sidelines where she stood with Holly, who was pregnant with a little brother or sister for Ava. Holly had promised not to go into labour at least until after the race.

'Come on, guys,' Maddie called over to her sister and Josh, who could barely keep their hands off one another. 'There's plenty of time for that afterwards.'

Jennifer had come to visit for Maddie's baby shower and had fallen for Josh the moment she saw him. Jennifer had moved back to Australia and now they were renting Maddie's old apartment until they could save up for a place of their own.

Maddie and Evan, Jennifer and Josh, joined the other runners at the start line beneath the blue banner.

Evan used a blue zinc stick to draw a line down Maddie's nose and then across the bridge spanning out to the cheekbones. 'You look beautiful.'

She grabbed the stick and did the same for him. Last year they ran the 5K given that Evan had only just got back into running following his operation and the chemotherapy, but this year Evan said he was going all the way and Maddie hoped she could keep up with him and make the 10K too.

'You ready for this?' Evan took up position next to her, ready for the off.

'Of course I am.' She hadn't run so far in a long time but hoped that any lack of fitness would be obliterated by her determination. She seemed to have plenty of that these days.

'Don't push it too much.' Evan adjusted his cap. 'You're still getting over having Sam. I'm proud of you just for being here with me.' He squeezed her hand in his. 'I'll do two laps, the 10K, but you can leave me after the first if you need to.'

She kept her focus straight ahead. They say that acceptance is the final stage of grief, and from now on Maddie was back on course, running towards her future. 'I'll never leave you,' she said.

He wrapped his arms around her waist, tilted her back and kissed her. 'From this day forwards.' He grinned, ignoring the catcalls from the crowd as the start gun fired.

Acknowledgments

As always, a huge thank you goes to my family for their patience and understanding. I would never have got this far without you all.

Thank you to Sue Moorcroft for critiquing Handle me with Care so that I could pull it apart and make it into a better story, and for reading my book and giving me a lovely cover quote.

My thanks goes to Rachel Daven-Skinner for her hard work and dedication in copyediting my manuscript. It was a pleasure to work with her and I've learned a lot during the process! Thank you too to Stephanie Box for proofreading my story and saying how much she enjoyed it.

The cover design stage was a lot of fun thanks to Debbie Clement and she did an amazing job … the only downside was having so many fantastic designs to choose from!

In writing Handle me with Care I undertook a lot of research into testicular cancer. I would like to thank Dr. Joe McKendrick of Eastern Health Victoria, Australia, for patiently answering my many questions in our interview and follow up emails. All the information I gathered enabled me to go on to develop my character, Evan, who follows his own individual journey with the illness.

Thank you to Amy Tyson, friend and physiotherapist who gave me enough information during our Pilates sessions to create a realistic work setting for my character, Maddie.

And finally, a huge thanks to Alison who, so far, hasn't resigned from her post as my beta reader. She's currently reading my next book …

Read on for an excerpt from my novel, The Friendship Tree, out now!

Chapter One

Tamara Harding wondered how she had managed to get roped into this when she had only been in Australia for ten days. She looked down at the friendship tree – a hand-drawn, landscape-oriented picture that held the details of every resident who shared the Brewer Creek postcode. Her task, as co-ordinator, was to update and redistribute the tree.

"I think there are already some updates waiting for you," her mum explained. "I know that Jake Manning's details still haven't been added, and he's been in town for a while now. I'll leave you to it." Katherine Harding kissed her daughter's cheek. "I'll see you after work."

Tamara waved as she watched her mum head off to her part time job at the local post office, but her smile soon faded when she thought again of Jake, the man who had come to town and set up a second veterinary practice. Tamara was fiercely protective of her stepfather, Bobby, and suspected that the new competition in town was making more of an impact than he was willing to let on.

The warmth of the tangerine sun that hung in the sky filtered through the fly-screen door as Tamara looked out over the garden, the orchard, and the paddock. She glanced back at the picture of the friendship tree which had been maintained in Daphne Abbott's miniscule Mrs-Pepperpot-style handwriting.

It had a thick trunk and sprawling branches heading up towards the top of the paper. More branches spread from those, holding up boxes containing the names and contact details of Brewer Creek's residents.

When Daphne had handed over the reins of the friendship tree to a still jet-lagged and bleary-eyed Tamara, she had done so with a look that left no doubt about the high standards expected of her from now on. But Tamara was ready to rise to the challenge; sitting around gave her too much time to dwell on the reasons why she had left London. Focusing on something new, like the friendship tree, would help her to settle in and feel a part of this town.

With her work hat on, she decided that her first task should be to bring this friendship tree into the twenty-first century. She booted up the computer in Bobby's study, and as the machine whirred into action she leant back in the leather chair and gazed out of the window. This sleepy town was as far removed from the London lifestyle and her job as a Public Relations Account Executive as you could get, but it also had the added bonus of being ten thousand miles away from Bradley Cox.

And that was exactly why she had come.

Since Bobby and Katherine Harding emigrated eight years ago, visits had been few and far between, with Tamara visiting Australia once and her parents making the trip home twice. The original plan had been for them all to emigrate as a family, but when Tamara's career took off in her early twenties she had made the heart-wrenching decision to stay in the UK. It had been her best friend Beth who had supported her in the early weeks when Tamara wondered whether she had made a mistake in staying put, but then Bradley came on the scene and everything in her world had been rosy… for a while.

Tamara studied the friendship tree with its scribbled alterations: one resident had married and changed surname; another had left the area; another looked as though he had moved with the times and added a mobile phone number. Daphne had also scribbled job descriptions: Bill "GP"; Derek "Mechanic"; Matthew "Dairy Farmer"; Len "Local Pub"; "Plumber" against a man named Flynn on the highest branch. She had never seen anything like this before. In the block of flats where she'd lived in England, you were lucky to know anyone else's name let alone their personal details.

Tamara found an image of the outline of a tree with a wide canopy and saved a copy onto Bobby's computer, then she added boxes to the branches and transferred all the details from Daphne's diagram. Once they had been triple-checked, she bumped up the number of copies to forty-five – the exact number of squares that she had on the tree to represent each property – and left the printer to do its thing.

Since her arrival on Christmas Eve, Tamara had functioned in a jet-lagged haze, falling asleep on any unsuspecting couch and fixing snacks in the middle of the night. But today her body seemed to have adjusted. Today was the first day that she could fully appreciate how different life was in this town, compared to London. She poured a glass of orange juice and looked out at the waxy sheen of the tops of the trees, the pineapple-like trunks, the rambling open spaces with an infusion of greens, mustard-yellows, and reds injected into the landscape. Her mum's Instagram photographs simply hadn't done Brewer Creek justice. It was a small town nestled in the Central Coast of New South Wales, and the feeling of space along with the vast expanse of seemingly limitless blue sky left Tamara satisfied that she had made the right decision.

Tamara checked her watch and quickly calculated the time difference, then reached for the phone and waited for the international call to click through. She hadn't spoken to Beth since she left the UK, and it was lovely to hear her voice again. They chatted about the perils of jet lag, sun versus snow, the latest night out in the trendy London bars that Tamara hadn't thought she'd ever miss until now. They joked about being thirty and living with your parents all over again.

"Bobby painted the annexe, so at least I'll be semi-independent in there," said Tamara. "I've been roped into organising a friendship tree for the town, too." She explained the intricacies. "I thought that sort of thing went out with wind-on cameras."

"Hey," said Beth, "never underestimate the power of the friendship tree."

"That's true. We probably would never have been friends if it hadn't been for the one at school."

"Exactly," said Beth, not bothering to conceal a yawn. "So come on," she groaned, "tell me what the weather's like? Do I really want to know?"

"It's sunny, twenty-five degrees and climbing."

"Oh be quiet," said Beth. "I'm so jealous! Surprise, surprise, it's freezing here. It snowed on New Year's Eve, too, not a bloody taxi in sight…"

Tamara wondered whether Beth had bumped into Bradley on New Year's Eve – they frequented many of the same bars and pubs. Did he even know yet that she had left the country? Somehow she had successfully avoided all contact with him since that awful night when she had realised she needed to get away once and for all.

As though reading her mind, Beth asked, "Have you heard from Bradley?"

The breeze outside picked up, and the rustling of plants and trees instilled a sense of calm in Tamara. "Not a thing," she said.

"Good." Tamara could imagine Beth's trademark glossy red lips and her serious frown, her razor-cut bob as she recited her sermon. "No offence, Tamara, but it's a good thing you're there, away from him. It's time to think of your own needs for a change."

"I know." Tamara still didn't understand how it was possible to love someone one minute and be so wary of them the next. Leaving the UK had felt like ripping off an extraordinarily stubborn plaster: quick and hugely painful, but ultimately for her own good. Leaving Bradley, with his classic dark hair and film star good looks, had been the easy part; the part that made sense. Leaving the solidity of her close friendship with Beth, which had stood fast for more than twenty years, had been the hardest thing of all.

"Promise me something, Tamara?" Beth's tired voice came from the other side of the world. "If

Bradley does get in touch, be careful. He seems to know how to wangle his way back in every time."

"I know what he's like."

To Beth, Bradley was a manipulative arsehole; to Tamara, he was a thirty-year-old man who had lost his way in life's maze, and at every turn he seemed unable to find his way out. Leaving him hadn't been easy. He had been through his own hell with his family, and until Tamara came along it had all been bottled up tighter than a jar of pickles. His past didn't excuse his behaviour, but it did give him a complexity to his personality which Tamara had tried her best to understand.

When they ended their call Tamara wondered briefly how long it would be before Bradley heard on the grapevine that she had left London. It was highly unlikely that he would jump on a plane and follow her. A London boy through and through, even the thought of relocating to the south coast last year when Tamara was head-hunted by an up-and-coming PR firm had rattled him.

She picked up the printed copies of the friendship tree and left them in a stack on the hutch in the hallway before trotting upstairs to get ready for the day. Unlike the world of PR where everything had to be done yesterday, the distribution phase of the trees wasn't urgent, and thanks to modern technology she was probably already well ahead of the game.

"Good morning, Bobby," she called chirpily as she passed the bathroom.

Bobby poked his head around the door, one half of his face freshly shaven and the other covered in the whipped-cream-like shaving foam. "Good morning, love." He still held the razor in his hand, a towel slung over his shoulder on top of a black dressing gown. "Were you talking to yourself again?"

She gave him a playful shove which barely registered with the tall, solid man whose head skimmed the door frame. Quite by chance, Bobby Harding had the same emerald green eyes as Tamara and Katherine, and aside from the fact that she always called him Bobby it was only Tamara's cocoa-coloured skin – a blend from her London-born mum and her biological, Nigerian father – that gave away the fact that he was her stepfather.

"That was Beth on the phone," giggled Tamara. "She says hello, by the way."

"Ah, that explains it. So I don't need to call the men in white coats yet then?"

"Not yet."

"So what's the news from London? Any snow there yet?"

"A bit on New Year's Eve apparently."

Bobby leaned against the door jamb, unconcerned that Tamara had interrupted his shave. "Still feeling a bit homesick, love?"

She rolled her eyes. "It's only been a couple of weeks. People go on holiday for longer than that."

He ruffled her shoulder-length, wavy hair with his free hand. "I know, but moving around is hard; I've done it enough in my time to know that you'll have some ups and downs. Remember this is your home for as long as you need."

Tamara hadn't revealed the reasons behind her sudden relocation to Australia; as far as her parents were concerned, she was here on an open-ended visit and nothing else.

Bobby caught the trickle of white, watery liquid that began creeping down his throat. "I'd better finish up. Those trashy UK magazines that you were after are still in the car, on the passenger seat."

"Thanks, Bobby." Tamara trotted downstairs in her pyjamas and slipped on a pair of flip-flops at the back door. Getting ready could wait; celebrity gossip and problem pages couldn't.

Outside, she aimed the remote at the small red hatchback to wake it up. She leant over to the passenger side to grab the pile of glossy magazines, but as she pulled her body back out she felt a firm hand swipe across the bare skin of her shoulder blades.

She screamed. The pile of magazines launched like confetti in the air as she clasped her chest, gasping for breath as she turned to meet the person responsible. "What on earth do you think you're doing?"

"Whoa, take it easy," said the man. He held up his hands as though he was the victim rather than her. "You had a spider on your back," he said matter-of-factly.

Tamara spun round on the spot like a dog chasing its own tail. Her arms chopped through the air like blades on a windmill as she attempted to detach any cobwebs that might still be lingering. Oh God, was there something in her hair? She swished at that, too; she felt itchy all over.

Cornflower-blue eyes looked down at her, a hint of amusement disguised beneath a wide-brimmed Crocodile Dundee-style hat, and a smile played on the man's smooth, pale pink lips which were surrounded by a light layer of manly stubble.

"G'day, I'm Jake Manning." A hand extended towards her as she looked up at him, moving into the shade created by his body so that she wasn't squinting in the sun.

"Tamara Harding." She found the warmth of Jake's rough, hard-working hand, which dwarfed her own and contrasted against her dark skin.

She bent down to gather the magazines from the dirt below and took one from Jake when he crouched down to help her. Suddenly aware of her barely-there pyjamas, she folded her arms in front of her chest when she stood up, using the magazines as added protection. She locked eyes with him, unsure whether she was more embarrassed by how little she was wearing, or the fact that he was drop-dead gorgeous and totally unexpected.

The corners of Jake's mouth curved upwards and parted enough to show a row of neat teeth. "Spiders sometimes sneak in that gap around the door frame," he said, gesturing towards the car. "Huntsmen aren't poisonous, but they could give you a nasty bite."

"Thanks. I'll try to remember that."

It was still early enough in the morning for the air to carry a chill despite the glow of the sun and the promise of an Australian summer's day, and Tamara felt her body showing outward signs of being cold. She hugged the magazines even tighter against her chest.

"I'm here to see Mr Harris's horse," said Jake, the same persistent grin on his face as he pointed to the fields running adjacent to the Harding property.

"Well don't let me keep you."

"Don't let me keep you either." He tipped his hat, smirked at the picture of Jennifer Aniston on the front cover of the magazine. "You look busy."

She walked away, frustrated at letting him have the last word. Up until her recent redundancy, she had worked incredibly hard and this was her first real bit of relaxation in eighteen months. She wanted to ask why he was here to see Mr Harris, who was one of Bobby's clients, but that wasn't something she wanted to tackle whilst wearing skimpy pyjamas. Instead, she stalked back into the house and turned around in time to see Jake saunter past the swaying branches of the eucalyptus tree at the foot of the garden, his faded Levis perfectly capturing his masculinity.

This wasn't why she had come to Australia; she didn't need another man to complicate things.

Chapter Two

Jake passed through the gate to Mr Harris's property. He couldn't shake off the image of Tamara, her skin silky-smooth to the touch as he'd knocked the spider away. He let out a breath as he thought of her dark hair that caught highlights from the sun and hung down between delicately-boned shoulder blades, and that sexy little toe ring that glistened in the light. As pleasant and well-meaning as Daphne was, she certainly wasn't a patch on this girl from London who had taken over control of the friendship tree, and he looked forward to coming face-to-face with Tamara again if she was as serious about keeping it up-to-date as Daphne was.

With noticeable hourglass curves, and cute, seductive, heart-shaped lips, Tamara was a welcome distraction in the midst of all the trouble in Jake's life right now, although he didn't doubt her ability to land a decent punch on him should he put a foot out of line. When she'd caught his gaze drop to the silky pyjama top which left little to the imagination, he'd averted his eyes quickly.

He knew he'd also raised Tamara's suspicions the second he mentioned that he was here to see Mr Wilson, and he admired that in her; looking out for your family was something very close to his heart. But if Tamara thought that he was here to cause trouble or muscle in on Bobby's clientele, then she was wrong. His reasons for being in Brewer Creek were far less callous than that, and he had chosen a place with country town safety that couldn't be mimicked elsewhere.

Soon after he'd arrived in town, Daphne Abbott had cornered him in the milk bar that she ran and requested his personal details for the friendship tree. From that moment he had been hooked on the place. It felt as though he had stepped into the pages of a children's book rather than an insignificant town.

Jake closed the gate to the paddock and waved over to Mr Harris, who was fitting a saddle to one of his horses. A quick glance at his watch reminded him that he didn't want to be out for too long, because April hated being left alone in the house.

Mr Harris pushed his greying hair back over to the other side of his head and Jake didn't have the heart to tell him that comb-overs really were a thing of the past. He followed the man past the stables and into the rear paddock where Solomon looked happy enough.

"The medication to clear up that abscess must've worked its magic," said Jake, gently inspecting the hoof which had been treated. When he patted Solomon and felt the horse tense, he took a closer look at the coat beneath the mane. "What's this?"

Mr Harris's face dropped when he peered at the injury. "He must've caught it on the fence; I can't believe I didn't notice."

Jake rummaged in his bag, deftly cleaned the wound, and then stitched the small area. "He'll be fine, Mr Harris, but you need to sort that fence out over there before any more animals get hurt." Jake pointed to a section of exposed barbed wire which had most likely been the culprit. "If there's grass over the other side, then Solomon's going to put his head over the fence to eat it. And next time he could do more damage."

"I'll get to it straight away. Thanks, Jake." Mr Harris shook his hand enthusiastically, an action which conveyed how welcome Jake was in this town. Already he felt part of the small community, and knew he and April had made the right choice in coming here.

With his bag repacked, Jake made his way across the paddock and looked over at the Harding property. He was settling in just fine in Brewer Creek, but Tamara Harding was a complication that he wished he felt ready to handle. In those few moments they had shared today, she had crept well and truly under his skin.

Chapter Three

"Here you go." Tamara plonked a pile of mail down onto the kitchen table beside Bobby. Despite the early morning wake-up call from the kookaburras, followed by a lengthy Skype call with Beth, she was full of energy.

"Thank you. Any creepy crawlies get you out there this morning?" Bobby teased.

"There was a nasty big cockroach scuttling across the lid of the mailbox; it must've seen me coming. God bless English postboxes, where the mail just lands on the mat."

Bobby ripped open a couple of utility bills and left them at the side of the table. "What did you think of my painting in there?" He gestured towards the annexe.

"I love it. Thanks." Tamara planted a kiss on his cheek.

The custard-coloured walls of the annexe were bare except for a framed picture of concentric circles in shades of reds and oranges, and some shelving above the bed. The annexe had its own kitchenette equipped with a fridge, toaster and a kettle, as well as a small shower room. "I really appreciate you making me feel so at home."

"No worries," Bobby replied in his best Aussie accent. "The paint smell will go in time, and feel free to put up some more pictures."

"You don't want to make me too comfortable," Tamara smiled. "I might outstay my welcome."

"Twaddle," Bobby slurped his tea. "We don't see enough of you anyway, so make the most of it. And you've got those concertina doors along part of one wall so you can open them up and enjoy the garden when you feel like it."

Tamara hugged him tightly. He had shown her the grand plans for the house renovations whilst she was still wobbly-legged from her flight, his enthusiasm bubbling over about the pool he wanted to put in, the cabana, and maybe a home theatre, too.

"Don't you have to get to work?" She looked at the clock as the big hand took it past ten o'clock. Bobby was still munching on the last mouthful of peanut butter on toast.

"Soon," he shrugged.

"Where's Mum?"

Bobby tipped his head of short, greying hair back to get the dregs of his tea in the bottom of the cup as he headed to his study, calling over his shoulder, "She's on the morning shift today, back at lunchtime."

Tamara pulled out a fresh loaf from the breadbin – why they couldn't buy bread pre-sliced she would never know – and cut a slice. When the slice tried without success to pop out of the toaster, she switched the machine off at the wall and used a knife to rescue it.

"I hear you met Jake the other day." Bobby reappeared in the kitchen and grinned at the sight of Tamara's toast, cut so unevenly that it looked like a ski run.

331

Trying to ignore the unexpected tingle that had zinged all the way up her spine at the mention of Jake, Tamara spread a generous helping of jam across the toast's bumpy, golden surface and said, "I thought Mr Harris was your client."

Bobby stashed a bowl and his empty mug in the dishwasher and sighed heavily. "Tamara, it's good of you to worry about me; about us. Jake is healthy competition, nothing more, nothing less. Times are tough for anyone these days and I'm no exception, and I'm guessing neither is Jake. Don't you worry, I still have my loyal customers."

"But some of them have left, according to Mum." Tamara knew that her stepfather wasn't the Rottweiler that he needed to be to keep his client base. Instead, he was the dog that rolled over and let you tickle its tummy, and that could threaten what he had built up over the years.

He smiled at her now. "When I'm booked up, some of them drift over to Jake and unfortunately it means that sometimes they don't come back. I expect Jake was here to check on Mr Harris's horse. I couldn't get out to him last week as I was dealing with Peggy Thompson – a litter of kittens arrived as a surprise one night in the corner of her laundry; she'd thought her cat was getting fat." His rounded belly jiggled as he laughed. "She had the poor thing on all sorts of diets before she even realised."

Tamara grabbed hold of his arm before he had a chance to fob her off some more. "You look tired."

"That's because I'm old."

"You are not old!" She nudged him, even though she had noticed herself that his eyes were more sunken and lacked their usual clarity, and his words harboured a definite lethargy whenever he spoke.

"When you get to my age, Tamara, going out to work each day becomes much like having the same dinner every night of the week. It satisfies you and means that you can function, but the excitement has gone."

She hesitated a moment, not wanting to speak out of turn. "You could always retire, or at least cut back a bit."

"One day," he said, and with that he left Tamara in the kitchen to wonder what this usually relaxed, happy-go-lucky man was holding onto so tightly inside.

She wandered into the front sitting room and watched Bobby's car slowly reverse off the drive, leaving her alone in the house. It was so quiet she could almost hear the grass growing outside. Tamara was used to living on her own in a one bedroom flat in Watford, not far from London, but the general noise that came with living in the same building as others and in such close proximity to shops and local businesses, must have kept her company.

She sat on the edge of the armchair and sipped from a glass of iced water, wondering how her parents could face their morning cups of tea or coffee when the weather outside was so warm. She looked out of the window at the landscape which her mum had provided a passionate rundown of when she arrived. Dappled with vibrant purple splashes of the jacaranda trees, and the creamy white sprays of fragrant flowers on the Fiddlewood that sat to one side of the driveway, it was the epitome of country living.

Restless, Tamara headed to the study and flicked on the computer. As it went through the motions of starting up, she let the sun warm her through the open window and carry the scent of the outside to the desk. She moved the mouse and prepared to live her life vicariously through the wonders of the worldwide web, flicking through her emails, deleting spam that asked whether she wanted to get laid more, something from EnlargeIt-Fast, and an invitation to have non-surgical fat reduction.

Her emerald green eyes played with the screen as she opened Facebook, unable to resist the opportunity to check-in with what was happening in the city she had left behind. She scrolled down the News Feed, giggling at Beth's post showing a photo of her on a narrow boat travelling along the Norfolk Broads with her brother Heath. Beth was the skipper and she looked as though she were driving a car in the Grand Prix rather than a vessel that was moving slower than a push bike.

When Tamara left the UK, she didn't think she'd miss her drab flat with its tatty Formica kitchen floor and the slightly torn wallpaper beneath the lounge windowsill. She never imagined she'd miss the smell drifting up to her paper-thin windows every morning from the cafe across the road, or the sound of the twin toddlers upstairs wailing as their mother tried to get through the witching hour. But now, seeing such scenes with only the whirring sound of the computer for company, she yearned for that type of familiarity.

The leather chair creaked as she leaned into its backrest and smiled as she saw her message inbox receive a new mail. It was from Beth:

Really missing you, mate, but DO NOT COME HOME YET! (I'm writing this because I know you'll see Facebook posts that make you feel as though you're missing out. Believe me, you're not!)
Trust me; I've always had your back, haven't I? Ever since that Darren Wallis picked on you by the friendship tree. Blimey, wonder what he's up to now? God, who cares!

Anyway, gotta go. I've got an early meeting in the morning.
Say a big hello to the parents. Love and hugs!

Beth x

Tamara manoeuvred the mouse ready to reply, but her eyes jerked to the other side of the screen. She felt her body go cold as she froze, because there staring back at her was a Friend Request, from Bradley.

She wondered why she hadn't seen this one coming.

"Pah... I thought Facebook was for Losers!" She held her thumb and forefinger against her forehead in an 'L' shape, remembering how he had used those very words when she'd signed up to the social networking site. She realised then that she was rubbing her temple, and even though the bruise had healed pretty quickly, the memories still lingered of that night.

She shuddered as her mind flitted to Bradley's solemn confession about his family a couple of weeks into their relationship: "I hid under my bed like a coward," he'd said, as he described his father's rage. "I should've protected my mum."

The breeze from the open window made Tamara shiver now. She couldn't deny that she missed Bradley, and she wondered whether things could've been different if she'd made him get help, or if she had supported him more. The answer from Beth would be easy: a resounding "no"!

Sometimes Tamara fought to forget the good times so that she could open her eyes to the bad. Was that what she needed to do now?

Of course Bradley had a nice side, but not everyone got to see that. Sometimes he'd bought her flowers "just because"; he'd driven around for hours one night to get her flu tablets when she couldn't sleep and her temperature had gone through the roof; he'd cooked her breakfast in bed when she had the hangover to end all hangovers.

Bradley had kind eyes, a soft voice, and all the vulnerability of someone with a shaky past which Tamara had found herself responding to. Could she really push him away when he was reaching out to her, the girl he described as his "best friend"?

Two rectangular-boxed options waited on the screen for her to make her choice:

Ignore.
Confirm.

Her eyes looked first at one and then the other, unable to settle on either. She rubbed her hands against her bare legs, biting her lip as she refused to let her hands anywhere near the mouse. This was her chance; her chance to let him know that it was really time for them to go their separate ways.

Her hand returned to the mouse, moving it from side to side as though it were some kind of Ouija board:

Confirm, Ignore, Confirm, Ignore.

Click.

Printed in Great Britain
by Amazon